The
Missing
Link

Charlyne Dickerson

Indigo is an imprint of
Genesis Press Inc.
315 3rd Ave. N.
Columbus, MS 39701

Copyright 2000 by Charlyne Dickerson

The Missing Link

ISBN: 1-58571-037-7

Manufactured in the United States

First Edition

They forgot about having a nightcap and made their way up the dark stairs to her bedroom where only a night light burned. The tension that had surrounded them dissolved into thin air the moment they faced each other in her bedroom. Craig drew her into his arms and held her tightly against his chest.

Shanna felt his heart thudding against her body and her knees turned to jelly. She reached up to draw his head down to hers, planting small kisses on his forehead, his cheeks, his chin. She surrendered her lips in a hot, passionate kiss.

Craig groaned. He silently started to undress her. Helping him, she kicked off her shoes and pulled off her panty hose. After he pulled her dress over her head and unclasped her bra, he looked at her in the moonlight streaming through the half-open window shades.

"You're truly incredible," he murmured ...

This book is dedicated with love and gratitude to R. Tuner Dickerson, my husband, who supports my dreams with unconditional love; to my daughter, Nancy Moten, who consistently offers words of encouragement and love; to my son, Larry Moten, who also believes in my dream and provides invaluable editorial assistance. My deep appreciation is also extended to my friends whose encouragement means so much to me.

CHAPTER ONE

The moment Shanna Taylor heard the door chimes, she quickly set down her morning coffee and rushed through the hallway to the front door. This had to be the person her boss had recommended to rent the studio she'd recently renovated above her garage. Her cheating ex-husband had moved out several months earlier, leaving her with their two teenage boys and a heavy mortgage. In spite of her misgivings about dealing with a stranger, she could think of no other way to survive in her present circumstances.

Opening the door, she took a step backward, startled to see a tall, gorgeous stranger facing her. Unable to get out a simple hello for a few moments, she finally found her voice. "You're...you're not a—"

"Uh...you were expecting someone else? Rick told me you had a studio for rent and I—"

"But you're a man!"

She stared up at the handsome stranger. That's the last thing she wanted in her space—hunk or not! "Rick should have known I was looking for a woman. He said a friend of his was hunting a place and I assumed he meant a woman."

"Well, I've been Rick's friend most of my life. I'm sure he wouldn't have recommended me if he thought there might be a problem. And I understand the studio is separate from the rest of the house, so I—"

Shanna held up her right hand. "What you don't understand is the fact that I have no intention of having a man in my space ... now or ever again." She hadn't meant to get so emotional. She awkwardly dropped her hand, a bit peeved at her reaction to the stranger.

Aware of Shanna's evident confusion for some unknown reason, he held out his hand to her. "Suppose I introduce myself. I'm Craig Boyd and I'm looking for a quiet place to live for the next few months."

Shanna just stared at him, mesmerized by his dark, intense eyes and deep, husky voice. His skin's the color of melted milk chocolate ran across her mind.

Craig hesitated, unsure of what to say next. After a few seconds, he continued. "I'm here from Chicago temporarily to oversee the financial affairs of our struggling loan offices in California, the San Francisco office being the first."

She swallowed hard before taking his extended hand, almost afraid to touch him.

He held her hand longer than she was comfortable with, and she rubbed the back of her hand when she got it back.

"Shanna...Shanna Taylor," she managed to get out.

Remembering her manners, Shanna stepped back, silently inviting Craig to enter her foyer. As he walked past her, she noticed the casual way he wore his obviously expensive dark gray suit, which fitted his broad shoulders like a glove. She judged him to probably be in his late thirties, perhaps only three or four years older than she. Why in heaven's name would such a man want to stay in a small studio above a garage rather than rent an apartment or stay in a hotel for a few months?

Shanna led the way into her living room. "Please sit down." Unsure of what to do next, she haltingly explained, "I...I have something in the oven I need to check on." She practically ran from the room, needing some time to untangle the thoughts running haywire in her mind. Uppermost was the reminder that she wanted no males in her life except her teenage sons. Yet the studio did have its own entrance, and he wouldn't have to have any contact with her. Also, her money problems would be solved for a few months until she could figure something else out or get a better paying job. Additionally, he had been recommended by her boss, so he must be a decent sort of guy. "Of course maybe after he sees it, he might decide it isn't what he wants," she said softly. That was a possibility, so the least she could do was to show it to him. Hurrying back to the living room, she found him studying the photograph of her sons on the mantel.

Craig turned as she entered. "These your young men?"

"Yes, the taller one is David and the other is Phillip."

He replaced the frame and walked over to the sofa, his thoughts straying to his own young son, Danny, about the age of the boys in the photograph. He was still trying to get shared custody of Danny, but so far had been foiled in his attempts by his lying ex-wife and her influential family in New York. There had to be a way he could share in his son's growing up, and he'd keep on doing whatever it took to have Danny with him part of the time.

Shanna failed to notice the disconsolate look on his face as he sat down.

She stayed near the fireplace, nervously twisting her hair above her ear.

Not understanding her silence, Craig cleared his throat before asking, "Changed your mind about renting the studio?"

"No...I...just have to get the key. The studio has a separate entrance through the garage. There's also an entrance from the upstairs rooms of the house. You would have to use the garage entrance," she emphasized. She was certain he would be discouraged with an arrangement like that.

Craig's face remained impassive while listening to her describe the rental. He unconsciously rubbed his hands together, still feeling the softness and warmth of her hand when he shook it. It had been a long time since such a warm feeling had swept through him. Her nearness slightly upset his cool in a way he didn't quite understand. Why did he feel so drawn to a woman he'd just met? Since his divorce, he hadn't wanted any woman to ever again become a part of his life. Yet he couldn't deny the chemistry that sparked between them with only a brief touch of their hands.

Afraid she wouldn't get rid of Craig so easily, Shanna reluctantly crossed the room to a small table and opened a drawer, pulling out the garage door opener and a key to the door of the studio. "I'll show it to you...but you probably won't be interested. It's comfortable but certainly nothing luxurious." Nervously twirling the keys around her forefinger, Shanna gingerly edged past him in the foyer. They stepped outside onto the porch and across the well-kept front lawn to the two-car garage attached to the right side of the house. "There's also a space for your car if you want to park it inside."

Craig was not listening, suddenly aware of her tight-fitting jeans, her shapely derriere, her small waist, and her auburn-streaked hair pulled back in a short ponytail...so absorbed in watching her stride in front of him, he was not aware she was talking to him.

"Uh...sorry...what were you saying?" he stammered.

Shanna threw a quizzical look back at him. "I was telling you that the studio upstairs used to be my ex-husband's office and retreat," she explained while opening the garage door. She crossed the garage to a staircase

located at the rear. Craig followed her up the stairs to a
large, sunny room paneled in knotty pine. He glanced
around the studio. At one end of the room he saw a com-
fortable-looking bed covered by an exquisite hand-made
quilt and several colorful pillows casually thrown against
the wall. Looking at a long leather cognac sofa and a
matching chair and ottoman, Craig visualized stretching
out in the long chair, his feet propped up on the ottoman.
He smiled as he admired the long, multi-colored area
rugs that lay in front of the sofa and along the side of the
bed. This would be an ideal set-up, a place of privacy yet
still connected to people not too far away.

Shanna watched apprehensively as Craig walked
around the studio, nervously shifting from one foot to the
other. Each time he passed near her, she inhaled his
heady aftershave lotion, a very pleasing but unfamiliar
scent and wondered what kind he used. Did he really
intend to take the place? Twisting the keys in her hand,
she halfway hoped he would think the studio too small or
not want it for some other reason. Yet she found his
presence very comforting. Shaking her head, she found
her contradictory thoughts too confusing as she watched
him surveying the room.

Craig stopped before a wide oak dresser with a long
mirror above it that sat on one side of the room. Opening
the drawers, he saw he would have plenty of space for
what he'd brought with him from Chicago. An oversized
desk, which took up most of the space below the wide
double windows at the front of the room, caught his
attention.

Walking around, Craig smelled the lemon polish she
must have recently used dusting the room. Waist-high
book shelves sat at each end of the long desk. A television set and VCR were on top of one shelf and a telephone attached to an answering machine sat on the
other. He pulled aside the cottage curtains and glanced

out of the double windows that overlooked the driveway and the small front lawn. Farther out he saw a portion of the San Francisco Bay, a very calming view.

Shanna watched Craig's deliberate inspection of the room, resisting the urge to tap her feet in her impatience to get him out of the studio. Instead, she pulled a few strands of hair from her short ponytail and started twisting them around her index finger while she bit her upper lip, an anxious expression on her face.

Craig pretended not to notice Shanna's unfriendly behavior while he continued to inspect the room. The more he saw, the better he liked the place. Walking across the room to the window on the opposite side, he looked down on a small fenced-in back yard with a well-used brick barbecue pit at the end of a stone patio. Lounge chairs and a couple of small round wicker tables were grouped a few feet from the pit. A large oak provided shade for a redwood picnic table and the two long redwood benches placed beneath it. A slight breeze ruffled the curtains in front of him, and he thought how nice it could be sitting in the shade of the tree.

The shrubbery and tall flowering plants around the sides of the fence looked healthy but needed trimming, he noticed as he surveyed the yard. In spite of that, he decided the whole area looked very homey and very inviting, a great place to relax in the evening.

Wanting to get Craig on his way, Shanna interrupted his survey, walking over to pull aside a tall, colorful screen revealing a compact kitchen area. "Here's a small refrigerator, and over there a hot plate and a microwave oven. They're usable but hardly sufficient to prepare meals."

He nodded his head as he glanced at the area. "This is just right for me since I seldom cook anything."

She turned and indicated a closed door. "That's the bathroom...it's kinda small but has a stall shower. And this other door leads to the upstairs bedrooms of the house. I keep this door locked from the other side."

Shanna paused for a few moments, apprehensively glancing over at him. "This whole space is rather small...you probably need a larger place if you plan to stay in San Francisco for any length of time," she suggested, again nervously jingling the keys looped over her index finger.

Craig returned her glance with raised eyebrows. The studio was perfect as far as he was concerned. *What can I say to erase that anxious look from her pretty face?* he wondered as he watched her edge toward the door leading to the stairway.

"Rick told me you insisted on keeping this house when you divorced. I can surely see why."

Shanna stopped suddenly when she heard Craig's voice again. *Darn that Rick. What else had her boss told this man about her?*

Another thought entered her mind. "My two rambunctious teen-age boys grew up in this house and love to play basketball in the driveway. You probably noticed the hoop above the garage door. Trying to dunk baskets is almost a daily ritual for them." *Surely that would turn him off.* She glanced at him apprehensively.

"Really? Maybe the boys will let me join them some evening. I shoot a pretty mean basket."

"You mean you actually want to—" Shanna started, suddenly feeling she was caught in a no-win situation. *Does nothing discourage this man? What else can I say?*

Craig held up his hand to stop her. "This is just what I want...just enough room and the privacy I need in the evenings. I usually bring work home with me." Confirming what he'd just said, he reached inside his jacket and withdrew his checkbook. "I don't know exactly how long I'll be in San Francisco, but I'd like to pay for the first three months. Is that okay with you?"

Stunned, Shanna could only nod her head. What else could she do? He really wanted the studio. She told him the monthly rental fee and watched nervously while he wrote out the check. She prayed she was doing the right thing.

Shanna remembered the disconnected telephone. "My ex had a private telephone line installed that I had turned off when he left. Would you like for me to call the telephone company to have it turned on for you?" That was the least she could do.

"I sure would appreciate it...if you have the time, that is."

"No problem. I'll call this afternoon and it'll probably be turned on right away."

Putting his checkbook back into his pocket, Craig stated matter-of-factly, "I'd like to move in tomorrow if that's convenient for you. I guess I can stand that hotel room for one more night."

He looked at her appealingly.

She felt as if his twinkling dark eyes were looking into her soul.

Unsettled, Shanna wanted to return the check; she wanted to tell him she didn't need the money and didn't want him anywhere in her life. But the fact that she DID need the extra income overruled her impulse.

Feeling ridiculous because of her thoughts, Shanna handed Craig the door key and garage door opener. "There's no reason why you can't move in tomorrow," she said curtly. Turning abruptly, she started down the stairs. After a final, satisfied glance around the room, Craig followed her.

They reached the driveway and Craig moved up beside her. "Thanks for getting me out of my hotel room."

Shanna merely nodded.

Craig offered her his hand, then remotely popped the

locks of his gray Mercedes parked in the driveway. He threw up his hand in parting as he buckled his seat belt and started the engine, slowly backing out of the drive-way.

A mixture of emotions overpowered Shanna as she watched Craig drive away. What a hunk! Tall and lean, he reminded her of her husband, but the resemblance ended there. This brother had skin the color of highly polished mahogany, close-cut, curly black hair and large twinkling eyes almost as dark as his hair. His broad smile emphasized the deep laugh lines on either side of his mouth, and his neatly trimmed mustache added sophistication to his whole face. Nor had his broad shoulders and narrow hips escaped her scrutiny. She shook her head, hoping to erase him from her mind. Get a grip, she told herself. You're a grown woman with teenage sons. You certainly can handle this.

❦

Craig drove slowly down the street; he could still see Shanna's lovely coffee-colored face. The last thing I need at the moment is to get tangled up with another woman, he thought. But Shanna's dark shining eyes... Dealing with his ex during the few years he was married had left him embittered. He didn't intend to ever again get involved in anything even slightly resembling a seri-ous relationship. Still, Shanna...he didn't want to think about her.

Straightening out the affairs of the California branch offices and getting back to his position as a financial ana-lyst at the Chicago headquarters was all he wanted to deal with for the next three or four months. Yet he could-n't deny the disturbing vibes that had passed between him and Shanna today whenever they passed near each other.

❦

Swallowing hard, Shanna realized she had watched

until Craig's car disappeared. She walked slowly across the lawn and into the house toward the kitchen. Uncharacteristically, she stopped before the oval mirror hanging above the small gilt-trimmed table in the foyer and peered into it. What she saw was the same face she always saw: a fairly attractive woman with skin the color of cafe au lait, auburn-streaked, relaxed hair now pulled back from her face, and wide dark brown eyes with thick lashes below naturally arched eyebrows.

Shanna leaned closer to the mirror and examined her full lips that turned up slightly at the corners. I should have smeared on some lipstick before he came, she thought as she peered at her makeup-free face. Well, it's too late now. She removed the rubber band holding her short ponytail in place. Why should I care what he thought? Tossing the rubber band onto the table, she childishly stuck out her tongue at the image in the mirror and made her way down the hall to the kitchen, determined to put Craig out of her mind. What was done, was done and I can't undo it now, she concluded. It's probably the biggest mistake I've made in a long time—other than marrying Paul, that is.

She continued to the kitchen and poured a fresh cup of coffee, taking it and the morning paper into her breakfast nook. The paper was soon forgotten, however, as she sipped her coffee and mused on her day. It had to be high on the one-to-ten scale of frustrating days. She only hoped the results of her decision would be good ones for both her and the boys. Her mind wandered to the day four years ago when Paul packed his clothes and other belongings and walked out. In the frustrating months after Paul left, she felt most of the time as if she were teetering on a high cliff with no one below to catch her should she lose her footing. Only time and the daily demands of her boys forced her to take control of her life. The worsening of her financial situation pushed her into a long overdue reality check.

After exhausting all the other possibilities she could think of, she'd come back to this one, which she'd at first refused to consider. Renting out the studio above the garage would increase her income. But the idea had been totally repugnant. Bottom line, she could think of no alternative. She needed no interference—certainly not a hunk like Craig—in the well-ordered life she had struggled to build with her two sons during the past four years. But what else could she do? Even with her own salary and the monthly alimony checks from Paul, she had barely been able to keep up the mortgage payments on the house she was granted in the divorce settlement. She needed money and needed it desperately.

Why did life have to be so full of difficulties? Dealing with monthly expenses was difficult. Dealing with unwanted would-be suitors was difficult. Work at the office sometimes became difficult when all the lawyers demanded her attention at the same time. Even the boys were occasionally difficult.

And having another human being living on her property would definitely be difficult, forcing one more major change in her life, whether she wanted it or not. She drew a deep breath, hoping to inhale some confidence and exhale some of the anxieties she had about renting the studio to a man.

"But it's all settled. No need to worry about it now," she told herself out loud. No need to cry over spilled milk, her mother always said.

Shaking her head to dispel her gloomy thoughts, Shanna remembered she had taken the day off to sign some papers at the bank and rushed upstairs to get her purse.

☙

Later in the afternoon, Shanna glanced at the clock above the refrigerator and saw it was almost time for her boys to get home from school. She got a few cookies from the jar and glasses from the cabinet and placed them in the middle of the table for their after-school snack. No sooner had she taken a casserole from the freezer for their dinner than she heard her boys running into the house, slamming the door behind them. Noise seemed to prevail regardless of where they were or what they were doing, yet they always lightened her mood.

David and Phillip bounced into the kitchen, threw their backpacks down in a corner and stripped off their jackets while heading for the table for their snack.

"Yo, Mom," the boys greeted her simultaneously.

Shanna snatched up the cookies.

David and Phillip smiled at each other.

"Hi, Mom."

Putting the cookies back on the table, Shanna poured tall glasses of milk.

"Better," she said approvingly. "So how was school today?" She looked at her two young sons, thinking of the ways they had grown in the past four years. They were at times endearing, sometimes exasperating, and sometimes downright funny, but always a joy to have around. Although there were almost eighteen months between them, they were about the same height.

At age fourteen-and-a-half, David was the spitting image of his father, the same coal black curly hair, smooth brown skin, sharp facial features and tall, slender build. He had also inherited his father's happy-go-lucky ways, which spilled over to his schoolwork; she continuously had to prod him to keep his grades up. He was a bright, naturally mischievous boy who sometimes got into situations that necessitated her talking to his teachers. Nothing serious, just bothersome at times.

She turned to thirteen-year-old Phillip, the quiet, studious one of the two. He also had a wide smile, a smooth brown complexion and eyelashes she'd kill for.

He was quick to smile and his laughter was a joy to hear. He always did everything he was supposed to do, yet there was just enough mischief in him to keep other boys from teasing him. He was by no means the perfect child, but he gave her fewer moments of anxiety than his brother.

All of her spare time was devoted to raising them the best way she knew how, so the boys were now her life. The thought that she devoted too little time to her own life crossed her mind occasionally, but she usually shrugged it off. Her job as a paralegal in a firm of lawyers and her boys' activities filled her time. She had no interest in forming any other kind of relationships. The bleakness of her social life no longer bothered her.

Shanna returned to the question she had asked. "So...guys, am I going to get an answer?" She took the makings for a salad out of the refrigerator, placing them on the counter.

Silence.

She turned around, sensing that all was not right. Neither boy was looking at her but at each other. Usually they freely recounted whatever happened during the day, and she usually told them about her day in the lawyers' offices.

"So...what's up?" She left the salad ingredients on the sink and walked over to the table. She sat down facing the boys, noticing a kind of sheepish look crossing David's face. Softly drumming her short nails on the table, she waited patiently for an answer. She knew one or the other of the boys would eventually tell her what was going on with them.

"David's got a girlfriend," Phillip finally blurted out. "And her name's Jessica." He threw a guilty look at David. "She gave me a note to give him after school today, and he won't tell me what it says...and that's not fair...I always tell him things that happen to me."

Shanna let out a slow breath of air. Is that all that this was about? She breathed a sigh of relief that it was nothing more serious, not wanting to have to pay another visit to their school because of some of David's shenanigans.

She then recalled that David had certainly become more meticulous about his appearance in the past few weeks. Recently she hadn't even had to remind him about taking showers, something he had formerly skipped whenever he thought he could get away with it. She looked at him closely and was surprised to see a faint fuzz on his upper lip. Careful to hide a smile that was threatening to break out, she looked at the blush that was now quite evident on David's face as he threw a dirty look to his brother.

"So why should David have to share his note with you, Phillip? Don't you think it might be rather personal when a gal writes a note to a guy?" She was relieved when she saw David's face light up as she continued. "Pretty soon you'll probably be exchanging notes with girls, too."

Phillip's eyebrows lifted. "Naw, not me. I don't go for that kind of stuff. Girls are a pain in the—"

"Phillip! Watch your mouth! You probably won't always feel that way. Things change, you know, as you grow older." Shanna rose and went back to the counter to prepare their salad. The boys, eyeing each other surreptiously, finished their snack and left for their rooms to start their homework.

Shanna faced the fact that they really were growing older. And there were so many things to talk about that they needed to know. Damn. Was she up to that task? What should a mother tell teenage boys? It would be easier for her, she admitted, if they were girls.

While she finished getting their dinner together, she concluded that maybe she would talk to Rick. Rick was older and had raised a son and daughter, both of whom were now in college. She was sure that Rick could give her some hints about what goes on in teenage boys' minds. She brushed the back of her hand across her forehead as another of her mother's sayings ran through her mind: If it's not one thing, it's another. Which was certainly true at the moment.

She called out to the boys and heard them noisily descending the stairs, evidently trying to beat each other to the kitchen. Phillip made it to the table first and gave David a sly grin when he sat down.

Halfway through the meal, Shanna remembered about Craig moving in. She hadn't told the boys. "By the way, guys, I rented the studio this morning to a Mr. Boyd. He came by earlier today to check it out...he's moving in tomorrow. He's working here in the city for three or four months, so this is not a long-term deal. He'll use the garage entrance, so don't unlock the upstairs door that leads to the studio."

She continued to eat when she heard no response and wondered how the boys were taking that news.

David and Phillip stared at her and then at each other a few moments, puzzled looks crossing their faces.

"But what about Dad's things? What did you do with them?" Phillip finally asked, twisting uncomfortably in his chair.

Leave it to Phillip to think about his father! David also looked at her expectantly. She knew that both boys deep down inside hoped that their father would return some day to live with them, even though she had explained to them in no uncertain terms that that was not in the scheme of things. Why couldn't they understand and accept that?

"Your father came by some time ago to get the rest of his belongings." She continued to eat her dinner, aware of the silence around them.

David laid down his fork before he spoke. "Can we

still play basketball with someone living above the hoop?" Shooting baskets was his favorite pastime. He was getting pretty good at the game and wanted nothing to interfere with his evening ritual.

"I mentioned that to Mr. Boyd, and all he said was that he could shoot a pretty mean basket himself. So I guess it won't bother him."

"Maybe he'll want to shoot some with us sometime," Phillip volunteered.

"He's not too old for that, is he?" David thought anyone over thirty was really old.

"He's probably about my age, maybe two or three years older. I didn't ask him his personal history, David." In the back of her mind, however, she had wondered about his age. Why, she didn't know...his age was really of no concern of hers. "I already mentioned that he'll be in San Francisco for only a few months, and he didn't want to spend that time in a hotel room. Other than that I know little about him, except Rick recommended him, and I trust Rick's advice implicitly. Otherwise I wouldn't have rented the studio to him."

"Cool," David said and Phillip nodded his head, as if the matter needed no further discussion. Much to her relief. The last thing she needed at the moment was resistance from them. Finishing their dinner shortly afterward, the boys rushed outside to the driveway to their evening ritual of trying to out dunk each other.

CHAPTER TWO

A few days later Shanna waited impatiently for Rick, her boss, to complete his business in court. As soon as he stepped into the office she cornered him. She wanted to know more about the man he had recommended renting her studio.

She greeted Rick as usual before launching into her questions. "By the way, Rick, Craig Boyd decided to rent my studio as you suggested. Have you known him long?" She made a pretense of shuffling some papers on her desk while waiting for Rick's reply.

"Let me think for a moment, Shanna." He walked over and set his briefcase on her desk. "I guess I've known Craig since grade school, and we've always kept in touch even though we went our separate ways after college. In my book Craig's one of the best friends I've ever had. He's been very successful in his firm and is one of the top guys. Guess that's why they sent him out here for a few months to straighten out the California offices." He rubbed his chin with the palm of his hand.

Rick was not providing the information Shanna was interested in. Taking a different tact, she said, "I just wondered why Craig was so taken with my small space. Seems like he would prefer something more—"

"More what, Shanna? You've got a great place."

"What I mean is—"

"Give Craig time to get acquainted. He's never been the most communicative guy, but it seems like he's really gone into a shell since his problems with his wife, though." Rick stopped for a moment.

Shanna raised her eyebrows. "So he's married," she stated rather than asked.

"Oh, he's been divorced for some time. After his wife took their boy to the East Coast, a mutual friend told me Craig just buried himself in his work in Chicago. Does little else as far as I know."

"How old is his son?"

"Probably eleven or twelve by now, I guess." Rick glanced sideways at Shanna, wondering about her sudden interest in talking about Craig. "Craig's evidently not interested in women. Since he's been out here he's refused to meet any of my wife's friends she was trying to hook him up with. As you already know, she fancies herself a matchmaker. It's funny how women are always trying to get us men married." He gave Shanna another inquisitive glance before asking her for his mail and then going to his own office.

For reasons Shanna didn't analyze, she brightened at this meager information from Rick, and the day passed more quickly than most of her days. Leaving her office later in the day, she stopped by the market on her way home.

Climbing out of her car, her arms full of bags, Shanna saw Craig pull into the driveway.

Craig noticed Shanna struggling to lock her car door while juggling her bags of food and walked over to her car.

"Here, let me help you," he offered, reaching out for the largest bags.

"Oh, I can manage."

Yet she didn't protest as he took two of the heavy bags from her arms and followed her across the lawn to the front door. Balancing the other bag, she unlocked the front door and set her bag on the small table in the hallway. She turned and reached for the bags in his arms.

"I'll carry them to the kitchen for you," he offered. "How in the world did you manage to get all of these in your arms? They're rather heavy."

Not answering, she picked up the bag from the table and led the way down the long hall to the kitchen. Following her, Craig's eyes were drawn to her curvaceous legs and the slim waist of her skirt belted around her middle. What is wrong with me? he wondered. Why am I suddenly interested in a woman's legs or her waistline?

Shanna turned to him when they reached the kitchen. "You can put your bags over there on the counter," she instructed him, momentarily in charge of the situation.

Craig deposited the bags and turned to face her, a wide smile on his face.

Shanna caught her bottom lip between her teeth when she felt a flush spread from her neck to her cheeks. His smiling dark eyes disturbed her composure. He looked very handsome in his conservative dark business suit and expensive silk tie with red diagonal stripes. She was sure she could have used his highly polished shoes for a mirror. What's the matter with you, woman? she asked herself. Cool it! All he did was help you with your groceries!

"Thanks for the help," she finally got out.

"Any time," he replied gallantly.

Craig noticed her flushed face and wondered why she seemed to be in such a dither. Maybe she wasn't used to having anyone except her boys help her. Were all the men in this city blind to her charms? But then, maybe she did have a relationship with someone. What did he know? However, in the few days he'd been living in the studio no male had come around—or at least he hadn't seen one.

"I guess I'll be going," he said in a low, husky voice, and headed for the door leading to the hallway. About halfway across the kitchen, he stopped and turned around, sniffing the air. "You must do a lot of cooking with spices. It smells good in here." He glanced around the bright yellow tiled kitchen with small plants on the window sills. "A kitchen is one of my favorite rooms," he added, "and your breakfast nook looks like a cozy place to eat."

"The boys and I spend a lot of time in this area. They sometimes do their homework here, especially Phillip when he needs some help or wants me to check his assignments." She thanked him again for his help—glad he was leaving—and followed him to the front door.

On her way back to the kitchen, Shanna reminded herself that she liked her present status, her independence. She was in control...she had to answer to no one and she liked it like that. Sharing her life with her boys suited her just fine.

Surveying the grocery bags to be emptied, she sighed. "Get busy, girlfriend," she told herself out loud. She quickly put away her purchases and started the evening meal before the boys got home from school.

❦

Climbing the stairs to his studio, Craig thought, "Whoa! Go slow with that woman, brother." He was conscious of how she affected him every time he was in her presence. He removed his clothes, carefully hanging up his suit and placing his loafers in the closet. He donned jeans and a sweat shirt before opening his attaché case to remove some papers that he wanted to study before the next day's meeting. After spending a few minutes on the reports, he found his mind wandering to his landlady.

Shanna's face kept appearing in his mind, and he finally gave up on his work and went into his small kitchen space to make a thick liverwurst sandwich. He spread the bread with plenty of mayo and then added sliced tomatoes and lettuce. He opened a can of beer and carried them both back to his desk.

Before sitting down, he opened the window that looked out over the driveway. He inhaled deeply when a light breeze wafted through the room. While eating, he thought about Shanna. He decided she was obviously a strong, independent woman who evidently could manage a job and a home as well as two young boys all by herself. However, he still couldn't pinpoint why she had seemed so turned off the day they first met or why she still seemed so stand-offish.

About halfway through his skimpy meal, Craig heard balls bouncing off the garage door. He quickly swallowed the rest of his beer, put his half-eaten sandwich in the refrigerator, and hurried down the garage stairs. He watched the boys a couple of minutes, each seemingly determined to beat the other.

"Hi, guys," he called out. "How about joining you for a few shots?"

Both boys stopped in their tracks and stared up at him. "Look, I really need the exercise, and I've got some moves, if I do say so myself."

Craig had seemed so distant the past few days they couldn't imagine him wanting to join them. He had introduced himself the first time he saw them after he moved in; otherwise they had said little to each other except in an occasional greeting. David found his voice first. "Sure, come on. But I'm pretty good, too. Think you can handle it?" he asked while expertly dribbling the ball down the driveway toward the hoop.

Craig smiled at the boy's bragging and deftly sidled over and quickly stole the ball, making a basket on his first throw. His mouth open, David stared belligerently at Craig. Phillip snickered but quickly swallowed his laughter when David threw his brother a dirty look.

Phillip, however, was not the least bit intimidated and continued to grin, glancing sideways at Craig, who nonchalantly ran under the hoop and captured the ball. He threw it in David's direction, but Phillip intercepted it and made a quick basket before David recovered his former aplomb. Not to be outdone, David rushed under the hoop and retrieved the ball, swung around, and dunked it with a flourish. Phillip jumped for the ball and threw it back to Craig.

"Not bad, kid," Craig encouraged David as he dribbled the ball in place. "You must practice a lot, or else you're just a natural."

Phillip put his two cents in. "Most of the time David's just lucky."

David threw a derisive stare in his brother's direction and totally ignored Craig, who, he thought, really wasn't that much competition. He hadn't yet decided whether he liked the guy or not. He surely didn't like the way Craig's eyes followed his mother whenever she was around.

After a few more minutes of playing, Craig knew he'd had enough though the two young boys hardly seemed winded. Tired and sweaty, he finally collapsed on the lawn, acknowledging to himself that he was a little out of shape to compete with two athletic teenagers.

"That's enough for me this evening, guys." Craig wiped his face with the tail of his sweat shirt.

"A little out of shape, huh, old man?"

David's sly grin was not lost on Craig. He wondered why David seemed to be rather antagonistic toward him.

Craig watched for a few more minutes as the boys continued to compete before he went back to his studio. He got the rest of his sandwich and another beer out of the refrigerator before returning to the material he had to finish reading before calling it a night.

A couple of hours later Craig decided he'd worked long enough. Getting up from his desk, he stretched his arms toward the ceiling, letting out a loud yawn. Maybe he'd sleep better if he went for a walk. Throwing a sweater around his shoulders, he hurried down the stairs. While locking the garage door, he couldn't make up his mind whether he wanted to go for a walk or to relax in a chair in the backyard for a while.

The backyard won out and he walked across the lawn to let himself in through the side gate. He lowered himself into a long lounge chair and adjusted the reclining back. Stretching out his long legs, he drew in a deep breath of the still night air, noticing that the fog was barely discernible, rather unusual for a San Francisco night.

A soft, cool breeze swirled around him and he lay back, enjoying the quietness of the early night, broken only by the occasional noise of a couple of crickets somewhere near him. He had been staring up at the few clouds floating across the star-studded sky for several minutes when he heard a door open and footsteps padding across the patio. Turning in that direction, he made out the form of his landlady in the darkness. His heart suddenly skipped a beat at the sight of her. How lucky could he be, he wondered as he sat up a bit straighter in his lounge chair, anticipating talking with her again.

Disappointment set in, however, when he saw she was only putting a small bag of trash in a can at the far side of the patio and did not look in his direction before returning to the kitchen and closing the door behind her. He heard the lock slide into place and watched as the lights in the kitchen went out. He let his breath out slowly, hardly realizing that he'd been holding it for several seconds.

Later, climbing the stairs to his quarters, Craig berated himself that he hadn't had enough nerve to call out to her.

CHAPTER THREE

Shanna hummed a tuneless melody while straightening up the kitchen. David and Phillip were in their rooms finishing their homework. The dishwasher's usual thump-thump-thump vied with her humming while sending out its lemony smell of steamy detergent. Another sound caught Shanna's attention.

Her next door neighbor, Angela Montgomery, called out. "Yoo-hoo, Shanna, it's Angela. Unlock the screen door."

Shanna and Angela had been close friends for several years. Angela had helped Shanna get over the shock of her husband walking out on her. She also had baby-sat David and Phillip many times when they were younger. Their husbands had once been friends, but their friendship cooled when Shanna's husband left her to marry his blond secretary.

Shanna unlocked the screen. She knew Angela was up to something the moment she marched into the kitchen and plopped down in a chair at the table without so much as a greeting. Looking at her well-dressed, attractive friend, Shanna saw that Angela had not changed from her office clothes. She was still in a designer's lavender silk suit over a purple, round-necked blouse and gold necklace that accented her dark brown

complexion. Her gold drop earrings matched her necklace. Her makeup highlighted her dark eyes and high
cheekbones.

Angela sat with crossed legs, slowly swinging one
high-heeled black patent pump...back and forth...back
and forth ... while looking out of the corner of her eye at
Shanna.

Shanna waited, thinking Angela must have found out
about Craig living in the studio.

"So..." Angela finally began. "What in the world are
you up to, girl? Who is that gorgeous hunk I see coming
and going from here in a gray Mercedes?"

Shanna pulled her hair back from her face and
reached in her pocket for a rubber band to hold it in
place. Ignoring Angela's questions, she smiled and
asked, "Would you like a cup of tea, Angela?" Not waiting for an answer, she walked to the stove to put on the
tea kettle. She took her time to gather the cups, saucers,
and cinnamon apple tea bags, Angela's favorite. For
some reason—one which she couldn't really identify or
justify—she didn't want to discuss Craig with anyone, not
even Angela.

"Yes, girlfriend, I'll take some tea if it doesn't take you
all day to fix it," Angela replied.

Shanna ignored Angela's sarcastic remark.

"And you haven't answered my question, Shanna.
Who is that guy I see traipsing around the yard and
what's he doing here? You know how I worry about you."
Angela tapped her long manicured red nails on the table,
a sure sign of her agitation.

"Oh, cool it, Angela. The man has a perfect right to
be here; he's renting the studio above the garage...and
his name's Craig Boyd, by the way."

Shanna brought the two cups of fragrant tea to the
table and deposited one in front of Angela, who immediately reached for the sugar bowl and put two heaping

teaspoons into her tea.

"You really believe in having tea with your sugar, don't you?" Shanna teased as she took a sip from her own cup.

Angela added another spoon of sugar and got back to her point. "You mean that hunk is living here? When did all this happen?" Angela's large black eyes grew larger as if she couldn't believe what she'd just heard.

Shanna drew a deep breath. She'd known all along that she'd have to deal with Angela sooner or later. "Drink your tea before it gets cold, and I'll tell you, Angela."

Shanna leaned back in her chair and took another sip of tea. "You know I've been strapped for money and trying to find ways to increase my cash flow the last few months. The only solution I could come up with is renting the studio, and I—"

Angela interrupted. "Did you have to choose a guy to live here that looks like that, girlfriend?" she asked, giving Shanna a you-must-be-crazy look. "Why couldn't you have gotten a woman to take the place? What do the boys think about that guy?"

"Well, to answer your first question, Angela, I asked Rick to help me find someone, expecting Rick's recommendation to be a woman. But when Craig showed up and really wanted the place, I didn't have the heart to deny him. He was living in a downtown hotel before he moved here. Felt too cooped there and wanted a place where he could feel a little more at home, and he—"

"Well, the guy certainly seems to be making himself at home here," Angela threw out to her friend. "I saw him shooting baskets with David and Phillip, and they all appeared to be having a rippin' good time."

"So you've answered your second question. At first both boys seemed to like having him around, but recently I've noticed that David seems to resent him." Shanna drew a deep breath. "Why David feels like that, I don't know, but I've seen him look at Craig in a peculiar way when he thinks Craig doesn't see him. But Phillip seems to get along great with Craig. Neither of the boys has said much else about him except that he's a 'neat guy'— whatever that means—and gives them a run for their money with the basketball, even though they think he's almost over the hill when it comes to age."

Angela circled the rim of her cup with her finger several times before she asked what was really on her mind. "Is he married?"

Shanna tried to suppress the smile that threatened to form on her lips. "I was wondering when you'd get around to asking that, Angela. Whether he was married or not didn't cross my mind when I rented him the studio. But since then I've learned he's been married, now divorced. Seems his former wife got custody of their son after the divorce and returned to her family on the East Coast."

"Did Craig tell you all that?" Angela looked askance at Shanna.

"Of course not, Angela, Rick told me—he's known Craig a long time. I guess Rick felt he owed me some explanation since he's the one who recommended the studio to Craig. Rick also said Craig has almost become a hermit since his divorce, seems he has no interest in meeting people, especially women."

Perplexed, Angela asked, "How does Rick know that, Shanna?"

Shanna sighed. Angela always wanted to know all the details! "Rick's wife has been trying to hook Craig up with some of her single friends since he's been here, but he refuses to go along with her match-making."

"Hmmm...so you and Craig are alike in that respect. You don't have an interest in men, and he doesn't want to have any thing to do with women. A very interesting

set-up, it seems to me," Angela observed slyly as she finished the last of her tea and walked over to the sink to
deposit her cup and saucer. "At least now I won't have
to worry about you. Thanks for the tea. I've got to go.
Clifton will be pulling in shortly, and I've got to throw
something together for dinner. She headed out the back
door, leaving Shanna to wonder about Angela's "worry
about you" remark.

Why would Angela even think she needed worrying
about? In the years since her divorce she'd learned
many ways to discourage unwanted advances from men.
She knew from experience there were plenty of brothers
who were perfectly willing to sleep with women, but
commitment wasn't in their vocabularies. She wasn't
interested in just having sex, regardless of a guy's physical appeal. Not that she even suspected that Craig
would show any interest in her. That was probably the
least of her concerns. He hadn't a clue that she always
got butterflies in her stomach whenever he was around.
She intended to keep that secret to herself.

Shanna finished preparations for the next day's dinner, put the casserole in the refrigerator and walked
down the hallway to turn off the lights in the living room,
a room that she had redecorated to suit her own tastes
soon after she married. She walked to the center of the
room and glanced around, enjoying the ambiance she
had created. Everything in the room was beautifully and
elegantly done, from the off-white walls to the pale gray
carpeting.

Deep pale pink chairs sat on each side of the wide
fireplace. Behind the chairs, built-in shelving housed
books and magazines and photos. A long white sofa with
wide, matching chairs faced the bookshelves. A long
glass-topped coffee table in front of the sofa held various
knickknacks and magazines. Everywhere splashes of
color provided a contrast in the fluffy pillows. Purple,

dark rose, and emerald green ones in various shapes
and sizes were thrown casually on the sofa and chairs.
Gold-trimmed tables held brass and crystal lamps and
small potted plants. Large green-growing plants filling
the air with their scents were placed strategically in the
room. She gave one last glance around the room she
had created and loved. Not a trace of Paul was anywhere in this room.

Shanna turned off the lights in the living room and
walked into the television room to straighten it up before
she went upstairs to check on the boys and their homework. Turning off the rest of the lights downstairs, she
climbed the stairs slowly, feeling a bit out of sorts but
having no clue as to why—unless it was her conversation
with Angela. She managed to put a smile on her face
before she knocked loudly on David's door. She heard
his television set going full blast.

"Come on in, Mom." Before she could ask, David
reached across his desk for the remote control to turn
down the volume. "Yes, I've finished my homework.
Want to check it?"

"Not unless you had a problem with it and want me to
look it over," she informed him. "Anything else?" David
shook his head. "Well, goodnight and turn off the television before you fall asleep." She placed a light kiss on
his cheek. "See you in the morning."

Shanna heard David's muffled "goodnight" as she
went out the door to check on Phillip. She found him in
his pajamas, curled up in bed and sound asleep while the
television played to a silent room. She turned off the television and walked across the room to his bed. She
tucked him in, kissing his cheek and pulling the blanket
up over him. He stirred slightly, but didn't awaken. She
rubbed his cheek lovingly before leaving his room, thinking how lucky she was to have two healthy boys as she

closed his door softly.

She walked down the hall to her own large mauve and white room. She glanced around at what she considered her haven, a place where she found comfort when the rest of her world went haywire. A chaise longue covered in deep purple to match the purple geometric figures of her bedspread sat near the front window. The white and gold-trimmed vanity, chest of drawers and night stands had been hers before she married and they still looked good. It was such a pleasant room now that she had it all to herself.

She picked up the remote control from her nightstand and switched through several TV channels, hoping to find a favorite old movie. Having no luck, she turned off the set and settled down in her favorite spot—her chaise longue—and picked up a mystery novel she'd been reading the last several nights. Though she was at a crucial spot in the book, she couldn't keep her mind on the plot and finally tossed it aside and threw a sweater across her shoulders, thinking the night air might help settle her down before she went to bed. She padded down the stairs and out the back door, intending to sit in the backyard for a while. She had almost reached one of the patio chairs when she uttered a soft cry and clamped her hand over her mouth. Someone was sitting there!

Craig saw her at almost the same moment he heard her muffled cry and rose to his feet. "It's me—Craig. I just came down for some air. It's a great night. Hope you don't mind," he added, almost apologetically. "Didn't mean to scare you."

Shanna walked closer when she recognized Craig. "You did give me a start for a moment. I just didn't expect to find anyone out here." For some reason though, she suddenly found comfort in his presence. "And, of course, I don't mind. Feel free to come down here any time you want," she added, lowering herself into a nearby chair.

They sat in silence for a few moments before both started to speak at the same time.

"This breeze is—" he started.

"The air feels like—"

Both burst out laughing at their attempted conversation and returned to silence. But both felt that a barrier between them had suddenly disappeared.

Each was very aware of how the other's presence somehow made the night more meaningful...the stars seemed to twinkle faster ...the moon shine brighter...the cool breeze blow warmer.

Shanna finally broke the silence again and turned toward him. "Rick tells me you're quite comfortable in the studio, and that you like shooting baskets with David and Phillip."

Craig stirred uncomfortably. What else had Rick told Shanna? Craig distinctly remembered telling Rick that he found Shanna very attractive and had asked where the boys' father lived. Surely Rick had not repeated that to her!

"You have two great kids. I'm sure it hasn't been easy raising them by yourself the last few years."

"Oh, the boys and I have had our ups and downs. Most of the time the boys are great to have around. I truly enjoy them. One-parent families are quite common nowadays, so I don't feel like I'm the only woman in this kind of situation." Her voice carried a tinge of defiance as if she dared him to disagree.

As far as Craig was concerned, she had put an end to that topic. He breathed in the fragrant night air deeply before he spoke again. "By the way, David and Phillip insist on showing me Fisherman's Wharf on Saturday. They couldn't believe I haven't been down there yet."

"Oh, is this your first time in San Francisco?" For some reason or other, she imagined he was probably very familiar with the area.

"Yes, and I was very excited when I found out I was coming here. I've heard a lot about the city from my friends, but until now I haven't had an inclination to explore on my own. So the boys' offer was right down my alley."

Craig noticed Shanna's silence. He hesitated before speaking again. "You don't mind if they spend the day with me, do you?"

"Of course not."

Craig hesitated before speaking again. "Or better still, if you're not going to be busy, why don't you come along with us?"

Shanna almost fell out of her lounge chair when she heard Craig's invitation...and suddenly she became tongue-tied. You're being idiotic, girl, she scolded herself. A few moments passed before she spoke.

Craig waited with in-drawn breath for her reply.

Twisting around in her chair, Shanna spoke hesitatingly. "At the moment...I ...I don't think I can make it. But the boys will be good guides. Fisherman's Wharf is one of their favorite spots. They would spend every weekend down there if they had their way."

Craig was glad it was dark. He was sure his disappointment at her answer was showing on his face. He hesitated a few moments before he spoke again. "Well, maybe you could show me some other tourist spots—grown-up ones—when you have some time."

It was now Shanna's turn to be glad Craig could not see her face when she felt the warmth spreading from her neck up to her cheeks. She suddenly felt all tingly inside. She would have to think about his suggestion. Noncommittally, she answered, "Perhaps you'll meet others who would be happy to show you some of the hot spots. I seldom go places that I cannot take the boys."

In the back of her head was the mind-boggling thought that it might be very interesting to show Craig anything

he hadn't seen. But she knew she should end the conversation before she made a fool of herself. Being
around him was getting to be a bit much for her to deal
with. She slowly rose from her chair.   "I think I'll call it
a night," she murmured, getting up from her lounge chair.
She headed for the kitchen door.

"I'm going to stay out here a while longer," Craig
called after her, sorry to see her leave and wondering
why he felt that way. Damn. Every time she was around,
he forgot all about not wanting a woman in his life. So
what was it with her? Maybe she seemed such a stand-
offish woman because she needed no one else in her life
either. She seemed to have complete control of her life
as well as the lives of her boys.

Thinking of Shanna's sons, Craig suddenly realized
he was actually looking forward to spending Saturday on
the Wharf with them. Maybe he could knock that chip off
David's shoulder. On the other hand, being with them
would make him remember how little time he'd spent with
his own son. But at the moment that was a situation over
which he had little control, and he refused to dwell on it
until he could find a way to change the circumstances.
His ex-wife called all the shots where their son was concerned, and there was nothing he could do about it at the
moment. He hoped he could keep up with all the energy
David and Phillip usually put into whatever they did.

Taking several breaths of the cool night air, Craig rose
and returned to his studio, hoping the short time outside
would help him get to sleep without thinking too much
about Shanna. What rotten luck! The one woman in all
of San Francisco he felt drawn to wanted no part of him.

Craig had no way of knowing Shanna was also at
odds with her feelings.

Shanna climbed the stairs and checked both of her
boys' rooms before going to her own. After undressing
slowly and hanging up each piece of clothing, she made

her way to the bathroom. She stopped at the cabinet above the sink. Studying her reflection in the mirror for several moments, she saw that her face was still flushed, much to her dismay. She removed her makeup and creamed her face with the moisturizer that was a daily part of her toilette.

After brushing her teeth, Shanna again gazed intently in the mirror. She stared at her wide-set dark eyes, leaning closer to check for any wrinkles. Who knew when wrinkles might appear as one approached her mid-thirties. Not seeing any sign of wrinkles around her eyes, she stared at her high cheek bones and generously curved mouth. Her eyes traveled to her long, smooth neck which also seemed to still be firm.

Everything considered, she decided she looked just like the person she was—a working mother of teenage boys who had little time or interest to spend on her own appearance. So why was she suddenly concerned about the way she looked? Refusing to even think about an answer, she padded back to the bedroom and pulled her short nightshirt over her head.

Ignoring her half-read novel, Shanna climbed in between cool sheets and pulled the blanket up to her chin with a happy sigh, thinking of the short conversation she'd just had with her roomer.

CHAPTER FOUR

Shanna awakened slowly early Saturday morning when the warm rays of the sun slanted across her bed. She rolled over to the side of the bed and sat there a few moments, stretching and yawning. She rose, walked over to the window and opened the half-closed shades. Not a trace of fog hung over San Francisco Bay, rather unreal for such an early hour. She wished the fog in her head would dissipate so easily.

Shanna again vacillated about going to Fisherman's Wharf with the boys and Craig. Do I really want to be near Craig all day and have those vibes every time I look at him? What's wrong with me? Have I completely lost my cool? Best to let sleeping dogs lie would probably be her mother's way of handling the situation. She halfway agreed and decided to definitely stay home.

Turning away from the window, Shanna walked over to get her robe. She made her way to the kitchen, careful not to awaken her boys so early. She measured the coffee and water, dumping both into the coffeemaker. While it brewed, she showered, threw on a pair of old white short shorts and an oversized turquoise shirt. Returning to the kitchen, she poured a large mug of the hot coffee and took it out to the front porch, retrieving the

morning paper from the shrubbery where it usually landed and taking it back to her lounge chair. Sipping her
coffee slowly, she leaned back and enjoyed the serenity
of the early morning.

A couple walking their dog waved to her. Three
teenagers jogged by and threw up their hands. She
basked in the peacefulness that surrounded her.
Looking out over the bay, she saw only one small sail-
boat out in the water, but in the part of the marina she
could see from her porch, several people were on their
docked boats, evidently readying for an early sail. For
several minutes she became engrossed in the scene in
front of her before opening her paper. Then she heard
David's and Phillip's footsteps in the hallway, signaling
the end of her quiet moments. Softly sighing, Shanna
threw aside the paper and went into the hallway. "So,
why are you two up so early? I usually have to drag you
out of bed on Saturday morning."

David and Phillip glanced at each other.

"Have you forgotten we're going with Mr. Boyd this
morning, Mom?" Phillip asked. "How could you forget
that?"

Shanna smiled. Of course she remembered. She
actually wanted more than anything to be near Craig for
a few hours but was afraid of the consequences his
nearness had on her. She gave each son a peck on the
cheek, and they followed her to the kitchen. She knew
the only other thing on their minds at the moment was
their Saturday morning breakfast, which was a large one
compared to the fruit, cereal and toast they had during
the week.

"So what do you two want this morning—pancakes or
waffles?" She opened the refrigerator to get the orange
juice, bacon and eggs from the shelf and set the orange
juice container on the table. "Pour your juice while you're
making up your minds."

"Waffles," Phillip decided.

"Pancakes," David said at almost the same moment. He scowled at Phillip. "We had waffles last Saturday, Phillip. Why can't we have pancakes today, Mom?"

"Pancakes seem to be a reasonable compromise, don't you think, Phillip?" she asked.

Phillip reluctantly agreed. "I guess so. Pancakes are okay. Just remember it's waffles next Saturday, David."

The boys helped themselves to another glass of orange juice while waiting.

The smell of bacon filled the kitchen, and Shanna soon had their breakfast on their plates. She sat down to enjoy her own food and her boys.

Halfway through the meal, David abruptly put down his fork and looked at his mother. "Why don't you want to go with us to the Wharf today? Mr. Boyd said you should—"

Shanna did not wait for David to finish. "There are some things I want to take care of today, David. You two can show him around." She dropped her head to escape the looks of the boys, not wanting them to see the flush on her cheeks at the mention of Craig.

"Aw, Mom, it won't be the same without you," Phillip put his two-cents in. "You always go with us."

Shanna stared at the two in amazement. They really wanted her to go. But what about Craig being there? She really couldn't spend most of the day in his company. A light bulb went off in her head. "How about having a picnic supper ready for all of you when you return?"

"Hey, that sounds good, doesn't it, Phillip?" David was eager to get started and rose from his chair. Phillip followed.

"Hold it, guys. What about your rooms? Beds made?"

"I thought the Emancipation Proclamation was signed in 1863," David slyly slipped in.

"It was. So you could stop making others' beds and make your own," Shanna retorted.

Not to be outdone, David announced, "That's why we went West and became Buffalo Soldiers. Who makes beds on the trail?"

"No," said thoughtful Phillip. "That was the white man sending the black man to fight the red man."

"Like in Vietnam. Only they were yellow," David added.

"Less history. More beds," Shanna chided, trying hard not to laugh.

The ploy not working, David and Phillip trudged back upstairs.

Finally, Shanna could laugh aloud while she cleared the dishes from the table, rinsed them and stacked them in the dishwasher. She walked into the laundry room to gather up the week's dirty clothes.

The first load of clothes were in the washer when she heard the chimes of the front door. Looking at her watch, she knew it was Craig coming for the boys. Before she could get to the door, David and Phillip rushed past and swung it open.

"Hi, Mr. Boyd. Come on in," Phillip invited.

"We've been waiting for you," David added.

Shanna walked out and watched Craig "hi-five" both boys.

"Okay, then let's go." Craig spied Shanna in the hallway. "Sure you don't want to come with us?"

"Not this time. But I promised the boys I'd have some food waiting when they get back. You're welcome to join us."

Craig brightened at Shanna's invitation. "That would be great. Want us to pick up anything while we're out?"

"No...on Saturday we usually just have some hot dogs or hamburgers and whatever else I can find in the refrigerator. It's my day off from really cooking."

Disarmingly aware of her skimpy shorts, Shanna
noticed Craig staring at her bare legs.

Unknown to either of the adults, David noticed the
focal point of Craig's eyes and turned away before Craig
could see the animosity on his face.

Craig raised his eyes to Shanna's face, feeling a
warmth steal over his forehead. He wondered whether
men actually blushed. Whatever it was, he knew it made
him feel uncomfortable. He couldn't understand why she
affected him in that way whenever he was near her. It's
probably best she isn't going to be around for several
hours, he thought as he turned his attention back to the
boys.

"Let's go, guys," Craig said in what he hoped was a
normal tone of voice. He was still rattled by Shanna's
long legs.

Craig waited until David and Phillip pecked their
mother on the cheek before heading out to his car.
Shanna followed them out to the driveway.

"All three of us can sit in the front," Craig announced,
hoping to prevent any argument about who was sitting
where.

"But I got shot gun," claimed David.

"Yeah. You're always shooting your mouth off,"
Phillip teased.

Shanna smiled at Craig's foiled wisdom. She stayed
in the yard until they all buckled in and Craig drove out of
the driveway before she returned to the house. As she
walked through the hallway to the laundry room, the
house seemed...empty. The washer had stopped and
she transferred the load to the dryer. Soon the fragrant
scent of Bounce filled the small room.

Anticipating Craig at their cookout, Shanna ran the
sweeper in the television room, dusted in the living room
and TV room, and watered the plants in all of the rooms.
Finishing that, she found her laundry was ready to be

folded. Taking her time, she hoped the day would pass quickly. She finished everything she could think of and decided to take a short nap. Maybe the house wouldn't seem so quiet if she were asleep.

Even with her long nap, Shanna thought the afternoon would never end. At last it was time to start the fire in the barbecue pit. She gathered the charcoal and lighter fluid and soon had the fire going. Glancing at the clock when she returned to the kitchen, she saw it was time to shower and she hurried up the stairs.

Quickly shedding her clothes, she padded into the bathroom, fitted her shower cap on securely, and turned on the water full force. Stepping under the shower head, she stood in one spot for several moments, enjoying the hot water pelting against her skin. She reached for her sponge and soaped her body for several minutes before rinsing off and stepping out of the shower. Wrapping herself in a long fluffy towel, she removed her shower cap and fluffed out her hair.

She looked through her closet and drew out a green short set and beige sandals. She was dressed in minutes. After giving her eyelashes a swipe with her mascara brush, she applied her favorite tangerine lipstick.

Humming along with the radio, she glanced in the mirror, deciding she looked okay. She hurried down to the patio to check the coals in the grill, hoping Craig and the boys were on their way home. Or was she mostly looking forward to having Craig join them? She refused to answer her own question.

✿

Early in the evening Shanna heard Craig's car pull into the driveway. The sun was low on the horizon and a faint cool breeze, typical of most San Francisco evenings, stirred the air. Checking the barbecue pit again, she saw the coals were glowing red, just right for the hot dogs and hamburgers. She hurried to the kitchen to gather up the tray of meat, foil-wrapped corn, and utensils.

Craig, David and Phillip entered the house, all three talking at once as they walked through the hallway on their way to the kitchen.

Shanna saw Craig and immediately put her hands to her face, hoping to stifle the laughter bubbling in her throat. Craig looked as if he'd just finished a fifty-mile hike! Sinking down into the nearest chair, he wiped his forehead with the back of his hand.

David and Phillip said "Hi" and continued on through the kitchen to the back yard.

"What in the world happened to you, Craig?"

"I'm really getting too old to even think I can keep up with teenagers," Craig complained. "The guys really put me through the hoops today. How do you keep up with them?"

"You just have to learn to say 'no' to some things," Shanna advised, still smiling at Craig's discomfort. "The food won't be ready for a few minutes if you want to wash up. There's a powder room next to the laundry if you don't want to go to your place."

"I'll take you up on that. I may not get back down if I go upstairs," Craig grumbled. He rose slowly and followed her directions.

By the time Craig walked out to the back yard, he found the grill covered with food. The table was spread with paper plates and paper cups as well as plastic knives and forks and paper napkins. He surveyed the scene. "Now this is my kind of way to spend a Saturday evening." He sauntered over to the grill. "Want some help, Shanna?" He noticed, however, that she had everything under control.

Phillip sidled over to Craig. "Want to shoot some baskets while we're waiting, Mr. Boyd?"

Phillip was rewarded with a loud groan from Craig.

"Where do you two get so much energy? I'm about to keel over and you ask about shooting baskets. No way!" Craig stated emphatically before he dropped down into a lounge chair. "In fact, the way I feel now I may never be able to shoot another basket in my life," he added, winking at Phillip.

"That'll be the day." David would not be left out.

The three gave Shanna an overview of their day, intermittently interrupting each other.

Listening to the three of them, laughing at some of their exaggerations, especially Craig's, she decided it was good that she hadn't been along with them. They evidently had developed a kind of camaraderie that might not have occurred had she been present. Even David seemed a little more at ease with Craig.

Shanna gazed at Phillip and David. The boys probably missed the companionship and guidance of a man, something she couldn't give them. That thought created a sadness that settled over her while she continued to turn the hamburgers and hot dogs.

"Isn't the stuff about ready? I'm starved," Philip complained, getting up and going to stand beside his mother while he checked the grill.

"Didn't you have lunch?" Shanna ruffled his hair, something he hated but silently tolerated. He immediately ran his hand over his head to smooth his hair back in place.

"I don't see how either of them could be so hungry. We finished off one of the biggest pizzas I've ever seen," Craig interjected. "You wouldn't believe the kind they ordered... mushrooms, black olives, onions, pepperoni, anchovies, extra cheese. I don't remember what else. And I lost count of the sodas they drank. Food must travel clear down to their toes. No normal stomachs can hold what they consumed."

"That's par for the course." She surveyed the grill.

"Everything is ready. Come and get it. I'll get the salad and drinks while you three fill your plates."

They all concentrated on their food for the next several minutes, saying little.

Finally Craig sat back, rubbing his stomach. "Now that's my kind of meal. I'm really stuffed." He turned to Shanna. "The next time maybe you'll let me do the barbecuing. It's one of the few things I can do with food."

David and Phillip rose and started to clean up, their job when Shanna barbecued.

Craig interrupted them. "You guys go on and practice your shots. I'll help your mother out here."

The boys disappeared from the backyard the instant Craig spoke.

Darkness settled in before everything was packed on the table and the fire doused.

On cue, David and Phillip appeared. "We're going inside to watch a movie, Mom." Turning to David, he announced, "And it's my turn to choose the video." They raced inside to the television room.

Shanna and Craig carried everything inside and quickly finished clearing the kitchen. Not wanting the evening to end, Shanna suggested, "Let's sit outside for a while."

Craig enthusiastically agreed and followed Shanna out to the patio.

Shanna sank down into a chair beside Craig and glanced over at him. "You know, sometimes I get tired just watching David and Phillip expend so much energy, so I can empathize with you about your visit to the Wharf. They didn't impose on you, did they?"

Craig shook his head. "To tell you the truth, I didn't realize how pooped I was until we got in the car to come home. That's when it hit me." For several moments he silently gazed into the darkness that surrounded them.

Shanna noticed a slight frown on Craig's forehead.

"You seem so far away. Is something bothering you?"

Craig sat up with a start and rubbed the back of his hand across his forehead. "What do you mean?"

"You seem so out of it."

"Oh...well...it's really nothing important, but..." Craig hesitated. He couldn't find the exact words to tell her what was bothering him. He thought about the couple of times during the day he'd noticed David looking at him with something akin to hostility in his eyes. Yet at other times David had been just as enthusiastic as Phillip in deciding what to do next. Maybe he'd just keep his thoughts to himself for the moment. No use worrying her about something he felt rather than knew.

Shanna waited, growing a little uneasy. Maybe he'd had a problem with the boys, even though she hadn't noticed any strain between them when they came home. She twisted around in her chair to face him.

"Well...ah, I was wondering..." Craig hesitated again, noticing Shanna playing with her hair. He was unsure whether he should mention other concerns he had about her boys. Because he really wanted to know, he decided to take a chance she would understand he wasn't meddling. "It's certainly none of my business, Shanna, but I was wondering about the boys' father. Do they ever see him?"

Even though Shanna hadn't expected that question, she answered very calmly. "Occasionally. Whenever Paul—that's his name—has the time, he will take them for a day or for the weekend. We have joint custody, but we don't have any set visitation times. So far it's worked out rather well, as far as I know. The only complaint I've heard from the boys is that Paul doesn't spend enough time with them when they're with him. Seems he lets his wife have the responsibility of planning things for them, and..." Her voice trailed off. Why is Craig taking this inquisitive interest in David and Phillip? she wondered.

Craig peered out into the night for several moments before he uttered a low, "Ummm."

Shanna waited.

Craig remained silent.

"What do you mean by 'Ummm'? Was there a problem today, Craig?" Shanna finally asked.

Craig assured her without hesitation, "Oh, no. No problems. But they did ask some...uh...rather interesting questions in round-about ways, especially David. He's fourteen going on fifteen now, isn't he? And that's a very difficult age for a boy."

Shanna knew what Craig said was oh, so true. She had spent many nights in the past questioning whether she could fulfill all the needs of her sons, especially David's since he was maturing so fast. Maybe she should insist that their father take a more active role in their lives. But how could she force that on a man not interested enough to talk to his sons on his own?

Seeing various emotions flitting across Shanna's face, Craig questioned whether he had trod on dangerous territory. After all, she probably had everything under control. Who was he to offer advice when he had failed in his marriage and had so little contact with his own son?

To make amends for his meddling, Craig insisted softly, "I really didn't mean to be critical, Shanna."

Shanna accepted Craig's half apology. "I didn't take it as a personal affront, Craig."

Craig shifted around in his chair a couple of times. "It's just that I...I overheard a couple remarks the boys made to each other, and I—"

Shanna held up her hand to stop him. Maybe he would understand her boys better if he knew something of the circumstances surrounding their father's leaving. She studied her hands a few moments, remembering how devastated she had been when she learned first-hand of her husband's infidelity. Her dark eyes glistened with unshed tears.

"You might as well know the whole story, Craig, since you'll probably hear many versions if you're around here long enough." She took a deep breath, exhaling slowly. "The bottom line is that I caught Paul and his blond-haired secretary in the act—right here in San Francisco in a motel not too far from here." She stopped speaking when she saw a look of disbelief cross his face.

"You've got to be kidding!" Craig exploded. "How did...you ...you know...find out about that?"

"Well, some of our so-called friends hinted on several occasions that something was going on between Paul and his secretary, but I just ignored the rumors, hoping they weren't true—or maybe not wanting them to be true."

Shanna leaned back against her lounge chair and stared up at the sky for a few moments.

Craig waited, somehow sensing there was more Shanna wanted to get off her chest.

Shanna bit her bottom lip. "Then Paul developed a lot of late evening clients—or so he said when I questioned him about not coming home until late at night. Even the boys complained to their father that they seldom saw him, but that didn't seem to bother Paul. Well, a long story shortened, I got an anonymous phone call late one evening that Paul and his blond secretary had checked into this motel. So I drove down to check it out. And sure enough, after handsomely bribing one of the maids, I learned the truth that—"

"I can't imagine you doing that!" Craig exclaimed, looking at her in surprise. "You mean you...you actually went to the motel room they were in?"

Shanna smiled at Craig's question. Sometimes she also wondered how she'd had the nerve to pull that off. "That's exactly what I did! I knocked on their door and

acted like I was room service. You should have seen
Paul's face when he opened that door."

Craig's mouth dropped open. He wanted to say
something but couldn't get the words out. He finally stut-
tered, "That's... that's incredible!"

"It wasn't the end of the world, Craig. At the time I
guess I was glad I finally learned the truth. In fact, outwardly I was rather cool during the whole confrontation
even though I was breaking up inside. After giving Paul
a piece of my mind in a few choice words which I won't
repeat, I told him he better not bring his cheating butt
home that night if he wanted to keep it intact."

Craig swallowed a smile, visualizing Shanna in a situation like that. He couldn't stop himself from asking,
"So what did Paul say, Shanna?"

"Paul didn't have a chance to say much of anything
because as soon as I finished with him, I lit into the
blonde, threatening to do her bodily harm if you can
imagine that. When I finally walked out and slammed
that motel door, her face was as white as the sheet she
tried to cover herself with." Shanna stopped and smiled.
"It's kinda funny now, but at the time I was as scared as
hell...I still don't know how I ever had the nerve to pull off
something like that."

"Didn't you give Paul a chance to explain...or anything?"

"You've got to be kidding! Paul didn't come home
until I left for work the next morning. When I got home
after work, I found that almost everything he owned was
gone from the house. It was days before I heard from
him. And only then because he informed me he was filing for divorce."

"I...I really don't know what to say. Do the boys know
what happened?"

"No, I didn't tell them the details. All they know is that
their father left and married shortly afterward. I didn't

want to prejudice their feelings toward him. Maybe someday they'll find out the truth. It's just not important at the moment. Only my friend Angela, who lives next door, knows the whole truth."

She glanced over at Craig. "I only told you so you'd maybe understand why David and Phillip might make some off-the-wall remarks sometimes."

Craig was deeply touched. He was really getting into this family deeper than he intended, but for some reason he was happy that she had shared that information with him. "Thanks for telling me, Shanna, and I'm sorry you had to go through something like that. I...I know what it's like to be hurt by someone you have a lot of faith in."

Shanna did not miss the sadness in Craig's voice.

"Thanks for listening, Craig. I really didn't mean to unload on you," Shanna said pleasantly as she stood up. "I think I'll call it a night. I'm going in to check on the boys. More than likely they're both sound asleep on the floor in front of the television."

"I guess I'll stay out here for a while. Have a good night, Shanna."

Craig watched her stride across the patio and enter the house, wishing she had stayed with him a little longer. He now felt more drawn to her but couldn't pinpoint why. The night now seemed dreary.

Entering the television room, Shanna did find both boys sound asleep, the television blaring. She turned it off and awakened them to go to bed. Both boys rose and staggered up the stairs without any fuss.

"Be sure to brush your teeth before you get into bed," Shanna called after them before she went into her own bedroom. She felt happier than she had been in a long time.

❦

The insistent ringing of the telephone beside her bed awakened Shanna early Sunday morning. She reached over for the receiver and muttered a groggy, "Hello."

She bounced up straight in her bed. It was her ex-husband's voice. What in the world did he want so early in
the morning?

Not bothering to return Shanna's greeting, Paul
asked, "Are the boys up yet? I want to come by and get
them for the day."

"Why didn't you let me know that yesterday, Paul?
They're still asleep and I don't know what they plan to do
today." Paul was being his usual self, never thinking
how his actions might affect others. Exasperated, she
drew her hand across her forehead. It was always an
ordeal when she had to deal with her ex.

"Can't you at least ask them, Shanna? I'll hold on."

Shanna reluctantly laid the receiver down on her bed,
threw on a robe, and padded down the hall. He's just as
arrogant as ever, she thought, going into David's room.
Shaking him awake, she explained, "Your father is on the
line, David. He wants to pick up you and Phillip to spend
the day with him and his wife."

David rubbed his eyes with his fist, still half asleep.
"Why is he calling so early? The sun's not even out yet."

"I have no idea, David. Do you or don't you want to
go?"

David shifted around and threw his feet over the side
of the bed before he answered. "I...I guess so. Does
Phillip want to go?"

"I haven't asked him yet. He'll probably do whatever
you want to do. So shall I tell your father to come by?"

"Okay...but I sure wish Dad hadda called yesterday if
he wanted us," he said grumpily.

"I'll tell him you'll be ready in about an hour. Will you
wake up Philip for me while I finish with your father?"

Back in her bedroom, Shanna picked up the receiver. "They will be ready in about an hour," she informed
Paul in terse tones.

"Why so long?"

"They have to shower, dress, and have breakfast, Paul. And they can't do that in ten minutes."

"Tell them to just get dressed and we'll have breakfast on the way to my house. I'll be there in about thirty minutes."

Sighing loudly, Shanna resisted the urge to bang down the receiver. Instead, she went into the bathroom and splashed cold water on her face. Why do I always let that man upset me? She brushed her teeth and then rubbed some toner on her face before going downstairs to start her coffeemaker.

Exactly thirty minutes later Shanna heard Paul slam the door of his silver BMW.

Going to the bottom of the stairs, she called, "Guys, your father's here."

David and Phillip were downstairs by the time Paul rang the doorbell. David opened the door. "Hi, Dad. We're ready."

Paul remained on the porch. "Okay. Let's go."

Shanna joined them on the porch. She would have preferred not to face Paul so early in the morning. Noticing he was his usual handsome, debonair self, she felt more tacky than ever. She wasted no words. "What time will you bring them back, Paul?"

"Around eight, I guess. They'll have dinner with me, so don't bother to fix anything for them."

Shanna followed them across the lawn.

The boys gave their mother a quick peck on the cheek before climbing into the car and waved as Paul backed out of the driveway.

"See you this evening, Mom," Phillip called.

Shanna stayed on the lawn until Paul turned the corner. A sense of loneliness descended on her. She seldom experienced such a desolate feeling. She turned and slowly made her way back into the house, her head lowered and her arms crossed against her chest.

Craig was working at his desk facing the front window. He had observed the activities on the lawn and didn't miss the forlorn look on Shanna's face when she turned to go into the house. He wished he could think of something to make her feel better.

CHAPTER FIVE

A couple hours later, after cleaning out some drawers in her bedroom and straightening out the closets in the boys' room, Shanna wandered outside. She swept off the patio and rearranged the chairs. Unwinding the hose, she watered the back lawn and plants, then turned on the sprinklers for the front lawn.

Finishing those chores, she walked back into the house. Within minutes she felt the walls closing in on her. "I'm outta here," she said aloud. She rushed back upstairs, changed into her jogging suit and shoes, and grabbed her purse and car keys. By the time she unlocked her car door and climbed in, she knew she had made the right choice in getting out of the house. She sat in the driveway for a few moments before figuring out where to go. "That's it," she said aloud when she decided on Cliff House, one of her favorite spots that faced the Pacific Ocean.

Nearing her destination, Shanna saw the area was crowded with the ever-present tourists. Driving slowly to find a parking space, she saw a car pull out some distance from the Cliff House. She pulled into the space near a pier, shut off the motor, leaned back in the seat of the car, and stared out at the waves crashing against the shore. The Pacific Ocean always mesmerized her.

Looking out over the great of expanse of water, Shanna watched a large cargo ship crawling slowly toward the Golden Gate Bridge, evidently heavily loaded since it rode so low in the water. Nearer the shore, a few brave surfers riding the high waves caught her attention. She cringed when one of the surfers lost his surfboard. Soon the seagulls, constantly dipping and soaring over the deep blue water, snatched her attention.

Feeling a twitch in her empty stomach, Shanna checked her watch. It was the middle of the afternoon. She got out of her car and stretched her legs, happier than she'd been earlier. Then she started the car and headed home.

Craig had interrupted his work several times to check the driveway while Shanna was gone. The sad expression on her face he noticed earlier stayed on his mind. Maybe she needed to talk with someone. He slowly worked up enough nerve to ring her doorbell when she got back.

❧

Shanna felt a coolness in the house when she walked into the living room. She put some kindling under the logs already in the fireplace, threw in a match, and in a matter of minutes the logs crackled and sent sparks against the fire screen. She got her book from her bedroom and curled up in the corner of her couch with her nearly finished mystery novel. She read only a few pages before tossing the book aside, unable to keep her mind on the plot. Staring into the flames, she wondered how her boys were getting along with their father.

Shanna jumped when she heard the chimes of the doorbell. When she opened the door, she drew back, astonished. Craig stood in front of her, an embarrassed half-smile on his face.

A prickly feeling went up and down her spine. She was too aware of how gorgeous he looked in his designer jeans topped by a light blue polo shirt, the open collar showing a hint of the hair covering his chest. Craig looked deep into her eyes.

Shanna drew in her breath sharply before she managed a muffled, "Hello."

"I...uh...I thought you might like some company since the boys are gone," Craig stammered.

Shanna stared at him. How did he know the boys were not at home?

Craig picked up on her confusion. "Uh...I...I saw David and Phillip leave this morning with, I guess, their father. I was working at my desk when he drove up. That was their father who picked them up, wasn't it?"

So glad to see Craig standing in the doorway, Shanna's first impulse was to pull him inside and cover his face with warm kisses. Wait. What was she thinking? A flush rose to her cheeks.

Craig looked at the peculiar expression on Shanna's face. "You feel okay?"

Shanna shook her head to dispel her disturbing thoughts and finally found her voice. "Oh...please come in, and, yes, the boys' father picked them up to spend the day with him." She stepped aside.

Craig walked in and closed the door. He followed her into the living room.

Feeling a bit embarrassed when she noticed Craig staring at the fireplace, Shanna explained, "I have a thing about an open fire and usually light the logs whenever it's the least bit cool. One of the things I like about San Francisco is that it's seldom very warm this time of the year."

"It does make it very toasty in here," Craig acknowledged. "I like fireplaces, too." He walked over to the mantel and surveyed the rest of the room. "This is a lovely room—yet it looks lived in. A person could really feel at home here," he added, inhaling the pine scent from the burning logs.

Craig's remarks made Shanna feel warm inside. Suddenly the lonely feelings that had haunted her most of the day flew out of the window.

"Sit down, Craig," she said as she plopped down on the end of the couch, drawing her legs up under her.

Craig walked across the room and sat down in the middle of the couch behind the long glass-topped coffee table. He felt uncommonly tongue-tied. How would she react to the proposition he was about to make?

"Would...would you like a glass of wine, or a soda, or coffee?" Shanna asked in a rush of words.

"If you'll have a glass with me, I'll take the wine."

"Red or white?"

"I'll take the red."

Shanna jumped up and headed to the kitchen, glad to have a few minutes to compose herself. Damn! Why do I act like a ninny every time he's around?

Taking two crystal wine glasses from the cabinet, she poured some Cabernet Sauvignon into the glasses and set them on a tray with two napkins. Reaching to the top shelf, she retrieved a can of mixed nuts that the boys luckily hadn't found and dumped the nuts into a glass dish.

Depositing the tray on the coffee table, she handed a glass to him. Their hands touched as he took the glass from her. Both tried to ignore the electricity that again sparked between them. Shanna curled up at the far end of the sofa, again tucking her legs beneath her. She hoped the confusion she felt inside did not show on her face. Taking a long sip of her wine, she turned her gaze to the fireplace, too aware of Craig's body not far from hers.

Craig turned his attention to his wine glass, trying to keep his eyes off Shanna so cozily situated at the other end of the sofa.

Moments passed while they sipped their drinks.

Shanna wondered why he'd chosen to come down at that particular time.

Craig wondered what she would say to his invitation.

She racked her brain to think of something intelligent to say.

He took another sip and set his glass down on the coffee table.

Several moments passed before Craig got up enough nerve to tell Shanna why he was there. "Uh...Shanna, I'm going out to the Cliff House for dinner in a little while and...and I thought since you're not cooking dinner for the boys you...you might like to join me." His words tumbled out.

Totally disconcerted, Shanna tried to speak. But no words came out—her mind must have stopped functioning. She was too aware of his closeness, and the way he was smiling at her, his deep, husky voice sending an unfamiliar excitement through her body.

Craig waited for her reply, afraid that she might refuse. "I've heard a lot about the view from the Cliff House since I've been here. There's not much fog this afternoon. I thought today would be a good time to see it."

Shanna detected a slight pleading tone in his voice. How ironic. But she certainly wasn't going to tell him she was at the Cliff House earlier in the day.

Should she or shouldn't she go with him? What the heck, it was just a friendly thing to do. She unfolded her legs from beneath her and turned to face him, amazed at her calmness since her mind was in such turmoil. "That sounds like a good idea. I wasn't looking forward to eating alone today. What time do you want to go?"

"How about in an hour or so? I'd like to be there at sunset. I've been told it's really something out there."

"I'll be ready. Be sure to take a jacket or sweater.

The ocean breeze out there in the evening is really chilly."

Smiling broadly, Craig rose from the sofa. Everything was coming up roses, he thought as he prepared to leave.

Shanna followed him to the door.

Before he opened it, Craig turned back to her. "And thanks for agreeing to go."

Shanna nodded, closed the door softly behind him and headed up the stairs. The afternoon suddenly seemed much brighter. Walking on air, she made her way to her bedroom to change out of her jogging clothes.

Searching through her closet a few minutes, she selected her favorite gray pants and a red striped top. She laid them out on her bed and added lingerie. She rummaged through her shoes until she found some loafers that didn't need polishing and threw them to the foot of her bed.

Hurriedly shedding her clothes, Shanna padded into her bathroom to dump a couple scoops of Estee Lauder bubble bath into the tub before turning on the hot water full force. A fragrant steam soon filled the room. Wrapping a towel around her head to keep her hair from frizzing up from the steam, she slowly eased down into the tub, grimacing as her body adjusted to the steaming water. She closed her eyes and lay back against the tile wall for several minutes, enjoying the soothing feeling of the hot water. When the water grew cooler, she reached for her sponge to complete her bath.

She was putting the finishing touches on her sparse makeup when she heard the garage door close. She quickly sprayed Estee Lauder cologne on her wrists and hair. Gathering up her purse, sunglasses, and a heavy multicolored sweater, she raced down the stairs. She hadn't felt so exhilarated in many, many months. She refused to question the reason for her elation.

Craig saw Shanna locking her front door and walked around to her side of the car to open her door and help her in. He threw his jacket to the back seat as he climbed into the driver's seat. "Buckle up, and we're off," he said pleasantly.

Shanna struggled with her seat belt. "I can't get this thing fastened."

Craig reached across to help adjust the mechanism, his arm brushing against the side of her breast in the process. Even though accidental, Shanna felt both alarmed and embarrassed. His touch did strange things to her. She glanced up into his dark eyes which flickered for an instant in a surprised expression. She felt heat spreading across her face. No way did she want him to see the blush creeping up from her neck.

Craig took her hand and showed her where to make the belt connection on her left side. She quickly completed the process. Reaching into her purse for her sunglasses, she put them on and then leaned back against her seat, relieved that he was now not so near.

"You know how to get to the Cliff House?" she asked.

"I know the general direction. You're probably more familiar with any shortcuts we can take," he replied, retrieving his sunglasses from the dash. He fastened his own seat belt before glancing over his left shoulder to back out of the driveway.

Shanna explained the route she usually took, while very aware of how debonair he looked in dark-blue slacks and light-blue shirt, its collar open and cuffs folded back. She thought the color did wonders for his mahogany complexion.

Craig followed Shanna's directions, glancing at her surreptitiously several times while driving to their destination. They said little on the way.

Craig detected a controlled anxiety behind Shanna's outwardly calm facade. Her unconsciously fiddling with her purse was a dead giveaway. Smiling, he admitted to himself that he wasn't the coolest guy at the moment either. He was glad when they pulled into a parking space at Cliff House.

Before she got her seat belt unbuckled, Craig was out of the car and around to her side. He helped her out of her seat and kept his hand under her elbow as they walked toward the restaurant.

That unnerved her more. His touch was the last thing she needed. She took several deep breaths, trying to get her equilibrium back.

Cliff House was crowded with tourists, some eating, some shopping for souvenirs, and some just wandering in and out of the building. After waiting several minutes, they got a table by a window that overlooked Seal Rock and the Pacific Ocean. After only a short wait, a waitress brought their menus and a server filled their glasses with ice water. Shanna ordered her favorite meal—curried shrimp—and Craig decided to have the same.

After giving their orders, they became absorbed in the antics of the seals frolicking out on the huge jagged rock jutting out of the ocean not too far from the restaurant. Neither seemed very comfortable, yet neither broke their silence.

Out of the corner of her eye Shanna saw Craig glance in her direction several times.

Craig thought he hadn't seen her looking so ... so what? He couldn't put his finger on it.

"I could watch them for hours," Craig finally said, pointing to the seals. "This is a real peaceful place."

Shanna nodded in agreement, unable to get any words out. Why does this man have such an almost overwhelming effect on me? she asked herself.

"No wonder my friends said I had to see this place," Craig added, thinking she evidently was as absorbed in their surroundings as he was since she was so quiet.

Both were relieved when the waiter brought hot rolls and butter and their large salads, which they dived into as soon as the waiter left.

At least this is something to do, Craig thought as he lifted a forkful of the salad, especially since he also seemed to have lost the art of polite conversation. He looked across the table and saw she was also devoting all of her attention to her salad.

Finally laying aside his fork, Craig broke their silence. "I'm glad you agreed to come with me today, Shanna. Sundays are usually such long, blah days for me when I haven't brought home a lot of work. After most week-ends—unless I have something special to do—I'm glad to get to the office on Monday morning."

"I sometimes feel the same way when the boys have their own activities on Saturday and Sunday. When they were younger, they were more dependent on me, of course. Then my weekends really flew by, not leaving me much time for myself." She fiddled with her silverware a few moments. "But...but recently I've hunted for things to occupy my time when they're out with friends or away with their father."

Craig detected a wistfulness in her voice. "Don't you have friends of your own?" he asked softly.

Before Shanna could answer, the waiter arrived to remove their salad plates and serve their entrees. Shanna was grateful for the waiter's brief interruption because Craig's question disconcerted her. She decid-ed to be very frank. "Other than my next-door neighbor Angela—who is also my best friend—I have mostly acquaintances now. I seldom go out."

Shanna hesitated, then felt the urge to confide in him further. "After Paul and I divorced, our married friends evidently decided that an extra single man at any kind of an affair was a plus. But an extra single woman posed a problem. None of them invited me to anything after Paul left."

Shanna looked down at her plate. "So my boys have become the center of my life. They take up most of my time one way or another. I like doing things with them, so I don't miss my former social life too much any more. When Angela can look in on the boys, I go to my sorority meetings and occasionally to the SF Chapter of the National Coalition of 100 Black Women." She played with her silverware while she spoke.

Craig felt a surge of sympathy for her.

Shanna finally took a deep breath, letting the air out slowly.

When she didn't continue, he leaned toward her. "But aren't you too young not to have a social life when—" He stopped when he saw an odd expression cross Shanna's face. Maybe he had overstepped his right by asking such questions. "I don't mean to pry, but...but you're too young to devote all of your time to your boys. Don't you expect to remarry some day?"

Shanna glared at him.

Craig leaned back in his chair as if he could escape the look in her eyes. He had to know more about this woman, and he was willing to incur her anger if he had to. He waited patiently for her reply.

Shanna dropped her head and fiddled with her water glass. She thought how naive about men and life she had been when she married Paul. She thought she knew it all at that time, but it was soon proved that she knew very little about life, about emotions, and—most of all—about Paul. She had learned, though, that nobody ever knows another person completely, not even a husband and wife. During the last two or three years she had lost her fairy-tale ideals about life in general and now tried to face the realities of living as best she could. That didn't include having a man in her life.

Craig squirmed in his chair as he watched various

emotions cross Shanna's face.

He waited.

She shifted around in her chair.

He took a sip of water and stared down into the glass.

She looked out over the ocean, almost as if he weren't there.

He waited.

Then Craig could no longer stand their silence. He was about to speak again when he heard her voice answering his question about remarrying.

Shanna spoke softly yet firmly. "It's been my choice the last few years to have my life revolve around the boys...and I have no intention of ever getting married again." She leaned back in her chair, satisfied with the positive spin she'd put on the muddle her life now seemed to be in. "I suppose I've met my share of wannabe male companions, but they just haven't interested me. I've finally found that I have an identity all my own. And I'm not interested in sharing my life with anyone—except my boys."

Craig studied her before he spoke. "But what about the time when the boys will be off at college or somewhere else, making a life of their own?" he asked gently.

"To use an old trite expression, I guess I'll cross that bridge when I come to it."

Thinking her answer a bit unrealistic, Craig turned his attention to the view. "Look, the sun has almost reached the horizon. Let's walk outside and watch it go down."

Shanna happily agreed.

Craig called for the check, took several bills from his pocket and left them on the tray provided by the waiter. Taking Shanna's hand, he elbowed their way through the crowd until they reached the stairs to a landing which overlooked the beach and the ocean. They stood in silence for several moments while the sun slowly slipped below the horizon in a blaze of red and gold.

"Now that's what I call a sunset!" He turned to her. "Ready to leave or would you rather go back inside for a drink?"

She thought for a moment. "Let's have one at the house."

"Sounds good to me," he agreed, and they made their way to his car. Little was said on the way back, but they were now more comfortable in the silence that surrounded them.

When they arrived home, Craig waited until Shanna unlocked the door and then followed her through the hallway into the kitchen. She opened the refrigerator to get a bottle of wine, but he stopped her. "If it's all the same with you, I'd just as soon have a cup of coffee."

Shanna returned the wine to the shelf and closed the refrigerator door. Smiling, she turned toward him. "I'd rather have coffee, too."

After starting the coffee, she reached up to get two coffee mugs. "Sugar and cream?"

Craig nodded his head in assent and walked over to the breakfast nook. He pulled out a chair at one end of the table. "Let's sit here," he suggested when he saw she was preparing a tray.

Shanna lifted an eyebrow. "I was going to re-light the logs in the living room."

"I can't stay too long. There's some work I have to finish tonight, or else my day will be a nightmare tomorrow."

Shanna hoped her disappointment didn't show as she placed hot, steaming mugs of coffee on the table.

"What time do you expect David and Phillip?" Craig asked, taking a slow sip of the hot coffee.

"I never know what time Paul will bring them back when he has them, but I hope it won't be too late tonight. They'll need to wind down before going to bed. They always insist on giving me a blow-by-blow account of their time with him, sometimes telling me things I really would rather not know." She gave him a lopsided smile as if he would know what she was talking about.

He could only guess what she was referring to.

"But there's nothing like keeping the lines of communication open," he observed candidly.

Shanna nodded in agreement. "I suppose you're right." She turned her attention to her half-empty mug.

Craig finished his coffee and rose to go.

"I really thank you for going with me this afternoon," he said as they walked to the front door. "Maybe we can do that again sometime," he suggested before leaving quickly. He knew if he lingered any longer he would be tempted to pull her into his arms and kiss her full lips until she cried "uncle."

CHAPTER SIX

With Craig's suggestion that they go out again ringing in her head, Shanna's heart beat faster after she closed the door. She hummed a tuneless melody as she padded down the hall to the kitchen to prepare for the next morning. She set a box of cereal and bowls on the table for the boys' breakfast. She got a small bowl and cut up some apples, peaches, and pears and poured a bit of honey over the fruit before putting it in the refrigerator.

Shanna was still in the kitchen when she heard a car in the driveway, followed by the slamming of car doors. The boys bounded into the house.

Shanna looked beyond them, relieved that Paul had not come in with them. He was the last person she wanted to see at the moment. She let out a slow breath when she heard his car backing out of the driveway.

David headed for the refrigerator.

"So...how was your day?" she asked, her usual question when they had been away.

"Dad wanted to know whether you'd gotten a new car—he thought Mr. Boyd's Mercedes was yours," Phillip informed her while he waited for David to get the sodas from the refrigerator. "And—"

David cut in. "And then he got pissed off when—"

"Watch your mouth, David," she interjected.

"And then we told Dad you rented the studio, and he asked a lot of other questions about what Mr. Boyd did and other stuff we didn't know, so we told Dad that we played a lot of basketball with him, and—"

"Slow down, David, you're losing me."

Phillip broke in. "And then he really got...I don't think he liked that so much."

"Didn't like what, Phillip? Mr. Boyd's playing basketball with you or my renting the studio?" She was more than a little confused by their conversation.

Phillip thought for a moment before he answered. "Both, I think. Wouldn't you say so, David?"

David agreed. "Then his wife asked a lot of questions while we were eating dinner as if our business is hers. I wish she'd just take care of her own. She's not our mother...I don't care if she is married to Dad."

"Now, be nice, David," Shanna cautioned. "She seems pleasant enough to me from what—"

"That's because you really don't know her," David interjected.

Phillip audibly agreed.

"Settle down, guys. I'm sure you were glad to be with your father for a while."

David and Phillip looked at each other a few moments before David finally asked, "Can I go to my room now, Mom? I just want to stretch out and watch television."

"Sure, if that's what you want to do. I'm not going to be up too much longer either."

Both boys gave Shanna a peck on the cheek before they headed upstairs to their rooms.

Shanna let out a long breath when they left, happy they hadn't asked about her day. For some reason, she didn't want to tell them how she'd spent her time. All she wanted at the moment was to sort out her feelings about her afternoon and evening with Craig.

A short time later Shanna got into bed with her novel, but Craig's face soon appeared between the pages. She finally tossed the book aside. She closed her eyes, but that didn't help. His image was imprinted on the back of her lids. She tossed restlessly on her pillow. She didn't want to remember the way he looked at her when he thought she wasn't aware of his scrutiny ...or how he looked when he smiled...or how his low, vibrant voice affected her when he spoke. Not to mention the electricity she felt when he accidentally touched her, and the alarming way she responded to his touch. His easy charm could have a hold on her if she allowed it. Which was the last thing she should let happen.

Shanna finally decided that the effect Craig had on her was because she was unaccustomed to being around such a devastating member of the opposite sex. She truly didn't know how to handle the emotions he produced in her, except not to be alone with him again. But would that solve anything when she knew deep down inside that she really wanted to be near him? Life was always full of complications, but this one she didn't need. She gave her pillow a savage punch, turned over and pulled the blanket up to her neck.

At the end of the hallway, Craig also had difficulty getting to sleep. It had been a long time since he had been so disturbed by a woman. The afternoon and evening forced him to confront the fact that he definitely was attracted to her and wanted her to be a part of his life. On the other side of the coin, he needed no woman in his life. But how could he deal with the longing he felt for her when he wasn't with her? Damn! What a dichotomy! The bottom line was that there was no way he could ignore the fact that each night she was in bed just down the hall from him.

❧

Late Monday afternoon, Shanna's day was interrupted by a phone call from the principal's secretary at David's school. The secretary made an appointment for Shanna to talk with one of David's teachers the following day. Hanging up the phone, Shanna quickly finished the work on her desk and left her office early. She wanted to be home when the boys arrived from school.

On the way home, Shanna wondered what David had gotten into now. He certainly wasn't a bad kid—he just always seemed to manage to be present when any confusion occurred. He had never been in any serious trouble and she fervently hoped the same was true in this case. Consoling herself with the thought that if the problem were serious someone at his school would have asked her to come in immediately, she felt less anxious.

A short while later, hearing the skidding of the boys' bicycles in the driveway and then a key in the door, she walked quickly toward the entrance.

David and Phillip stopped in their tracks when they faced their mother in the doorway. Their surprise at her being home clearly showed on their faces.

"What're you doing home, Mom? Are you sick or something?" David asked, concern spreading over his face. Phillip just stared at her.

"I'm okay, David. It's you I'm concerned about at the moment." She turned to Phillip. "I want to talk to David, Phillip, so why don't you go upstairs and start your homework after you get some cookies and milk. I'll call you when I'm finished with David."

The boys followed her into the kitchen. Shanna sat down at the table and waited until the boys got their afternoon snack.

Phillip, thinking David was in some kind of trouble, glanced anxiously at his brother before picking up his snack and his backpack. He left the room with a worried

look on his face. He loved his brother and always hated
it when David got into trouble.

Shanna rose from the table and walked to the refrigerator to get a soda. Taking a deep breath, she sat down
to deal with whatever problem she now faced. She waited patiently for David to come to the table.

David took his time pouring his milk and putting a
handful of chocolate chip cookies on a napkin. He
glanced surreptitiously at his mother several times in the
process. He finally dropped down sideways into a chair
facing her, seemingly concentrating on his snack. He
didn't look at her.

Shanna quickly got to the point. "Do you know why
I'm supposed to have a conference with your math
teacher tomorrow, David?"

David glanced at her and then turned his attention to
his cookies again.

Shanna waited patiently, thinking how embarrassed
he must feel. Her heart went out to him. He really is a
good boy, she thought. Just trying to deal with being a
teenager.

David finally spoke up. "Yeah, I guess I know."

Shanna studied her son. He was always so free with
words and affection, but now he had suddenly clamed
up. She could tell from the tight expression on his face
that he didn't relish talking to her.

Shanna spoke softly but firmly. "Suppose you tell me
why, David. I'd like to hear your side before I talk to your
teacher in the morning." She reached up to twirl a strand
of her hair. David watched his mother wind her hair
around her finger and knew that was a bad sign. She
always did that when she was upset about something.

"What did they tell you when they called?" he asked,
plopping a cookie into his mouth before gulping part of
his milk.

"That's the problem, David. The school secretary

only asked that I talk with your math teacher tomorrow."

"Well...uh...Miss Hanford—she's my math teacher—"

"I know her name, David. Remember I met her during Parent's Night," she informed him. "So what about her?"

"Well...uh...she doesn't like me...and every time she gets a chance she tries to put me down in front of the class. And today she really pissed—sorry—really dumped on me and I took up for myself. I couldn't help it if everybody in the class laughed." David looked up pleadingly at his mother.

"But you must have done something to upset her, David."

"I told her she should pick on some of the dumb kids because I had one of the highest grades in the whole class...and that some of the things she did were real dumb and..." His voice trailed off.

"And what, David? What else did you say?"

He swallowed hard. "Uh...I called her a dumb-ass teacher."

"David! What possessed you to say some outrageous thing like that? That doesn't sound like you at all!

"I know, I know. But this wasn't one of my best days." He ate a couple more cookies before he spoke again, a frown on his face. "I had a lot on my mind."

Shanna sipped her soda and waited.

David shuffled around in his chair, his eyes on the floor.

"What, David?"

"Well...yesterday Dad didn't even ask us what we'd like to do, just took us to his house and we sat around listening to him and his dizzy wife most of the day. That's no fun. They don't even have a basketball hoop." He finished in a rush and drank the rest of his milk. He put down his glass with a thud.

A bell sounded in Shanna's head. So there was

something behind his actions in school today. Another problem. If it wasn't one thing, it was another.

"Hmm...I'll talk to your father. He probably doesn't know how you feel when you're there."

"Won't do no good," David mumbled.

"We'll see. I need to mention a couple other things to him as well." Shanna rose from the table. "Why don't you do your homework while I start dinner?"

David was only too happy to end their conversation. He gathered his napkin and took his glass to the sink before he hurried from the kitchen.

Shanna had their dinner together in a short time and called upstairs. "Come on down, guys. Dinner's ready."

Entering the kitchen first, Phillip sidled up to his mother. "Is David in trouble again at school, Mom?" he asked in a low voice.

"Take that worried look off your face. Whatever it is, I'm sure it's not life-threatening." She was glad the boys were so close, but David was a worry for Phillip at times.

During dinner the boys recounted more about their day with their father, ending with Phillip asking, "Why does Dad's wife always hang onto him—all that kissing and slobbering gets on my last nerve, and—"

David butted in. "And Dad never has much to say to us. Usually he asks how school is or something just as stupid, but he doesn't even listen when we try to tell him."

Both boys looked at their mother as if she had all the answers.

Shanna merely shook her head. At a loss, she tried to inject a positive note. "Your father is probably very busy adjusting to his new life while—"

"Humph! They've been married long enough for it not to be too new, Mom!" David injected.

"Yeah, that's right, David," Phillip added.

Well, my idea went over like a lead balloon, Shanna thought to herself. She racked her brain for a way to put a positive spin on the whole situation. Nothing earth-shaking came to mind.

"Maybe if you two spent more time with your father and got to know his wife better, you might feel different-ly." She looked from one boy to the other.

Neither boy spoke for several moments. David final-ly sputtered, "That'll be the day!"

Shanna changed the conversation to a more pleas-ant one. "It won't be too long before school is over. Do you two want to go to Camp Atwater again this year?"

The boys' faces lit up. "Yeah!" they uttered in unison. They began recounting some of the antics they had pulled the past summer.

Shanna held up her hand. "Enough of that! I received a brochure and applications a couple of weeks ago. Do you want to go for two or three weeks?"

The boys looked at each other. "Three weeks?" David asked Phillip. Phillip gave him a thumbs up.

"Okay, I'll send back your application in a couple of days to make sure you have reservations for three weeks."

What she was going to do without them around for that length of time, she didn't know. But she would cross that bridge when she got to it. She turned back to the boys. "Have you guys finished all your homework?"

Phillip nodded.

"I've finished most of mine," David informed her. "But can we go outside for a while first?"

This she had expected. "Don't stay out too long."

They were out of the room before she finished her sentence.

※

Later in the evening Craig pulled into the driveway a little earlier than usual, his briefcase bulging with work he wanted to finish. As soon as he reached his room, he quickly changed into jeans and a loose-fitting shirt and spread some folders on his desk. He worked for almost an hour before he heard the basketball bouncing off the garage. Looking out of his window, he saw Phillip dribbling and tossing the basketball. David sat on the step, his chin resting in his hands, a gloomy expression on his face.

Ummm, Craig thought to himself, I wonder what's wrong down there. Did the boys have an argument? He turned back to his work, the boys still in the back of his mind. Finally, he threw aside his pen and went downstairs. He crossed the lawn and sat down beside David. He laid his hand on David's knee. "Bad day, big guy?"

David did not reply.

"Why all the doom and gloom?" Craig asked softly, determined to get an answer. "You look like you've just lost your last friend."

David remained silent, his chin still in his hands.

Craig waited a few moments. "Don't want to talk about it, huh? Well, how about me beating you a few rounds at the hoop?"

David brightened slightly at Craig's suggestion. He got up and intercepted a ball Phillip tossed in the air, dribbled it a couple of times, then sank it through the hoop. Before David could retrieve it, Craig pounced on the ball, made a smooth basket of his own, and got the rebound. He looked triumphantly at David, who took on the challenge, and for the next hour or so the three had a rough and tumble game.

As usual, Craig was the first to give up. "I've got work to do, guys. See you," he called out before leaving them.

Before entering the garage, Craig glanced toward the front porch, hoping to see Shanna there. He wasn't that lucky. He entered the garage and slowly walked up the stairs, a letdown feeling deep in his gut.

CHAPTER SEVEN

Shanna's anxiety rose the closer she got to David's school. She didn't look forward to her conference with David's math teacher. By the time she found a parking space, her hands were sweating. She composed herself momentarily in the car.

When she walked into the principal's office, the school secretary recognized her. "Please have a seat, Mrs. Taylor, and I'll call Miss Hanford's room."

Shanna had barely sat down when the secretary informed her, "Miss Hanford doesn't have a class this period. Do you know where her room is?"

Shanna nodded and hurried down the hall, anxious to get the matter settled. She knocked on the door before walking into the classroom.

Miss Hanford rose from her chair behind her desk and held out her hand, cheerfully greeting her. "Glad you could come in, Mrs. Taylor. Please sit down," she said, pointing to a chair beside her desk.

Shanna barely returned the teacher's greeting, anxiously waiting for Miss Hanford to tell her about her problem with David. Shanna consciously resisted the nervous habit of twisting a strand of her hair, holding tightly to her purse with both hands instead.

Miss Hanford shuffled some papers on her desk and

cleared her throat before speaking, almost apologetically. "I'm sorry you had to take time off from your work,
Mrs. Taylor. But I wanted to talk about your son's behavior in my class." She paused for a few moments.

Shanna's anxiety level rose higher before Miss
Hanford continued.

"Actually, David is a good student—and one of the
brightest in my class—but lately he seems to have lost
interest and disturbs other students when he finishes his
work. I've spoken to David several times, but he has
ignored my warnings. His behavior yesterday was the
straw that broke the camel's back, so to speak." She
stopped for a few seconds. Shanna glanced at the
teacher with a question on her face. "To be more specif-
ic, David made some very rude remarks to me in front of
the class. He even called—"

Shanna held up her hand. "David told me his side
last evening. It's hard for me to believe David really
acted so uncharacteristically."

"I was quite taken aback myself, Mrs. Taylor."

Removing and wiping her glasses carefully, Miss
Hanford sighed. "I really feel that David regretted his
words the moment they were out of his mouth, but he
didn't want to lose face in front of the class, so he didn't
apologize." She was silent for a moment. "I think something else was going on with David yesterday. I noticed
a sullen expression on his face when he entered the
room. He's usually so outgoing, kidding around with
other students before class begins. It was obvious he
wasn't in a good mood. I'm sure the other students
noticed his unusual behavior also as some kept peeking
around at him. It was near the end of class when his
outburst occurred, and that's when I decided I needed to
talk to you and his father. By the way, I hoped you would
have his father here, also." She looked expectantly at
Shanna.

Shanna studied her nails for a few moments. Oh,
how I wish Paul had come with me, she thought. "I didn't
contact his father, since the secretary didn't mention
there was a serious problem." Paul was seldom around
to deal with problems when they were married, she
remembered, so why should it be any different now. Still,
she felt very much alone. She hoped she was making
the right decisions for both boys, especially David at this
crucial point in his young life. She became aware that
Miss Hanford waited for her to continue, and Shanna
drew her mind back to the problem at hand.

"But I'll talk to his father about this. We certainly will
not condone David's disrespectful behavior." Shanna
clasped her hands tighter in her lap, a gesture Miss
Hanford did not miss. "Did you put David on any kind of
punishment, Miss Hanford? He didn't mention you had
given him detention or anything."

Miss Hanford brightened. "No, yesterday I informed
David that we would talk about his behavior when he
cooled off. I've been thinking about an alternative which,
I think, will help David in a more positive way than having him spend time in detention. However, I wanted to
run my idea past you first." She hesitated a few
moments, looking at some notes on her desk.

Shanna waited, twisting a tissue in her hands and
wondering what was coming down next. Why couldn't
David be more like Phillip, who seldom had any difficulties at school. She looked up when she heard Miss
Hanford speaking again.

"I'd like to have your permission for David to tutor
some students in math after school a couple of days a
week. We only have a few weeks left in the semester.
There're several students in his class who are doing
poorly, and I think David could really help those students
prepare for their final exam."

Shanna leaned forward. "Really, Miss Hanford?"

"David's very good in math, and taking on that kind of responsibility might help his attitude in my class if he felt I had the confidence in him to recommend him to other students. If he agrees, it means he would be about an hour or so later getting home on his tutoring days. I know he always goes home with his younger brother. If David agrees with my suggestion, would that be a problem for you or your other son?"

"I can make some arrangement for Phillip."

Shanna suddenly felt better. "David has a tendency to look out for others. I think tutoring students will appeal to him." She was silent for a moment. "However, I'd prefer that you talk this over with David before I speak with him again, Miss Hanford, since he seems to think you don't like him, and feels—"

Miss Hanford held up her hand. "Not like him? That couldn't be farther from the truth, Mrs. Taylor. I have no idea why he thinks that. In fact, I'm quite fond of David; he's one of my favorite students. But I can't let him disrupt the whole class. He's quite popular with the other students, and if I can just channel his energy in a more positive way, everyone will benefit. Shanna's respect for Miss Hanford rose considerably. She knew David was in good hands in that particular class. She was now sure that David's last disappointing visit with his father had something to do with his behavior.

Miss Hanford did not miss the relief that spread across Shanna's face. She felt a bit of relief herself. "David is coming in to see me during his lunch hour today. I'll tell him about our talk and of my decisions. Tutoring is not an easy job. Many times it can become very frustrating. But I think David can handle it." She rose from her desk, signaling to Shanna that their conference was over.

Shanna stood up, relieved and happy that the meeting had gone so well. "Thank you for your interest in

David. If there's anything I can do, please call me. I'm sure your plans for him will work out. He really is a good boy."

Miss Hanford looked at Shanna with sympathetic eyes. "I understand, Mrs. Taylor, but sometimes it's especially hard on a teenager growing up in a single-parent home." Shanna nodded, shook Miss Hanford's hand, and took her leave.

She hurried to her car and drove to her office, relieved that David wasn't in any serious trouble. But Miss Hanford's last statement bothered her the rest of the day. A single-parent home. What was a person to do, she wondered, when she couldn't control the circumstances under which she had to live? She unearthed no answers to her questions. When she got home later than usual that evening, she learned her boys had finished their snack and started their homework at the kitchen table.

"Hi, Mom," they greeted Shanna when she walked into the kitchen.

Shanna noticed immediately that David looked happy and thought that was encouraging. Evidently his talk with Miss Hanford had gone well. She put her bags down on the counter and started putting her purchases away in the pantry. David's voice stopped her. She turned around to face him, her eyebrows raised.

"Guess what, Mom?" David called out and didn't wait for her reply. "Miss Hanford wants me to tutor some kids in math after school, and I'm going to help her with some kids during our math class. Isn't that great?" he ended enthusiastically, a broad smile on his face.

Shanna's heart lightened, happy that everything was going to work out for David.

Phillip saw his chance to speak. He had worried ever since David told him what Miss Hanford wanted him to do. "But what about me when David stays after school?"

He looked up at his mother. "Do I have to come home by myself, Mom?"

Before Shanna could answer, David spoke up. "Why couldn't you shoot some baskets in the gym while I'm busy, Phillip? It'll only be two days a week. The gym teacher stays there with some kids until six o'clock every evening, and I'll be through way before that. Then we could come home together."

Phillip beamed at his brother. "Yeah, that'll work," he stated with a smile on his face as if David had just solved all the problems of the world.

David's suggestion also pleased Shanna. She was glad David was taking responsibility for his brother without her mentioning it.

"And, guess what, Mom?" David continued. "Jessica told me this afternoon that she wanted to come to my tutoring sessions."

"Humph," Phillip snorted. "Girls! I bet she doesn't have any trouble with her math. She just wants to be there to look at you, David, and you know that."

David blushed and walked back to the table, punching Phillip on the arm before he sat down. Phillip punched back.

Shanna looked at David and raised her eyebrows. "Isn't Jessica the girl who gave Phillip a note for you a few days ago, David?"

"Oh...yeah...that's the same girl." His voice lowered and an embarrassed look crossed his face. "I think she likes me."

Shanna decided to let that information go right over her head for the time being. She glanced sideways at David again, thinking how tall he had grown during the past year. Tall and gangling and awkward. She looked at his upper lip again and confirmed the fact that he really did have the fine fuzz she recently noticed. Maybe he would soon start filling out and his awkwardness would be less noticeable. She smiled as she thought of how he seemed to stumble when there was nothing to stumble over.

During dinner, Phillip abruptly inquired about Craig. "How much longer do you think Mr. Boyd will live here, Mom?"

Shanna started. It was uncanny. At that very moment she had been thinking about Craig. "I really don't know, Phillip. He hasn't discussed his plans with me. Why do you ask?"

"Uh...I was just wondering. It's kinda neat having a man around to help with things. Last week he fixed my bike handle, and he's been showing David some things about his car, hasn't he, David?"

"Yeah. But he's still just a roomer. Not like he's related to us or anything, Phillip."

Shanna glanced over at David, thinking his last remark sounded rather terse.

"Ah...you're just jealous of the way Mr. Boyd looks at Mom. You think he likes her, and you know that's the truth. You told me so, David."

Shanna's mouth dropped open.

David glared at his brother. "You sure got a big mouth, Phillip. I'm never going to tell you anything else."

Flabbergasted, Shanna stared from one boy to the other, incredulity clearly showing on her face. "Stop it, you two. I'm sure Mr. Boyd doesn't dislike me, and of course he can't...can't just ignore me whenever I'm around."

David did not let the conversation end there. "But you two sat out in the back yard a long time the other evening."

Shanna hoped the heat she felt inside didn't show on her face.

"Adults usually talk to each other, David. There's nothing unusual about that."

David had no reply. He just looked at his mother with doubt in his eyes. He wanted to believe her, but he still didn't like the look in Craig's eyes when his mother was around.

They soon finished their dinner, and Shanna rose to clear the table. "I'll take care of the dishes. If you two want, you can shoot baskets for an hour or so before getting started with your homework. Just watch the time."

The boys rushed out the front door, glad to end the dinner conversation. However, they left their mother to contemplate what had been said...and not said.

While clearing the kitchen, Shanna's mind turned to Craig. Was she also as obvious as David thought Craig was? She'd have to cool it when Craig was around. Easier said than done, though.

Lucky for Shanna, Craig spent long hours at his office the rest of the week. She didn't have to see him.

CHAPTER EIGHT

Late Saturday evening Shanna breathed a sigh of relief as she sank down on the bed. It had been a busy day. While the boys were with their friends on an all-day hike, she had finished all her chores in the house, gone to the cleaners and then to the market, as well as doing a couple more errands which took more time than she expected. She had stopped on the way home to grab a quick sandwich for her dinner since the boys were having a cookout for theirs.

Now all she could think of was having time to herself for a leisurely soak in the tub before the boys returned. She threw off her clothes in a rush and went into the bathroom to fill the tub with hot water and her favorite bath salts.

While the tub was filling, she creamed her face, and then held a hot towel to it for several seconds before removing the cream. Even that small amount of attention to her skin was refreshing. As steam from the bath tub slowly filled the room, she slipped down into the steamy, bubbly water, heaving a sigh as her body adjusted to the temperature.

She placed a heavy towel behind her head and lay back for several minutes, soaking up all the soothing effects. When she felt the hot water losing its warmth, she reached out and grabbed a handful of bubbles and blew them softly into the air, watching the multicolored balls float around until they burst. She played with the bubbles a few moments before reaching for a sponge and scrubbing vigorously until she felt her whole body tingle from her efforts. Sighing, she wished she could scrub Craig out of her mind as easily.

When she finished, she went back to her bedroom and sat down at her dressing table. She took several minutes brushing her heavy, slightly wavy hair, and then patted in a moisturizer on her face and neck. Totally refreshed, she threw on a shorts outfit and some flip-flops to sit on the patio until her boys returned.

Unconsciously humming softly, Shanna's mind turned from the confines of her bedroom to the studio apartment. She would have to try harder to maintain a facade of indifference toward Craig whenever he was near. She took a deep breath and exhaled slowly, hoping she could control her feelings from now on.

She picked up her novel and headed for the backyard to read until darkness took over. Closing the kitchen door, she abruptly stopped. Craig was sitting in one of the lounge chairs.

"Hi," Craig greeted her and looked away when he saw the flush appearing on her face.

"Uh...I didn't know you...were out here," Shanna finally stammered. His vibrant, husky voice sent shivers up her spine. She drew a deep breath and exhaled slowly to maintain her cool on the outside.

"Thought I'd enjoy the quiet with the boys away. At least I don't have to dunk basketballs this evening!"

Shanna smiled. "I was going to have a glass of wine. Would you like one?"

"That sounds good," Craig replied.

On her way back to the kitchen Shanna thought how comfortable it was to have someone to have an adult conversation with, something she hadn't had too frequently lately. Wow, she chided herself, let's not go too far with that kind of thinking. After all, Craig is merely a roomer. And he may not be around too much longer. That thought caused a little pang in her heart.

Little did Shanna know that Craig felt it was his lucky evening. He wanted nothing more than to sit outside with Shanna and learn more about what made her tick. He felt much closer to her since their conversation about her ex-husband. He surmised there was more behind her cool exterior than perhaps even she was aware of.

Shanna handed Craig the wine before sitting down in the lounge chair near his.

Craig took a sip of his wine. "Ummm. This just hits the spot." He lifted his glass in her direction. "I'm becoming attached to your back yard. It's so peaceful out here this time of the evening." I also seem to be getting attached to you, he wanted to say.

They sat in silence a few moments. Shanna studied her flip-flops, thinking of the first time she met Craig. She remembered the chemistry that had sparked between them when he touched her hand during their introduction, how she'd felt something powerful happening even then. Now just thinking about that made her shiver.

Craig noticed her movement and asked huskily, "Are you chilly?"

Shanna shook her head. "No, it's okay out here now, but it'll probably get cooler in a short while." What an inane conversation, she thought, glancing over at his relaxed body.

Craig looked out into the night and then up to the sky where the moon was emerging from behind a cloud. He thought it looked as alone and forlorn and lonesome as he felt at the moment. Something else caught his attention. "Look," he said, "the stars over there look like little white Christmas tree lights." He pointed toward a cluster of twinkling stars high in the sky.

Shanna turned her head in the direction he was pointing and agreed the stars really did twinkle like tiny tree lights. They continued to look out into the darkness. It was a beautiful night with not even a hint of fog and only a slight breeze moving around them.

A leaf floated down to Shanna's head. She reached up to pick it out of her hair at the same time Craig reached over to brush it away. Their hands touched in midair and each felt the warmth of the other's hand.

Her smile faded as she looked at him.

He wanted to jerk his hand back. But that would tip off his growing feelings for her, and that was the last thing he wanted to do. He proceeded to pick the leaf from her hair.

Her tension doubled at his touch and a warm feeling quickly spread to her face, causing an unwanted blush on her cheeks. They stared at each other, each aware that the other was experiencing the same physical reaction.

Shanna rubbed her hand across her face, hoping to erase the flush she felt there.

Craig looked down at the leaf in his hand as if it were the cause of his discomfort. He had never felt quite like this about a woman, not even when he was married. No one had ever affected him as she now did. Never.

When Shanna glanced over at Craig, she saw a slight smile lifting one corner of his mouth. She turned away, unwilling to play his game, if that's what it was. She was unsure about the rules of flirting nowadays and certainly didn't want to learn at this stage in her life. Twisting a strand of hair around her finger, she wished she could think of something profound to fill the yawning silence. Why did she feel so ill-equipped to make small talk?

Finally, in an attempt to curb her nervousness,

Shanna leaned toward Craig and asked, "Would you like another glass of wine?"

"Maybe later."

Craig turned to face her. His gaze moved from her eyes down to her lips. His lips parted and he drew his tongue over them as if to moisten them. He now knew there was no way he could have a platonic relationship with her. He felt too drawn to her, and he wondered how his attraction to her could have become so strong after only a few hours alone with her. That in itself was a revelation to him since he had avoided women the last few years. But she'd been on his mind all week while he tried to convince himself that he should keep his distance from her, yet wondered how he could see her alone again. What was wrong with him?

Shanna drew back slightly in her chair, entranced, yet slightly intimidated by Craig's gaze. She suddenly wondered how his full lips would feel on hers. All evening she had unconsciously watched him peripherally...the way he looked in his tight-fitting jean shorts...his firm thighs and legs...the way he moved around the grill...the way he seemed to be so much at home. She was forced to confront the fact that she was more than attracted to him and that it wasn't going to be easy to keep him at a distance. They would probably be in close proximity many times during the next three or four months that he occupied the studio.

But physical attraction isn't everything, she thought. Maybe she would find out things about him she really didn't like, though she had her doubts about that at the moment. And with his interest in the boys, she realized it would be impossible to just ignore him. Was it fear of becoming involved in a relationship that bothered her?

The bottom line, she decided, was the fact her pulses raced whenever he was around, and he seemed to be around more and more. So it was up to her to put a stop to it before things got out of control. It might take a Herculean effort to feign indifference to him, but she must. On the other hand, there was the possibility she was over-reacting to the whole situation, that he had no designs on her, and her life would remain as humdrum as it had been for a long time. That thought didn't add to her comfort zone. Her head was telling her one thing but her heart another. God, she was so confused. Her reverie was broken when she heard his voice, low and quiet.

"It's so peaceful and serene out here," Craig mused. "Like there're no problems to solve, and everything's right with the world."

Shanna looked at him quizzically. "That's rather naive thinking, isn't it?"

"Perhaps, but we all deserve such moments every once in a while, even when we know we're only fooling ourselves."

Craig clasped his hands behind his head and slid forward in his chair, stretching his long legs out in front of him. Shanna waited for him to continue talking, but he just stared out into the darkness, evidently comfortable in their silence.

Curiosity finally got the better of Shanna. She knew so little about him. Reaching up to unconsciously twist a strand of her hair, she took a deep breath. "You mentioned earlier that this week had been a rough one for you. Where is your office located?"

Craig turned abruptly to face her. "Oh, I thought you knew. It's on Bush Street, almost the center of the financial section near—"

"Oh," Shanna interrupted. "That's very close to where I work." What an inane statement she realized when she remembered he was Rick's close friend, and that he certainly must have been in to see Rick.

"I know," he replied. Perfect timing, he thought. "Maybe we could have lunch one day next week."

Hedging, Shanna explained, "I usually send out for a sandwich or take some fruit with me for lunch. Most of the places near where I work are usually so filled with the noisy lunch crowd that I prefer the quietness of my office." She didn't mention the fact she hated to sit at a table for two when she was alone.

Craig refused to be put off by her reply. "I know a small out-of-the-way place not too far from my office where the food is excellent and the service is fast. I usually call a couple hours ahead when I know I'm going there, and I've never failed to get a table. Would you like to try it? I could give you a call some morning to see whether you can make it."

Hesitating for a few moments, Shanna finally agreed that having lunch with him would be nice, all the while rubbing her sweating palms on the side of her shorts. What she was really letting herself in for, she didn't know, but at the moment she didn't give a tinker's damn.

With that settled, Craig proceeded to tell her some of the problems he was facing in straightening out the agency. He ended by saying, "I may have to stay in San Francisco longer than I thought."

Before Shanna could comment on that announcement, her boys came through the kitchen door. After telling about their day, David announced, "We're going to bed, it's almost eleven o'clock."

"Aren't you guys chilly out here?" Phillip asked, hugging his sides.

Shanna realized that she did indeed feel a little chilly, something which she hadn't noticed until now. "You're right, it is a bit cool, Phillip." She stood up and glanced around at Craig, who immediately rose to his feet also but made no attempt to leave. His remark about having to stay in San Francisco longer than he'd first expected must have gone right over her head, he decided.

Both boys gave Shanna a peck on the cheek and

said goodnight to Craig before they went back inside the house and up the stairs to their rooms.

Shanna started toward the kitchen door. She turned to Craig. "You can go through the house if you like. No need to go way around the yard."

Craig followed her silently through the house to the front door, again noticing her shapely form. She's really got it going on and doesn't even know it, he thought to himself.

"I enjoyed the evening, Shanna." Standing close, he looked down at her as if he had something else on his mind. The palms of Shanna's hands grew warm again as she looked up at him. She felt very confused standing so close to him. Shanna wondered whether he was going to kiss her. What would she do if he did? She didn't have to make that decision as Craig bid her goodnight.

❦

For the next few days Shanna dressed with special care to go to the office, something she had previously given little thought to. Most mornings she just pulled out the nearest skirt and top without giving her clothes another thought. Now she took more time with her makeup, and selected clothes that she seldom wore from her closet. And each morning she wondered if that would be the day Craig would ask her to lunch.

Shanna smiled self-consciously when Rick complimented her one morning. "You've been looking great recently. Sure you don't have a new interest in your life?" her boss teased.

Blushing, Shanna turned away from him. "Mind your own business, Rick," she said softly.

During the mornings while she worked Shanna started each time the phone rang, hoping it was Craig, yet feeling anxious in case it was. He was always gone by the time she left in the mornings and usually had not returned by the time she got home in the evenings, so she had not seen him.

Little did Shanna know that Craig had made a point not to be at home, stopping to have dinner when he left the office. Cooking for only himself was not one of Craig's things, but he usually managed to have something in the refrigerator to put in the microwave when he needed to. But now eating alone in his studio was unappealing when he could hear sounds from the other part of the house. It only made him feel lonely, wondering what Shanna was doing.

It was early Thursday morning that Craig finally called Shanna's office.

"How about lunch today, Shanna? Can you make it?"

When Shanna replaced the receiver, she raised both arms in the air. The rest of the morning sped by.

CHAPTER NINE

To the amazement of her co-workers, when lunchtime arrived on Thursday Shanna rushed out of her office, a glow on her face they seldom saw. They looked at each other when she sallied by, dressed in a suit they'd never seen.

Shanna caught the first elevator down to the street level and quickly walked the short distance to the restaurant where she was meeting Craig.

Craig stood up when he saw Shanna enter the restaurant, a feeling of elation surging through him as he watched her walk sedately through the crowd toward him. He admired the stunning way she looked in her smart dark blue suit over a simple white round-necked blouse. Her shiny auburn-streaked hair framed her face, a few strands escaping to her broad forehead. He noticed she wore little jewelry, just gold drop earrings. And her plain blue pumps added to her height and set off the legs he had been admiring since the first time he saw her.

Shanna spied Craig immediately and made her way through the crowd to his table, becoming more apprehensive with each step she took toward him, yet feeling a thrill deep inside as she looked at his tall, dark, handsome presence. He stood out among the other diners.

She hoped her face didn't reveal her inner turmoil as she greeted him with a breathless "Hello."

Craig looked down adoringly at Shanna from his towering height when she sat down in the chair he pulled out for her. He inhaled the faint scent of her cologne which she had worn before. It seemed to suit her personality, slightly elusive. A small smile tugged at his lips when he took a seat to face her across the table, aware of the stares of other diners. He knew they made a very handsome couple, and he was happy that, at least for a short while, he would have her all to himself.

"I'm glad you could make it." Craig gave her one of his broadest smiles. He looked across the table at her, feeling better inside than he had in a long time. The things she did to him were unbelievable.

"It's really good to be out of the office for a change." Shanna really wanted to say what was in her mind—how good it made her feel to have lunch with him— but of course she didn't.

A waiter appeared immediately. Shanna glanced over the long menu, trying to decide what to order, changing her mind a couple of times.

Noticing Shanna's indecision, Craig lowered his menu. "The crab-stuffed prawns are great here, and a glass of white wine really tops them off," he announced.

Shanna decided to take Craig's suggestion. "Perfect. That sounds good to me." She carefully laid aside her menu, feeling very inane. She glanced over at him and became more embarrassed when she saw him looking at her with a half-smile on his face. She felt her inner temperature slowly rising before he finally spoke.

"I'm getting hungrier by the minute...I was even thinking of taking a bite of your hand." With a twinkle in his dark eyes, Craig teasingly reached across the table for her hand, raising it towards his lips and planting a soft kiss on her palm. He smiled when a slow blush crept up from her neck to her forehead. He couldn't remember any of the women he knew blushing so easily.

Shanna felt her heart pounding, the touch of his lips on her palm sending electrical currents coursing through her veins. She withdrew her hand slowly, his eyes still holding hers as if she were hypnotized. She couldn't deny the effect Craig had on her whenever he touched her, nor was she sure she wanted to. What was it about his touch that caused her hormones to go berserk, making her feel that her body was suddenly aflame?

Luckily the waiter arrived with their lunch, and they ate ravenously, covertly glancing at each other between bites and making a few mundane comments as they concentrated on their food.

Craig finished his lunch before Shanna. He lowered his eyes and started fiddling with his fork, slowly moving it around in circles. He was again silent as if in deep thought. A couple of times he shifted slightly in his chair before he finally lifted his head and looked directly into her eyes. "Look here," he began, "you...you're becoming something of a distraction in my life. And at a time when I don't need or want to be distracted." His voice was low and soft, almost as if the words were being forced from his mouth.

Shanna's eyes widened and she blinked rapidly, trying to make some sense of what she had just heard. She waited for him to continue, totally disconcerted. She supposed he was showing an interest in her, and she didn't know how to handle it. If she'd had more casual relationships with men since her divorce, she would probably now know how to react to his words.

To make matters worse, the wine seemed to have sped directly to her brain. She hoped it was the wine that was causing such turmoil with her emotions. What had happened to her world, her safe world with her boys? Shaking her head gently, she tried to concentrate on his deep, baritone voice as he continued to speak.

"...and I can't believe the way you entered my thoughts at the most inopportune times this week. I can't seem to get you out of my mind." Craig leaned back in his chair, aware of the confusion that was flitting across Shanna's face.

Shanna set down her almost empty glass abruptly. What was he talking about? She again shook her head to clear up whatever was interfering with her thought processes. "You...you what?" she asked stupidly.

"I said I can't seem to get you out of my mind," Craig repeated softly.

"You mean me?" Shanna asked, as if it were incredulous that he meant what he'd just said. "You hardly know me. How can you say that?"

Craig raised his eyebrows. "Are you always so practical-minded? I'd like to know your secret. Haven't you ever just followed your intuitions?"

Shanna stared him wide-eyed. Little did he know he had hit a sore spot. She had learned to trust her intuitions since her divorce from Paul, and that hadn't been the easiest thing she had ever done. She'd learned to become an expert at keeping her intuitions in the right perspective...that is, until now. Could she handle what presently seemed to be happening? The confusion in the back of her mind overwhelmed her.

Craig noticed Shanna's hesitation and continued in a low, quiet voice. "Maybe it's best if you ignore what I just said. You're evidently satisfied with your life the way it is, and I certainly don't want to upset it." He saw that she was looking past him, staring into space while twisting a few strands of her hair around her finger. Did she really hear what I just said? he wondered. He waited.

Shanna finally looked over at Craig with a sigh. "I don't think you understand where I'm coming from. You're right, I am satisfied with my life the way it is now...and I don't want to get involved with anyone. I like talking to you, and I like the way you handle the boys, but that's about it since—"

Craig interrupted. "Are you afraid of being hurt again? Is that why you seem so aloof most of the time?"

Shanna felt the tears forming behind her eyelids but willed them to stay there. She knew that her life had certainly been empty without a man around. In truth, she really liked men, but she knew what could occur if she let men into her life—they would try to take over. And that was something she didn't want.

She shrugged her shoulders. "We barely know each other, Craig, and I'm not too sure but that we should keep it that way."

"You might find that I can be a very good friend, Shanna, and if you're like most people, I'm sure you must need a broad shoulder at times." He was silent for a few moments while he watched various emotions flit across her face.

Shanna finally answered. "I guess I'd like to be your friend, Craig..." Her voice trailed off before she continued. "But I'm not ready to even think of anything else, and I..." What she really wanted she was unwilling to admit, even to herself. She seldom thought of her own needs and desires; she was too tied to the lives of her boys. And her life had been more peaceful and a lot simpler without any serious involvement with a man. If she were wise, she'd keep it that way. She turned away from his piercing eyes, hoping he had no inkling of the thoughts running around in her head.

Craig waited for Shanna to continue. When he realized he wasn't going to get any other answer, he suggested, "Let's get out of here." He pulled his wallet from his inside coat pocket and placed some bills on the table. Walking around to pull out her chair, he led the way for her out of the restaurant.

"Thanks for lunch," Shanna said shyly when they reached the street.

"The pleasure was mine." Craig wanted to take her in his arms and wipe that scared feeling from her face, but he merely nodded before they parted to get back to their offices, each having serious private thoughts.

He wondered whether he had scared her off for good.

She wondered how in the world she could deal with what he'd casually presented to her during lunch. Did he really mean what he'd said?

The rest of the day passed slowly for both of them.

☙

Shanna slowly walked back to her office. She soon discovered she couldn't keep her mind on the work piled in front of her and found herself staring out of the window more than she worked. Craig had upset her more than she wanted to admit.

Craig had a long staff meeting that afternoon, the outcome of which disturbed him to no end; he had to spend a few days at the home office in Chicago, leaving as soon as he could get airline reservations. The last thing he wanted to do was to be away from Shanna at this particular time. He thought he might be making a little headway with her, and he didn't want his so-called progress interrupted. But he also had his work to consider, and if the firm wanted him in Chicago there was nothing else he could do but comply.

Later in the evening Craig knocked on Shanna's door to tell her he had to return to his Chicago office for a few days. He saw the disappointment on her face when she learned his news. Before he turned from her to go back to his studio, he asked softly, "While I'm away, will you think about what I mentioned at lunch today, Shanna?" He hesitated when she didn't reply. "And tell the boys to get in some extra practice as I expect to take them on when I get back."

Shanna smiled and nodded her head. "Have a good flight. See you when you get back," she called after him as he crossed the yard. How could she not think about what he'd said? she asked herself as she closed the door and went to the kitchen to check on the boys' homework. She found them arguing about what television program they wanted to watch later.

"Hold it a minute, guys." Shanna turned to David. "I talked with Miss Hanson and she informed me you're doing a bang up tutoring job."

David lowered his head, embarrassed by the compliment.

Phillip piped up, "Yeah, and now more girls think they need tutoring. You should see them looking at David, Mom—all bug-eyed and—"

David stood up. "Why can't you ever keep your mouth shut, Phillip? What do you know about—"

"I know what I see," Phillip retorted.

Shanna stepped in. "Cool it, guys. I'm just glad your sessions are going well, David."

Phillip knew when to stop teasing David. "So let's flip for the TV movie, David."

"Neither of you will see anything if you don't finish your homework," Shanna informed them as she set about clearing the kitchen and preparing a casserole for the next evening. She barely heard their grumbles as she went about her work. Her mind was on her lunch with Craig, wondering for the hundredth time whether she had heard him correctly. Had he truly meant what he'd said?

❧

Although Shanna's life went on normally for the next few days while Craig was away, she felt a bit out of sorts for no particular reason. She drove the boys to baseball practice, did her usual marketing, and piddled around the house over the weekend while the boys were with friends, but something seemed to be missing.

She was more at odds with herself than she had been during the time of her emotional divorce. But she refused to admit to herself that perhaps Craig's absence had something to do with her mood swings.

Late Friday evening of the next week Shanna sat on the patio sipping iced tea and feeling alone and lonely. Paul had picked up the boys for the weekend soon after they came home from school. She knew they should spend as much time as possible with their father, but for some reason she also resented the fact that he only took them when it was convenient for him. He'd promised to take them sailing on the bay on Saturday. She hoped he kept his promise. So many times in the past she had to deal with his disappointing the boys for various reasons.

Shanna was considering taking a short run before going inside for the night when the sound of a car door closing interrupted her thoughts. She rose and went through the house to the living room window. Looking out to the driveway, she fervently hoped she was not having unexpected company; she was in no mood to entertain anyone. She saw Craig's long legs climbing out of the car. Her heart skipped several beats and her hands began to sweat. Wide-eyed, she watched as Craig reached into the back seat to get his luggage and briefcase. He closed and locked the car door and put the keys into his pocket. She watched him stand still for a few seconds and stare in the direction of her door before he proceeded to open the garage door to his studio.

Shanna's steps were lighter when she returned to her chair on the patio. She reached over for her glass of tea, deciding she really didn't want to go for a run after all.

Craig spent some time unpacking and putting away his clothes before going to the refrigerator for something to drink. Passing the window that looked out over the backyard, he saw Shanna sitting on the patio, a glass in her hand. Maybe she has more of whatever she's drinking, he thought, and hurried down the stairs to join her. He tried to hide his elation at seeing her. He'd missed her like hell every day he was away.

Shanna had almost finished her drink when she saw the gate to the backyard swing open. She swallowed hard, trying to contain the happiness that welled up in her.

Craig strode toward Shanna, a big smile on his face. "Hi, there," he called out. "Mind if I join you?"

Her heart was beating so loudly she hoped it didn't affect her voice. She drew a deep breath. "You're back," she said inanely, setting down her glass with a clatter.

Craig settled down in one of the lounge chairs.

"Would...would you like some iced tea?" Shanna stammered, hating the way her voice sounded.

"Thanks. I do feel a little thirsty," Craig acknowledged, "and your tea looks too good to pass up."

Shanna rose and headed for the kitchen, glad to have a few moments to compose herself. Her heart was beating fast against her chest, and her fingers had turned into thumbs. She took her time getting his tea, hoping to gain some control over her raging emotions. She avoided handing it to him, carefully setting it on the table beside him.

Craig picked up the glass and drank several swallows before returning it to the table. "This is some good stuff," he said gratefully, smiling in her direction.

They sat in silence for a few moments, sipping their tea.

Shanna finally asked, "So how was your trip?" His trip was not what she really wanted to hear about, but it seemed a safe subject at the moment. Deep inside she wanted to know whether he'd missed her as much as she'd missed him. But she could not possibly ask him something like that.

Craig leaned back and told her briefly why the trip had been necessary, ending with, "It seems I'll be out here a little longer than I mentioned last week." He glanced at her to see her reaction to that news, but her face showed no expression one way or the other, and he turned away, slightly disappointed. "I hope that doesn't interfere with anything you and the boys have planned for the summer." Looking around, he asked, "By the way, where are David and Phillip?"

"Their father picked them up earlier this evening to spend the weekend with him. And your being here longer than you first planned won't be a problem for me or the boys. They usually go to a camp in Massachusetts for three weeks as soon as school is out, and I have no definite plans for my vacation at the moment."

Had Shanna been looking at Craig, she would have seen the elation that crossed his face.

Craig picked up his glass, swallowing the rest of the tea before setting the glass back down. "That tea really hits the spot."

Shanna noticed Craig's glass was empty and went to the kitchen. She brought back the pitcher and refilled his glass, which he emptied halfway in just a couple of swallows.

They sat in silence for a few moments before Craig suggested, "Since the boys won't be around this weekend, maybe I can persuade you to go over to Alcatraz with me on Sunday...if you've nothing better to do. I've wanted to go over there ever since I've been out here but didn't really want to go by myself. I'll be at the office most of the day tomorrow to get a head start on next week. But it will free up Sunday for me."

Shanna's body went berserk at the thought of spending several hours with Craig. She had difficulty finding her voice, but finally said, "I think I'd like that. I've taken the boys over a couple of times, and each time I saw things I hadn't seen before. What time would you like to go?"

Craig thought for a moment. "Why don't we leave early enough to have breakfast on the Wharf and get the eleven o'clock ferry. So we should leave here around nine. Is that too early for you?"

Shanna shook her head. Too early? This evening wouldn't be too early. Tomorrow at that time wouldn't be too early, but surely she could wait until Sunday. Speaking in as casual a voice as she could manage while her emotions were going haywire, she replied, "No, that's not too early since we're having breakfast. I'm an early riser, even on Sunday. Must be a habit left over from getting up with the boys when they were younger."

For him, it was mission accomplished...or at least it was a start.

For her, it was something to anticipate in place of spending a long day alone. Or perhaps something more.

They exchanged a few more pleasantries before parting, each knowing it would seem like a lifetime until Sunday arrived.

🍁

The sun was barely above the horizon Sunday morning when Shanna stretched languorously before rolling out of bed. She was eager for the day to start; she wondered whether Craig was up. She threw on a robe and padded down the stairs. While the coffee was brewing, she showered. Then she got the paper from her porch and took it and a mug of coffee out onto the patio.

Sipping her hot coffee slowly, Shanna enjoyed the quiet of an early Sunday morning. Before catching up on the news, she became engrossed for several minutes in looking around her small yard, thinking she needed to do some pruning before the shrubbery got out of hand. The grass also needed cutting, something she must remind the boys to do the following week.

A short time later Shanna noticed the sun was much higher in the sky. Checking her watch, she was amazed at the time and jumped up, gathered her paper and mug, and hurried to her bedroom to get dressed. She was determined to be ready to step out of the door when Craig rang her doorbell. She gathered her clothes and dressed in record time. She'd just finished putting on the little makeup she used when she heard her chimes. She grabbed her purse and a sweater and rushed down the stairs, stopping for a moment to compose herself.

When Shanna opened the door to Craig's dark smiling face, her heart did a flip-flop. He looked as if he had just stepped out of an advertisement for sportswear she often saw in magazines—like the centerfold in *Ebony Man*, she thought.

"Hi," she finally got out.

Hi, yourself," Craig responded. "Ready to go?"

Shanna nodded. After locking the door, they hurried out to his Mercedes to start their day.

Craig had little trouble finding a parking spot on the Embarcadero near the restaurant where they were going to have breakfast. The tourists were just beginning to arrive and only a few people were in the restaurant. They finished their meal hurriedly, eager to get to the Ferry Building to pick up their tickets for Alcatraz.

It was almost ten-thirty by the time they reached the ticket office on the pier. Rows of tourists were already lined up. While waiting to board the boat, they watched the sailboats battling the choppy waves of the Bay.

"I've never been crazy about sailboats. Seems like so much trouble to handle. Give me a motorboat anytime," Craig declared.

"But sailboats are so...romantic, Craig."

"Sure, if you're just sitting back while others do the work."

"Hmmm...I've never looked at it that way," Shanna admitted.

They turned back to look out over the bay again until it was time to board.

The short trip across the bay to Alcatraz Island was over before Shanna had time to complain about the choppy waves. They followed the crowd off the ferry when it docked. They stopped at some tables displaying literature about the island and took several minutes selecting leaflets and brochures before starting up the hill to the buildings. Locating their guide, they spent the next few hours listening to him point out various parts of the prison and give the general history of the Island.

Throughout most of the tour, Craig held Shanna's hand in his warm one. Both were more aware of each other than what the guide described as they moved through various parts of the former prison. The time passed too quickly and both were disappointed when their guide pointed out that the ferry was on its way across the bay to pick them up. Craig did not let go of her hand until they boarded the ferry in single file.

Craig drove into their driveway as the sun was nearing the horizon. Opening Shanna's car door, he walked her to her front door and waited until she inserted the key in the lock.

Shanna turned back to face him. "Thanks for a lovely day, Craig," she said softly. "The day went by so fast I didn't even have time to miss the boys, who should be coming back shortly."

Hearing that, Craig changed his mind about asking whether he could come in for a few minutes, something he had looked forward to. He was loath to part from her but picked up on the information that the boys were expected.

Clearing his throat from the emotion he was feeling, he merely stated, "You made my day also. Maybe we can visit some other places when you have time to yourself." With that said, he leaned down and gave her a sound kiss on her cheek before turning abruptly to make his way to his studio, silently cursing the desires coursing through him.

Astonished, Shanna put her hand to her cheek, staring at his back before closing her door with emotions similar to Craig's. She walked through the house and up the stairs to change into her pajamas and robe, her mind going around in circles when she tried to analyze her reactions to Craig. She was glad the boys had not yet returned because she needed time to remember every word he'd said, and the way he'd looked at her most of the afternoon. And now her cheek still felt warm from his kiss. In one way he frightened her; in other ways he attracted her. For several moments she vacillated between uneasiness and hope. The bottom line, she knew, was that she couldn't simply ignore the emotions he aroused in her.

Shanna finally went downstairs to the living room, lighting the logs before she settled down on the couch to catch up with her magazines. She'd glanced through only a couple before she dozed off, Craig's face floating around her in her half-dream state.

She started when she heard the boys burst through the front door, both noisily talking at the same time. They would definitely take her mind off Craig while she listened to their weekend experiences with their father.

"You two seem to be at loggerheads. Why all the grumbling?" Shanna asked.

David spoke up. "Can you believe Dad didn't take us sailing yesterday? And he promised he would!"

"Yeah," Phillip chimed in, "and all because that wife of his didn't want to go!" He flopped down in a chair, disgust written all over his face.

"Calm down, guys. It's not the end of the world, you

know. There will be other days to go sailing."

"That's not the half of it, Mom. They took us to one of their friend's house who had two second-grade brats and we had to spend the whole afternoon playing those dumb kid's games!"

"The whole weekend—a total bust," Phillip added. "I'm going to watch TV—something else we didn't get to do. Come on, David. Let's go upstairs."

After the boys left, Shanna checked the fire screen around the fireplace and turned out the lights downstairs before slowly climbing the stairs to her room. She knew she would replay the whole day in her mind before she settled in for the night.

CHAPTER TEN

Duke uring the next three days Shanna heard Craig drive in after she was in bed and leave before she went to work in the morning. Was he was deliberately avoiding her? Her previous optimism waned. Maybe he'd had second thoughts about the things he told her. Maybe he really hadn't meant any of them. Maybe he... She finally refused to speculate any further about his actions and tried not to think about him.

David and Phillip inquired about Craig a couple of times, missing the basketball bouts they had with him.

"Oh, Craig is probably busy, guys," Shanna told them shortly. She didn't want to hear anything else about him.

Shanna was clearing the kitchen Wednesday evening when Angela phoned. "I'm coming over for a few minutes...if you're not busy, that is."

Shanna brewed more coffee and got down two mugs while waiting for Angela. The minute Angela stepped into the kitchen, Shanna knew she was ticked off about something. Her friend and neighbor usually didn't waste time in being subtle about anything.

"Hi, Angela," Shanna greeted her when she came through the kitchen door. "Haven't seen you for a few days. How's everything with you?"

"Oh, girlfriend, I'm okay," Angela informed her. "It's

you I'm worried about."

"Well, sit down, Angela. I'm sure you're going to tell me why you're looking so put out."

Angela pranced across the kitchen. She pulled out a chair in the breakfast nook and sat down heavily.

Shanna raised her eyebrows. Worried about me? What in the world is she talking about? Shanna poured coffee into the mugs and sat down at the table opposite Angela.

Angela picked up her coffee, glaring at Shanna over the rim of her mug. She took a couple of sips before getting to the reason for her visit. "I heard you toured Alcatraz with a tall black Adonis last weekend. And the boys weren't with you."

Angela knew she'd hit a vulnerable spot when she saw a blush slowly spread over Shanna's face. "So what gives, Shanna? You haven't mentioned you had a boyfriend. Who was he? Anybody I know?"

Shanna lowered her mug to the table and turned it around several times before she spoke. Feeling that a discussion about Craig would somehow bring out what she actually felt for him, she hedged. She had worked hard at shutting out the memory of Craig's attentions and the emotions he loosed in her. Or was it just her hormones acting up? She certainly had no intention of discussing that with Angela, even though they often shared confidences about almost everything.

Angela waited, impatiently glancing over at Shanna several times while taking small sips of her coffee.

"Oh, you must be talking about Craig." Playing down her day with Craig, she absently added, "He wanted to tour the Island since he'd not been there, and I agreed to go with him while the boys were—"

"Craig? You mean your roomer?" Angela asked, her eyebrows moving up in disbelief. "You went out with that hunk?" She set her mug down and stared at Shanna.

"Look, Angela, we toured Alcatraz together. Okay? You make it sound as if we were carrying on a torrid love affair." Shanna realized her voice had risen slightly.

That fact was not lost on Angela.

Slightly chagrined at her own reactions, Shanna smiled at Angela. "There's no need to make something out of nothing, Angela. He asked me to go because he didn't want to go by himself. And I had a good time. I enjoyed talking with him. He's also very interesting to listen to."

"So why did he ask you? Gossip around the city has it that there're dozens of women in San Francisco who would give their eyeteeth just to go out with him for an evening, not to mention spend the day with him."

"How would I know why he asked me? I suppose because he knows me better. I don't know. Maybe because I'm just a friend he wouldn't have to deal with all the rigmarole that goes on in a real dating situation." She hoped Angela believed her explanation.

Angela raised an eyebrow. " Hmmm. You've never shown any interest in the guys I've introduced you to the past couple of years. Yet you tramp all over Alcatraz with someone you hardly know. Are you sure you're not asking for trouble? After all, you two are very accessible to each other."

Shanna could not hold in her laughter. "Don't even go there, Angela. That's such a ridiculous idea...I'm certainly old enough to take care of myself. If push comes to shove, I'll sic the boys on him."

Shanna's half-hearted joke fell flat.

Angela did not share her laughter. "That's not funny, Shanna. You really don't know that much about him, do you?"

Angela's remark elicited a sobering thought in Shanna. No, she admitted to herself, she really didn't know him that well, but that didn't stop her heart from beating rapidly when he was near her. Nor her knees from turning to jelly when he touched her. Not to mention what his just being close to her did to her emotions. But Angela certainly wasn't going to know about that!

"You're right that I don't know much about Craig, Angela, but he seems to be a decent sort of guy. My boss surely wouldn't recommend a cad to live in my house." Shanna stopped talking for a few moments and thought of her conversations with Rick. "After all, Rick has known Craig most of his life, so he must not have a past to be ashamed of. I told you the last time we talked that Rick said Craig has been married but is now divorced. Remember?"

But Angela was not to be put off so easily. "You just can't tell about guys nowadays, Shanna. And you have to admit you haven't had much experience in dealing with them," she reminded her friend.

"I'm sure what you say is true about most guys, Angela, but Craig seems different—he's mostly interested in his work. And he spends what free time he has in the evenings shooting baskets with the boys." She didn't know whether she was defending Craig to Angela or to herself.

"I hope you're right, Shanna. Frankly, you're a pretty good catch, so to speak. I guess I worry that some no-good guy will come along and sweep you off your feet."

Shanna looked askance at Angela. "You've got to be kidding! I haven't had any trouble with guys breaking down my door the last few years. And the few that I've talked to certainly didn't impress me enough to even give them the time of day!"

"Well, you've got to admit you really didn't give them a chance to prove themselves one way or the other, girl-friend."

Shanna knew her friend was right on that score and told her so. "I just haven't met any one who I would even go to lunch with, much less go out on a date."

Shanna felt the conversation was going nowhere and changed the subject. "Did David tell you he's tutoring some of his classmates in math two evenings a week? His teacher thinks he's tops in the subject. He even helps her with students during class."

"No, David hasn't mentioned that to me. But I'm not surprised; he's one smart young man. By the way, he's really growing up. I noticed some fuzz on his upper lip, and you know what that means. Does he have a girl-friend?"

Angela's question threw Shanna for a loop. She hadn't even thought that David might be interested in having a girlfriend! Remembering the note Phillip had given David ... It didn't mean that she was his girlfriend! She knew the girls liked him, or so Phillip always teased him about girls liking him, but she hadn't considered whether he had a special girl.

"Uh, I don't think he likes any special girl but—"

"Don't bury your head in the sand, Shanna. David's going on fifteen, isn't he? Have you talked to him about the birds and the bees, as old folk used to say?"

From the expression on Shanna's face, Angela knew she hadn't.

"Maybe you should mention the subject to Paul, Shanna. Maybe they've already had this much-touted father/son talk."

Shanna's blood pressure rose a few points. Her boys were really growing up too fast for her comfort. Since she hadn't grown up with brothers, she had no close males to compare them with. Another problem to deal with! She would mention it to Paul the next time he picked up the boys for a weekend.

The two friends talked on for several minutes before Angela took her leave with a parting shot. "It still would-n't be a bad idea to keep your distance from Craig,

Shanna. At least until you get to know him better," she
cautioned before she closed the kitchen door.

Shanna smiled to herself when Angela left. "I wonder what you would do if you were in my shoes?" she
asked an absent Angela, and went upstairs to check on
the boys' homework and lay out her clothes for the next
day.

❧

Shanna's phone rang shortly after she arrived at
work on Thursday. She almost dropped the receiver
when she heard Craig's voice.

"Hello...Hello...Shanna?"

She swallowed hard a couple of times before finding
her voice to answer.

"Hello, this is she," Shanna finally got out, wondering
why he was calling.

"I've just got a minute. This place has been a mad-
house this week. But I wanted to know if you and the
boys would like to go to our firm's staff picnic on
Saturday. There'll be other young people there, so the
boys will have something to do, and—"

Shanna cut in. "That sounds like a lot of fun, Craig.
I'll check with David and Phillip, of course, but I think
they'd like to go."

"Great! I'll tell you more about it when I get in this
evening. At least I hope to make it in before you turn out
the lights. Got to go now," Craig stated before hanging
up his receiver.

Shanna stared at the telephone thoughtfully a few
seconds after she hung up the receiver. She certainly
hadn't expected this. Somehow she knew the rest of her
day was going to be just fine.

❧

Shanna rose early and opened the bedroom shades
to check on the weather Saturday morning. There was
little morning fog over the Bay, which always portended

a great day. Craig told them to be ready by noon. She glanced at the clock. She wanted to have time to finish her Saturday chores before they went to the picnic. She would get the boys up after she had her first cup of coffee over the morning paper. They had been very excited since she told them about the invitation from Craig a couple days earlier.

Shanna threw on a light robe after her shower and went down to the kitchen. While the coffee was dripping, she got the paper from the porch. She was almost finished with her second cup when the boys came out. She knew they were expecting their usual Saturday morning breakfast of pancakes or waffles, but she dispelled their hopes. No way was she going to cook a big breakfast this morning.

"Get some orange juice and cereal, guys. That will hold you until we get to the picnic. And then do your chores. Craig said we should be ready to leave about eleven-thirty."

Both boys rolled their eyes heavenward at having to settle for cold cereal but got their cereal and bowls without voicing their displeasure. Shanna heard them arguing about whose turn it was to do their bathroom, and for once Phillip got his way. "So I'll run the sweeper," he informed David.

All three had completed their chores and were dressed and ready with time to spare when they heard Craig out in the driveway. The boys rushed out to help him put some balls and bats and a volleyball set into the trunk of his car.

"Sorry, guys, but I don't think there's a hoop, so we won't take—" Craig stopped in mid sentence. When he spied Shanna walking across the yard, his heart skipped a beat and he stared at her pale yellow shorts with a shirt to match. "... the basketball." All of a sudden his hands felt as if he had five thumbs on each as he turned back to arrange the equipment around the other things he always carried in his trunk. With the help of the boys, he finally had everything in place. He closed the trunk with a thud and greeted Shanna.

"You're looking like a ray of sunshine this morning," Craig observed, consciously not letting his eyes drift below the shorts. He smiled inwardly when he saw a slow blush starting on her cheeks.

"Uh...thanks," Shanna managed to get out. She sure hoped her boys didn't see her face.

Walking to his side of the car, Craig opened both doors. "How about sitting in the front with me, David?" he asked, which thrilled David no end as he went around to the other side and opened the doors. Phillip climbed in beside his mother, happy to have her in the back seat with him.

"Buckle up, everyone," Craig instructed before he started the engine and backed out of the driveway.

"Where is the picnic?" David asked. "Mom said she didn't know."

"I guess I forgot to tell her. It's over in Mill Valley. One of the firm's powers-that-be has a large place and the office has its picnic there each year."

"My father lives in Mill Valley," David informed him.

"Oh?" Craig replied. "Maybe he'll be there as some-body's guest. I understand Mill Valley isn't too large of a place. So you'll probably know some of the kids."

Had Craig glanced in the rearview mirror he would have seen a shadow cross Shanna's face. She hadn't given a thought to the fact that Paul might be at the pic-nic, and her anticipation dulled slightly when she thought of the possibility of running into her ex-husband and his blond wife.

Having followed a map the office supplied, Craig soon pulled into a long, wide driveway. Several small groups were scattered about on the spacious lawn beyond the large, sprawling house.

"Quite a layout, isn't it?" Craig remarked, climbing out of the car and opening Shanna's door, while the boys got out on their side of the car.

"You're right," Shanna answered, very impressed with the sight in front of her. "Seems like a perfect place for a picnic. I haven't seen so much lawn in a long time."

"Come on, guys, help me carry the equipment while your mother admires the scenery," Craig instructed the boys as he opened the trunk. They soon had everything under control and walked across the wide expanse of lawn to join the crowd. Craig unloaded the bats and balls near a spot where someone was busy organizing a softball game.

A youngster recognized David and Phillip and called out to them. "Come on over here, guys," he called. "We're trying to get a team together. You two can be on my team."

Craig smiled at Shanna, as if to say she needn't worry about their having a good time. As he watched the boys tear across the lawn to join a group, Craig turned to Shanna, happy to have her all to himself. "You're looking really great today," he said as he reached for her hand. "Let's go and meet some of the people." B o t h were aware that their touching hands produced sparks. Shanna glanced up at Craig while slowly pulling her hand out of his and putting it into the pocket of her shorts.

Craig smiled down at her. His eyes seemed to gaze into her very soul. He understood her feelings and shoved his hands deep into his own pockets. They continued walking toward the early arrivals.

Walking across the lawn, Shanna glanced toward several tables with umbrellas and other uncovered tables that surrounded the pool. She smiled at the antics of some small children splashing around at the shallow end while some teenagers were showing off on the diving board at the other end of the pool.

"I wish I'd known there was a pool," Craig said, apologetically. "We could have brought our swim suits."

"I'm sure we'll find enough to do without going swimming." Shanna glanced around at some people playing cards, others with scrabble boards or backgammon sets between them, while some were just sitting and talking.

Craig wondered what Shanna looked like in a bikini and felt a flash of heat go through him.

Shanna wondered what Craig looked like in tight swim trunks and turned her head from him when her heart skipped a couple beats.

They passed long tables loaded with food: many kinds of salads in addition to large bowls of potato salad, pasta, cole slaw, baked beans, trays of deviled eggs, platters of thick sliced ham and cold cuts, various kinds and sizes of rolls, pickles, and olives. Chips surrounded various kinds of dips and salsa. Other platters were piled high with cut-up fruit on ice, and small trays of several kinds of cheese dotted the table. Large containers of soft drinks on ice were placed strategically near the tables. Several barrels of ice contained beer and small bottles of wine coolers. Men in long white aprons tended grills piled high with barbecued ribs and chicken while other grills held hamburgers and hot dogs cooking slowly.

"There's nothing like the smell of barbecue," Shanna observed, inhaling deeply.

They approached a long table where several guests just chatted. They joined that group at the end of the table. Craig knew most of the people and he introduced her to those sitting nearby. Soon they were all engaged in a political conversation about the coming election for the mayor of San Francisco. Craig listened as if he were a permanent resident. When Shanna expressed her views of the present mayor and some of the problems with the present council, Craig was slightly surprised by her cogent remarks and silently agreed with most of her basic criticisms of how the city was governed.

While Shanna and Craig talked, Phillip ran up to claim Craig for his softball team. Shanna excused herself from the group and walked across the lawn to watch the game. She found a spot under a tall tree and sat down on the lush grass.

The game went on for almost an hour before the hosts announced the barbecue was ready. Shanna eagerly followed Craig and the others to fill their plates and claim a place at a table. She noticed that her boys joined kids about their age seated at another table. She occasionally glanced in their direction as the teenagers noisily kidded each other about how much they could eat. She was happy to see her boys interact so confidently with other young people and thanked her lucky stars that so far they had given her so little trouble. With all the news on television and in the papers about drugs in schools all across the nation, she felt blessed that so far she hadn't had to deal with that in her own home.

Shanna brought her attention back to the people she and Craig were sitting near. Even though they exchanged pleasantries with the people around them, they were really more interested in each other as they sat close together at the crowded table, making it impossible not to touch while they ate ravenously.

Shanna admired Craig's ability to be at ease around his staff. She discerned they all seemed to have respect for Craig's position, plus admiration for him as a person. Craig sent her occasional smiles as he chatted about happenings at their firm. She covertly looked at him as he talked with others. She felt a rush of heat at how great he looked in his shorts that showed off his long, well-formed legs and narrow waist and his fitted golf shirt that emphasized his muscled arms and broad chest. She prayed she wouldn't start squirming on her bench.

As she raised a rib to her mouth, Shanna's hand stopped in midair. Craig looked at her quizzically when she uttered a soft, "Oh, no."

"Is something wrong, Shanna?" he asked. He saw her looking in another direction, and he followed her eyes to Phillip who was talking to a tall man who had a vaguely familiar face.

Shanna placed the rib back on her plate and carefully wiped her hands on a large napkin before she answered. "I'm okay," she replied.

Craig detected a change in her tone of voice. Then he remembered the man who'd picked up David and Phillip one weekend. He turned back to Shanna.

"That's Paul, the boys' father, that Phillip's talking to. His wife is standing next to him. I really didn't expect to see them here, even though I knew they might be." She didn't add that was all she needed to spoil her day.

"Does that bother you, Shanna?" Craig asked, watching the emotions crossing her face as she watched Paul and his wife heading toward their table.

"It doesn't actually bother me, it's just that I..." Shanna's voice trailed off as her ex-husband got nearer.

"I just talked to Phillip and David," Paul said, not really looking at Shanna but at Craig.

Shanna remembered her manners and introduced Paul and his wife to Craig, not mentioning, however, that Craig now lived in the garage studio. The two men merely nodded while eyeing each other speculatively.

Paul turned back to Shanna. "I didn't know you and the boys were going to be here," he said inanely.

"I could say the same for you. It just so happens that Craig is heading up his firm's San Francisco office at the moment. He invited us." Despite Shanna's best intentions not to let her irritation show, she knew her remark would get to Paul as he always wanted to be the top guy at any affair.

Paul barely glanced at Craig as he asked, "Are you going to be in San Francisco long?"

"I came out here for two or three months, but it now looks like I'll be here much longer than I expected," Craig explained. He suddenly developed a dislike for the man facing him for some reason he could not put his finger on.

They exchanged a few more words before Paul and his wife wandered in search of the couple who'd invited them. Shanna heaved a sigh of relief when they walked away from the table. For her, the afternoon had lost some of its luster.

During the remainder of the afternoon Shanna and Craig talked, snacked, and sipped beer or wine while they watched the teenagers' softball game. Craig occasionally eyed her surreptitiously, thinking how he would like to have her all to himself. But he made no romantic gestures in front of his friends, other than to throw his arms around her shoulders when she leaned across him to speak to others.

It was early evening before the ball game ended, and most of the guests prepared to leave. Shanna rounded up her boys while Craig gathered the equipment he'd brought. Making their rounds, Shanna and Craig told everyone good-bye and thanked their hosts.

On their way back to the city Shanna and Craig said little, just listened to the boys recount the events of their day. As soon as they reached home, David and Phillip bounded out of the car and raced into the house to watch their favorite Saturday television program.

Shanna walked to the back of the car while Craig opened the trunk to remove the equipment. "Thanks for inviting us to your picnic. I don't get to many adult events. I really enjoyed the day with your friends. Would you like to come in for a cup of coffee or a nightcap?" She wanted to have him to herself if only for a short time.

Craig looked at her with longing in his eyes, but merely answered, "Not tonight." He wanted to take her in his arms and cover her with kisses and hold her close to his chest. But he turned away, hoping she hadn't seen the passion he was sure showed on his face. In a husky voice he added, "I'll take a rain check, though."

"Anytime," she replied, and turned away, not wanting him to see the disappointment flitting across her face. She walked across the lawn and into the house. She closed the door slowly. She felt more alone at that moment than she had in a long time.

Feeling restless after she entered the house, Shanna piddled around for the next couple of hours, watering her house plants, checking the refrigerator and pantry for items she needed to pick up the following week, and making out a list of things to do. Since it was too early to go to bed, she finally settled on looking at a television program in the living room. Before curling up on the couch, she lit the logs in the fireplace and turned out all the lights except one in front of the window. She saw little of the television program because in a matter of minutes she fell asleep. David and Phillip awakened her when they went to bed, and she bid them goodnight after reminding them to brush their teeth, but she didn't move from her spot and soon drifted back into a light sleep.

In her dreams Shanna heard the chime of a doorbell. She didn't realize her own doorbell had actually chimed until she heard it the second time. She sat up and rubbed her eyes with the backs of her hands. The chime sounded again. Sleepily, she wondered who could possibly be at her door and tiptoed to the peephole to check. Surprised yet elated, she quickly opened the door and drew Craig inside, hoping he hadn't disturbed the boys.

Speechless, Shanna looked up into Craig's face, seeing his embarrassed half-smile.

"I couldn't sleep...so I went for a walk...and I saw

your light from the driveway, and I—"

"Come on in," Shanna interrupted. "I fell asleep on the couch, and I thought I was dreaming when the doorbell first chimed." Closing the door softly, she led him into the living room.

"Sit down while I put on another log."

Before Shanna made it to the fireplace, Craig reached over and got a log from the box, opened the fire screen, and placed the log carefully on the coals. It caught fire immediately and the dry wood crackled as flames shot up around it. Satisfied that the fire was burning as it should, he walked around the coffee table and took a seat on the sofa beside her.

"Let's have a glass of wine," Shanna suggested. "Or would you rather have coffee?"

"I'll take the wine."

Shanna quickly rose and headed out of the room, glad to have a moment to get herself together. She had to stop the fast beating of her heart and do something about her sweaty palms. What his mere presence does to me should be against the law, she thought on her way to the kitchen.

Shanna took her time in opening the wine bottle. She took down two crystal glasses and placed them and the bottle on a tray. Thinking Craig might like a snack, she cut up some cheese and apples and placed them on the tray, along with small cocktail crackers and napkins. Shanna was ready to carry the tray to the living room when Craig appeared in the kitchen. "Oh," he said as he looked at her loaded tray. "Now I see why it took you so long." He took the tray from her and headed back to the living room.

Shanna moved some magazines aside on the coffee table so Craig could set the tray down. Reaching for the wine, he poured it into their glasses and handed one to her. Holding his glass up before he took a sip, he toast-

ed, "To many more days like today." He looked at her
with a twinkle in his dark eyes.

Silently, Shanna touched her glass to his, hoping
what he said would actually be what the future held as
she took a small sip of wine.

They sat slightly sideways on the sofa, only a short
distance apart, and they looked into each other's eyes as
they chatted about the day they'd just spent together.

After a few minutes Craig set his glass down and put
his arm on the back of the couch. "I feel happy when I'm
around you, Shanna," he said softly.

"I'm glad," she said shyly. "I enjoy your company,
too."

Craig was silent a few moments. "I think friendship
and respect for each other are the most important
aspects for a lasting relationship between a man and a
woman." He took another sip of his wine and ran his finger around the edge of the glass several times before
setting it down again. He moved closer to her so that his
arm still rested on the couch but now his hand touched
her shoulder lightly.

Craig looked at her thoughtfully. "I think that's one
reason why my marriage failed—Ann and I certainly
weren't friends at the beginning, and we didn't try to
become friends later on when all the early passion wore
thin. Nor at any time did we have respect for each
other's differences, which were certainly many, but we
could have gotten through that, I think, if we'd really
wanted to. Even after our son was born, our relationship
didn't get any better." He turned from her and stared into
the flames.

Shanna waited. What could she say? She knew so
little about him, other than the way he affected her.

Craig turned back to her. "I made up my mind when
the divorce was final that I wouldn't pursue another
woman until I had my priorities straight, knew what I had

to offer a woman and what I wanted from her. Life's too short to be unhappy. That's why I've dodged all the women my friends thought were right for me. My work is very demanding, and I pour myself into it. That's also probably why I haven't missed the company of women enough to seek any out...that and the fact that casual sex doesn't appeal to me."

Craig stopped talking for a few seconds before moving still closer to her and taking her face between his hands. "But now I'm really puzzled at the way I'm attracted to you. And it isn't just something physical—although that has its place in any relationship—it's...it's...it's like I've found the other half of me," he stammered, ending in a rush of words, still holding her face between his hands.

Shanna squirmed in her seat. It took all of her willpower not to press her lips against his in a kiss she had yearned for all day. But she had lived with caution too long to bow out now. If anything came of their relationship, it certainly was worth waiting for. She withdrew his hands from her face.

Craig recognized her reticence and backed off. "Can't we just give ourselves a chance that a relationship might work, Shanna?" he asked softly.

Shanna studied her nails for a few moments. She finally raised her head and looked into his eyes. "Let's be sensible about this, Craig. I have two teen-age sons to raise. I can't let anything get in the way of that. I can't carry on a casual affair on the side. That just wouldn't work for me." Her heart ached as she said those words, knowing she wasn't being honest with herself. Deep inside she knew what she really wanted was to make love with him. She drew a deep, ragged breath just thinking about it.

Craig smoothed back her hair gently and pulled her closer to him. "I'm not asking for anything you don't want to give, Shanna. But I am asking for a chance for us to get to know each other better. And if nothing happens, well, so be it. If we remain platonic friends forever, I'll at least know I've given it my best shot." He looked deeply into her eyes, detecting her warring emotions. "I've laid my cards on the table—the rest is up to you." He took a deep breath to restore his diminishing control, as he wanted her more than he had ever wanted any woman. He suspected that she wanted him almost as much but was unwilling to admit it. No way she could escape feeling the passion that enveloped them whenever they were together.

"I have some hurdles to get over before I can commit to anything, Craig, and I need a little time." Shanna looked at him pleadingly.

"That you've got," Craig said softly. He got up to leave. "Now maybe I can get a good night's sleep."

Shanna rose to walk to the door with Craig. Before she opened the door she lifted her arms and lowered his face down to hers in a long, passionate kiss. Dropping her arms, she opened the door, practically pushing him through it, afraid she would lose her willpower and entice him to stay. The consequences of such an action could be...she drew in a deep breath; she didn't want to think about that.

Shanna considered herself a practical person. She didn't believe in fate, the full moon, the stars, horoscopes, crystals, or numerology. None of that kind of stuff. Yet there was something inevitable about his renting the studio. For a few hours he'd made her feel like a woman—desirable, wanted, a little fascinating perhaps, and certainly alive in a way she couldn't remember. She had never felt about a man the way she now felt about Craig, and it scared her pants off.

Checking the fireplace before she put out the light, she made her way to her bedroom, intending to reminisce about the day and the evening. She wanted to think about his smiling dark eyes and his handsome face and the way he looked when he said he'd found the other half of himself. Remembering the camaraderie that existed between them the whole day and evening, she decided everything about him fascinated her.

CHAPTER ELEVEN

Shanna had a hectic week and saw Craig only in passing. It was the last few days of the school year for David and Phillip. Her boss gave her a few hours off during the day to attend some programs at their school. A couple of evenings she took David and Phillip shopping for their three-week stay that started the following week at Camp Atwater in Massachusetts. Since this was their second year at the camp, both boys were anxious to get back to see the friends they'd made the previous year.

In addition to overseeing the packing of their trunks, Shanna had so many little odds and ends to take care of for them that by the end of the week she was completely frazzled. She didn't have time to think about Craig or missing her boys while they were away. Last year she'd taken her three-week vacation while they were at camp, but this year she decided to vacation later in the summer when the boys could accompany her.

Late Saturday evening Shanna was making one last check with the boys and their trunks when Craig appeared on the lawn below her bedroom, calling her name. She opened the window and peered down at him, wondering why he hadn't rung the doorbell.

"Shanna, I know you're busy," Craig called up, "but I

wanted to let you know I'll take you and the boys to the airport tomorrow morning."

"Hey," she called down, "that's nice of you, but I don't think you know what you're letting yourself in for. You should see the stuff they're taking with them, claiming they can't do without any of it."

"All the more reason why you could use my help," Craig insisted. "What time do you want to leave?" He could tell from her face that she was happy he made the offer.

"Around eight o'clock, I think."

"See you then," he called back, making his way to his car parked in the driveway.

For Shanna the rest of the evening flew by as she and the boys completed their last minute checks. When they finally locked the trunks, it was almost midnight.

"You guys better get to bed. You have to get up much earlier than usual in the morning if you expect to make that plane." That admonition sent them to bed without any fuss.

A bit weary now that everything was done, Shanna settled down for the night. How nice that Craig had suggested helping them, she thought, grateful she didn't have to deal with it by herself.

Almost asleep, Shanna suddenly sat straight up in the bed. She and Craig would have the house to themselves for three weeks! The boys wouldn't be around to act as a buffer! She twisted and turned for a while before falling into a dream-filled sleep—dreams mostly about Craig.

❧

Shanna and Craig waited in the terminal until the boys' plane was lost in the clouds before starting back to his car. Embarrassed, Shanna wiped the tears that she was able to hide from the boys but which now insisted on seeping from the corners of her eyes.

Craig glanced down at Shanna with compassion, knowing how much she would miss them since her life revolved around her boys. He took her hand and held it tightly until they reached the parking garage and climbed into his car.

Before starting the engine, Craig reached into his car pocket for some tissues and handed several to her. "Go ahead and cry. I understand."

Craig's sympathetic words went straight to Shanna's heart.

Between sniffles, Shanna explained, "Massachusetts is so far away."

Craig didn't have the words to comfort her as his mind drifted to Danny, his own twelve-year-old son also across the country. He wished he knew what had been planned for him during the summer months. Was his mother sending him to camp where he could be with other boys his age? Danny hadn't mentioned any plans in his last letter. Craig ran the back of his hand across his forehead, thinking how useless his wishful thinking was. He forced his mind to deal with the things he now had some control over. His son's activities were not in that category.

Neither Shanna nor Craig spoke on their short drive from the airport back to the city.

Her mind was on her boys.

His mind was on her.

Craig had parked his car in the driveway before he got enough nerve to approach Shanna about an idea he had. Turning to her before she got out of the car, he spoke softly. "I'd like to take you to dinner tonight...some place special...a place where we could feel we're having a real date." He glanced down at his sweating palms before he continued. "I want you to feel like you're some-one special. I'm not taking you out just to make you feel better, although I hope you will." He drew a deep breath as he ended his short stammering speech which had no resemblance to the one he'd planned to make.

Shanna stared at Craig as if he had suddenly grown two heads. "A...a real date?" she asked inanely, having no idea what else to say.

"A real dinner date," Craig repeated. "Where would you like to go? What's your favorite spot?"

Shanna hesitated. It had been so long since she'd been out with anyone that she had to think. "I...I guess I'd choose the Top of the Mark Restaurant."

"That's in the Mark IV Hotel on Nob Hill, isn't it? I've heard some of my staff rave about it, but I've not been there. So, the Top of the Mark it is. How about making it a Sunday night supper? I'll call for reservations when I get upstairs and let you know the time we should leave. Is that okay with you?" He was wishing it was time to leave right then as he wanted nothing more than just be with her.

Little did Craig know that Shanna was thinking that a hamburger at a fast food restaurant would have tasted just as great as long as they were together.

"Sure," she said. "I didn't get too much sleep last night and I'm going to take a nap. If I don't answer right away, leave the message on my answering machine." She got out on her side of the car and walked around to the front of it.

He met her before she reached the sidewalk and pulled her in his arms, caressing her shoulders. "Now don't worry too much about the boys. They'll be in good hands. I know one of the counselors who's a swimming instructor there during the summer months, and I talked with him. I didn't tell the boys because I didn't want them to expect any special treatment."

"Really?" Shanna asked, surprise in her voice. "Why didn't you tell me that sooner?"

"If you remember, all week you were running around

like a chicken with its head cut off. The closest I could get to you was to say hello," Craig reminded her.

Smiling at his description of her—which was much too accurate—she pulled away and went across the lawn to her now quiet but empty house.

❧

Shanna vacillated between being almost deliriously happy and extremely despondent. She had already let Craig know she didn't want to have a casual affair since she knew he would be leaving San Francisco eventually. Yet here she was agreeing to go on what he called a "real date." She really must be losing her cotton-pickin' mind!

Throwing caution to the wind, Shanna found herself making preparations for their date a couple of hours before he would call for her. Going through her closet, she laid out several outfits she'd had no occasion to wear for a long time. She surveyed each one closely, settling for an understated little apricot silk number which though plain on the hanger did wonders for the body. With simple lines and a split up the left side, the dress flattered her and its color heightened her complexion. She remembered all the compliments she'd received the one time she'd worn it during her marriage. Especially compliments from men, which had irked Paul no end. Holding the dress up in front of her body, she hoped it still fit, even though she knew she had not gained any weight since her divorce. In fact she might have lost a couple of pounds.

Shanna returned all of the other clothes to her closet, and pulled out a long unused small bag and matching strap sandals. She searched out sheer panty hose and a black bra from the bottom of her lingerie drawer and laid them on her bed. A fringed beige shawl with gold threads running through it was next. She laid it beside the other articles.

Satisfied with her selections, Shanna turned her

attention to taking a long, hot soak in the bathtub. She went through the ritual of filling up the tub and dumping in a couple of caps of expensive bath oil that she hadn't used in ages, saving it for special occasions. In her book, this was definitely a special occasion.

Smiling at the way she was pampering herself, she decided to go all the way and went down to the kitchen to get a glass of wine to drink while she soaked. Setting the wine glass within easy reach, she lowered herself very slowly into water so hot it made her body tingle. When her body adjusted to the heat, she reached for her glass and took a long sip of wine, then leaned back in the soothing water, closing her eyes and willing her mind to become a blank.

When she finished the rest of the wine, she sighed and climbed out of the tub. There's nothing like a long, hot bath to feel like a new person, she thought. Good for the body as well as for the soul. Feeling renewed, she reached up for a long fluffy towel to dry off.

She caught a glimpse of herself in the mirror and turned away. She didn't want to argue with an image that she knew would say she was about to do the most stupid thing she'd ever done in her whole life. C'est la vie! It had been so long since she'd been on a so-called date that at the last minute she was getting butterflies in her stomach just thinking about it.

Shanna shook her head vigorously and padded to her bedroom to apply her makeup. She looked through all of the paraphernalia on her dressing table that she seldom used and selected eyeshadow and mascara. A soft blush she applied brought out the coloring of her cheeks. She worked with pinning her hair into a French roll a few minutes before she got it just right. Turning from side to side to look in the mirror, she hardly knew the woman who stared back. She turned away, afraid she might want to change everything back to the more comfortable way she always looked.

Checking the time on the clock on her bedside table, Shanna saw she had only a few minutes to get her clothes on. She drew on sheer panty hose, then leaned over to position her breasts in her bra. Picking up the simple pale apricot silk dress from the bed, she drew it over her head and smoothed it down over her hips, marveling at the way silk always made her feel...and very relieved that it still fit her perfectly.

Opening her jewelry drawer, she examined several pieces before finding one which would glamorize the simplicity of her dress. She fastened a long silver pendant, then clipped matching earrings on her tiny ears, and finally a heavy silver bracelet on her wrist. Seldom used and very expensive perfume scented the insides of her wrists, between her breasts and behind each ear. A last look in her floor-to-ceiling mirror on her closet door assured her she'd achieved the desired effect—sensual but definitely not sexy.

Glancing at the clock again, Shanna quickly dropped her lipstick and comb into the small bag, along with what she called her "mad money." She just finished closing the bag when the doorbell chimed. Hurriedly grabbing her bag and shawl, she rushed downstairs to the front door.

Craig stared at Shanna a few seconds before letting out a low whistle. "You look incredible," he murmured, surveying her from head to foot. "What have you done to yourself? You're absolutely stunning!"

That was all Shanna needed to hear. He was pleased with the way she looked. She knew it was going to be a great evening.

"You're looking rather handsome yourself," she returned his compliment as she took in his soft gray suit over a light blue shirt and gorgeous silk tie. "But we can't stand here admiring each other. Our reservations are waiting," she said walking through the door as regally as a queen heading a parade.

"You're right," Craig agreed and followed her to the car, too aware of the way her hips moved in her silk dress. He opened her door and helped her inside before he walked around to the driver's side.

On the short drive to Nob Hill they said little. But each stole glances at the other, very happy with what they saw as they listened to the soft mood music on his stereo.

Craig pulled into the circular drive of the Mark IV Hotel and the valet opened her side of the car. Walking around to join her, Craig placed his hand on her elbow. Looking down on her, he broke into a wide smile. "You really do look incredible, Shanna."

Shanna returned Craig's smile, grateful for all the pains she'd taken in dressing. The appreciative looks from people they passed in the lobby on their way to the express elevator for the Top of the Mark reinforced her confidence.

When the elevator stopped at the restaurant level, Craig slid his hand down to the back of her waist and effortlessly guided Shanna through the entryway to the restaurant.

They were seated immediately at a window table with an awesome view overlooking San Francisco's Financial District. Even though the city seemed wrapped in a soft blanket of fog, they could make out the car lights on the streets below and the lights of the tall buildings around the city. A few blocks away they saw the TransAmerica Pyramid Building with its top penetrating the fog-shrouded sky. Stars sparkled here and there in the night sky, and a waning silver moon moved slowly above them as they looked out into the night.

Shanna let out a soft sigh. "This is an incredible view. I feel the same way every time I look at the Golden

Gate Bridge." For her the view was doubly incredible tonight because Craig shared it.

Craig looked at her with raised eyebrows. "I'm glad I followed your suggestion. I like this place, too. Every day I learn there're so many things to do and places to go in San Francisco. I know now why so many people who visit here fall in love with the city."

Neither was aware of the subdued voices around them nor the clink of ice as glasses were raised to the lips of other guests. They were enchanted with being together and had eyes for no one else. But neither spoke of their feelings.

A hovering wine steward approached their table, and Craig turned his attention to the wine list handed to him. Shanna glanced around at the softly lit tables while he studied the numerous wines for a few moments.

Craig finally selected a chardonnay and asked if that was okay with her before he handed the wine list back to the wine steward, who returned almost immediately. He held up the wine bottle for Craig to read the label. Craig nodded his head and the steward proceeded with his reverent ritual of opening and decanting the wine.

Pouring a small amount into a glass, the steward handed it to Craig, who took a small sip. "Excellent," Craig said, and the steward solemnly filled each of their glasses.

Craig raised his glass to Shanna. "To a gorgeous woman and a beautiful evening," he said huskily, leaning across the table and looking deeply into her eyes.

Blushing, Shanna smiled and nodded to him over the rim of her glass, her eyes as sparkling as the glass she held. She found it difficult to appear calm. Every time she looked at him her heart beat faster while heat suffused her body.

When the waiter brought their menus, Craig ordered for them since they both had settled on the poached salmon. While waiting for their food, he led her to a small space where another couple was swaying to the soft music of a small group in the background playing the soft, romantic music of the 1950's. The music was as elegantly romantic as the surrounding atmosphere, and they moved around the space in perfect harmony. She rested her cheek against the smooth textured lapel of his coat, inhaling the pleasing scent of his cologne. He didn't fail to notice that her body seemed to fit into his arms in all the right places, just as he'd thought it would.

Feeling the tenseness leaving her body, Shanna moved closer to Craig, thinking what a wonderful dancer he was, very light and graceful on his feet for such a tall man. She drifted along in his arms, feeling as light as a feather as he led her loosely around the floor. It wasn't long, however, before she felt his arm tighten around her waist, pulling her body closer to his. They danced in companionable silence until the waiter served their entrees. During the meal they said little, attacking their food with relish and very aware of each other.

"Dessert?" he asked, finally pushing his plate aside.

"Just coffee, please," she replied.

Taking a sip of the fragrant brew, Shanna glanced at Craig over the rim of her cup and became unnerved when she saw him staring intently at her. She set down her cup noisily when he spoke.

"Have you always lived in San Francisco?" Craig suddenly asked.

"I moved here when I finished college to work in Rick's law firm, met Paul shortly afterward and married him. David was born during the first year and about eighteen months later Phillip arrived. I went back to work when Phillip was old enough to put in nursery school." She paused and twirled her cup around in its saucer. "That's about it in a nutshell, I guess," she finished and glanced across to him, almost as if to say it was now his turn.

When he didn't speak, she asked, "Is Chicago your home?"

"No. After Ann and I married, I lived on the East Coast before moving to Chicago. I couldn't refuse the offer the firm made if I transferred to Chicago, so I relocated. Ann was a typical New Yorker, and I think she felt like a fish out of water from the beginning of our stay in Chicago. She tried to adjust, I guess, but she was too unhappy being away from all her family and lifelong friends, so one day she just packed up and took off with our son. She left me a note saying she wanted a divorce as soon as possible, that she'd fallen in love with someone else. But it must have fizzled out soon after that, because she didn't marry the guy."

Craig paused for several moments before continuing. "After Ann left, I threw myself into my work...and it's been that way ever since. Funny thing is, even though I like women, I've never had the urge to have any lasting relationship with another woman. I guess I don't want to be burned twice." In the back of his mind he was thinking how very much he wanted to tell her that being with her was different, that she was the first woman who had appealed to him, even more so than Ann ever had.

Shanna took another sip of coffee, hoping he would tell her more. When he didn't, she refused to pry.

"You mentioned you hadn't considered remarrying," Craig reminded her.

Shanna slowly shook her head from side to side, giving him a short answer. "I've never even thought about marrying again," she said tersely, "not even if the man were the last one on this earth. I have other priorities."

"But 'other priorities' can't take the place of another person's warm body next to yours in the middle of the night," he pointed out softly.

She refused to acquiesce. "You said you have your

work. Why can't I have my priorities?"

Craig had no reply to that.

Shanna glanced at him before she added, "In the last four years and for the first time in my life I'm doing what I want to do, not what someone else wants or expects me to do."

"But what about the boys? Have you ever thought they needed a full-time father?" Craig wanted to swallow his words the minute he saw the emotional changes flitting across her face.

Shanna looked down into her coffee cup for a few moments. "Their supposedly 'full-time father' was not around too much even when we were married. They probably see him almost as much now as they did when he lived with us. The boys were not that high on Paul's list of priorities." She paused before she explained, "You see, Paul has always been quite a womanizer. I knew that before we married, but I thought he would settle down once he had a family...how wrong I was. He always had to go somewhere, so he didn't spend very much time with us."

Craig's heart ached for Shanna when he heard that. How could any man go for other women when he had Shanna all to himself? Her ex was certainly a fool in his opinion, and Craig developed a sudden resentment toward him. He reached out his hand to her. "How about another dance before we go?"

He walked around and pulled out her chair, putting his arm around her waist when she rose. He pulled her in his arms again when they reached the small dance spot. She reached up and put her arm across his broad shoulders, almost as if it belonged there. He smiled down at her and they glided around the floor for the next few minutes, their bodies fitting together like pieces of a jigsaw puzzle. She floated in his arms with closed eyes and wished their dance could last forever.

When the small band stopped for a short intermission, they went back to their table, gathered their things and made their way down to the lobby to wait until his car was brought around. On the way home they listened to mood music his stereo seemed to be playing just for them.

Although they hadn't finished the bottle of wine during dinner, Shanna felt a little drunk from the happiness bubbling inside. When Craig parked in the driveway, Shanna turned to him and asked shyly, "Want to come in for a nightcap?"

Not daring to let himself speak, Craig nodded his head and walked around to help her out of the car. He kept her hand in his as they walked across the lawn. Taking her key, he opened the front door and dropped the key into her hand when they stepped inside. He closed the door, and they got no farther. He pulled her into his arms, his self-imposed control disintegrating as he held her tightly to his chest. She awakened something in him that he thought he'd forgotten, something he'd tried not to think about the last few years.

A shiver ran through Shanna. Everything was happening too fast and she lacked the control to stop it. She pressed closer to him.

"Oh, Shanna, I've wanted so much to hold you and kiss you since you met me at the door a few hours ago," Craig said softly, looking down into her dark sparkling eyes. "You've been driving me crazy every time I looked at you this evening and..." He lowered his lips to hers in a long, breath-stopping kiss. He moved back slightly when his body threatened to show her what was running through in his mind.

Trance-like, Shanna lifted her head to stare into his eyes, an aching yearning deep inside her. The masculinity he radiated overwhelmed her. Throwing caution to the wind, she reached up and placed her hands on each side of his head, pulling his lips toward hers again, kissing him passionately. She decided at that moment to have a deliberate, casual affair with him until he returned to Chicago.

CHAPTER TWELVE

They forgot about having a nightcap and made their way up the dark stairs to her bedroom where only a night light burned. The tension that had surrounded them dissolved into thin air the moment they faced each other in her bedroom. Craig drew her into his arms and held her tightly against his chest.

Shanna felt his heart thudding against her body and her knees turned to jelly. She reached up to draw his head down to hers, planting small kisses on his forehead, his cheeks, his chin. She surrendered her lips in a hot, passionate kiss.

Craig groaned. He silently started to undress her. Helping him, she kicked off her shoes and pulled off her panty hose. After he pulled her dress over her head and unclasped her bra, he looked at her in the moonlight streaming through the half-open window shades.

"You're truly incredible," he murmured, pulling her into his arms and gently fondling her breasts. Then he quickly removed his clothes. Taking his billfold out of his pocket, he removed a small foil-wrapped packet and laid it on the night stand.

Lifting her gently, he placed her on the bed and fell in beside her. He felt like a person who, dying of thirst, is suddenly offered a cool drink of water. He pelted her with kisses...her face, her breasts, her stomach until she moaned from the pleasure he gave her.

Shanna felt emotions awakening in her she had no idea she even possessed. She wrapped her arms around him tightly and returned his passion.

Craig tried to restrain himself but gave up when Shanna became an eager partner.

Shanna's surrender only drove Craig to greater heights as he continued to explore every inch of her body. He reached over to the nightstand for the packet.

When she could no longer stand his hot kisses, she arched her hips toward him. He put his hands on her bottom and pulled her up to his pulsing loins.

For the next few minutes they were stunned by their passion. Both were amazed when all their pent-up emotion exploded in unison, sending them to heights neither had ever before reached. They slowly drifted back down to earth. He did not move from inside her but held her tightly to him until her breathing returned to normal and his heart stopped its throbbing. They lay together for a long time, not speaking, just holding each other tightly until they fell into a sound sleep.

Both jumped when her alarm clock on the table beside her bed sounded, at first not remembering they had to go to work.

Turning her toward him, he kissed her softly. "Good morning, sleepyhead."

Shanna stretched languorously, remembering the night—his hot passionate kisses, the feel of his hands stroking all parts of her body, the incredible lovemaking. She now had no intention of ignoring the chemistry between them, regardless of what the consequences might be.

"I didn't know lovemaking could be like this," she whispered softly.

"Really something, huh?" He pulled her to his chest,

holding her tightly for several minutes before gently
pushing her from him. Groaning, he got out of bed. "Why
couldn't this be Sunday? Then we'd have the whole day
to do more exploring! Guess I better go shower."

"My feelings exactly!" she informed him and blew him
a kiss as he walked out of the door.

☙

Still floating on a cloud on her way to work, Shanna
swore the sun was shining brighter and the birds chirping
louder than they ever had. What a difference he'd suddenly made in her life! She had a hard time keeping her
mind on her work, jumping every time the phone rang. In
one way she wished it was Craig; in another way she
was apprehensive at seeing him again. Would he still
feel the same about her?

By the end of the day, Shanna was still walking on a
cloud and her heart skipped a beat when she passed
Craig's car in the driveway. Opening her front door, she
frowned when she saw a note lying on the floor in the
foyer. Reading it, she felt the gods were giving her time
to straighten out her thinking. Craig and other staff had
gone to the Monterey office in the company car and
would be gone a couple of days.

Out of habit, Shanna went through the hallway to the
kitchen before she remembered the boys would not be
there. Still feeling at odds with herself, she put aside all
thoughts of what she would have for dinner and hurried
upstairs to get into her jogging clothes. She drove to a
spot in Golden Gate Park and parked her car where she
knew there would be other joggers. She soon felt invig-
orated from her running and the cool, brisk air she drew
into her lungs.

It was almost dusk by the time Shanna returned to
her car and drove home to take a hot shower before
making a tuna fish sandwich for her dinner. She put the
sandwich, a glass of iced tea, and a cup of custard on a

small tray and carried it to her bedroom. Watching the news while she munched on her sandwich, she'd almost finished when the phone rang.

Happy to hear David's voice, she talked to him and then to Phillip for several minutes. The most she got out of them was that they were having a good time, and that most of their friends from last year were also there.

Only minutes later, Craig called. "Hi, sweetheart! How are you? Did you get my note? Sorry I didn't get to contact you before I left. But things here were in such turmoil, a couple of guys and I left as soon as we got some records together."

"I'm okay," she replied, happy he couldn't hear the pounding of her heart. "How's Monterey? How long will you be there?"

Craig hesitated a moment. "Longer than I thought. Probably until the end of the week, but I was thinking tonight that...that maybe I would stay over the weekend and see some of Monterey while I'm here, and then—"

Even though Shanna's heart fell to her toes when she heard that, she managed to say brightly, "That sounds like a good idea. You might not have another chance to visit there before you leave San Francisco. Monterey's a really famous tourist attraction."

"Well...well, what I was thinking is that...that maybe you could drive down early Saturday morning...and we could have the weekend to explore the city together," he spilled out.

Her heart suddenly rose from her toes, and she drew in a deep, ragged breath just thinking about spending the weekend with him. As calmly as she could manage, she agreed. "That sounds like a great idea, Craig."

Before hanging up the receiver, she assured him she could easily manage the drive by herself, already thinking about the scenic drive down the coastline that she had made a couple of times with her boys.

As soon as they finished their conversation, Shanna raised her hands above her head and let out a loud, "Yes!"

They talked several times during the week. Each time they spoke, their anticipation of spending the upcoming weekend together was uppermost in both their minds.

CHAPTER THIRTEEN

In Monterey Craig couldn't totally concentrate on his work. Staff members looked at him skeptically several times during the week when they noticed his mind wandering while they worked. One guy finally spoke out near the end of the week. "You've really been out of it the last couple of days. Something wrong, Craig?"

Craig appreciated their concern and apologized for his frequent preoccupation. "Sorry, guys. There's something on my mind...but it'll be cleared up in a day or so." He looked at them sheepishly, feeling a bit foolish that he'd let his daydreaming become so public. "By the way, I'm not going back with you guys on Friday. I'm staying here until Sunday."

Little did his associates know that Craig's mere thinking about the upcoming weekend with Shanna made his pulses race and muddled his mind. He saw her face everywhere he looked. He wanted to do nothing during the weekend to disrupt the harmony slowly developing between them.

Saturday morning finally arrived. Craig awakened early in an anxious frame of mind. "Maybe I'm worrying needlessly," he said aloud while shaving, trying to convince himself once more that the weekend would go smoothly. He purchased a newspaper and found a chair

near the front of the hotel lobby. It went unread because
he couldn't remove his eyes from the front door of the
hotel. With each passing minute, he grew more impatient.

※

Saturday morning Shanna rose very early, eager yet
a little apprehensive about spending the weekend with
Craig. After a quick shower, she hurriedly packed, threw
her small bag into the back of her car, and headed down
the scenic route to Monterey.   She usually stopped at
vista points to view the Pacific Ocean crashing against
the rocks far below the road, hoping to catch sight of
seals basking on the narrow stretch of beach in some
places.

Today her mind was on getting to Craig. The view
was wasted on her.   She kept her eyes on the
speedometer since that route was heavily patrolled. The
last thing she wanted was a speeding ticket. Luckily, the
traffic was light, and she reached the outskirts of
Monterey in record time. The nearer she got to her destination, the faster her heart beat.

By the time Shanna reached the hotel, her excitement was at its peak. She drove into the circular drive
and stopped her car at the front door, unbuckled her seat
belt and reached to the back seat for her luggage.
Before she could open her car door, Craig appeared. As
soon as her feet reached the ground, he drew her into his
arms for a quick kiss and reached for her bag.

Shanna's heart pounded crazily as she followed
Craig through the lobby to the elevator and then down a
long hall to his room.

Craig nervously unlocked the door.

Shanna glanced around the spacious room while
Craig set her bag on one of the luggage racks. "What a
lovely room," she said inanely. "It's just like one of—"

Craig pulled her into his arms for a long, passionate

kiss. He finally released her and she sank into one of the deep chairs near the wide expanse of glass. Her heart pounded like a sledge hammer against her chest. Cool it, girl, you've got the rest of today, tonight and tomorrow with him, she reminded herself.

The phone rang and Craig walked across the room to answer it. He listened for a moment, then hit his forehead with the heel of his hand. "I'll be there in about fifteen minutes," he said before replacing the receiver.

Turning to Shanna, Craig looked at her apologetically. "The auditor has run into a snag at the office. I have to meet with him for a little while. I'm sorry about this, but I need to deal with this before I leave and—"

"Oh, no problem, Craig. I'll just have a short nap while you're gone...I really didn't sleep too well last night."

I can identify with that, ran across Craig's mind. I had the same problem. He walked across to her chair and pulled her up into his arms, holding her tightly for a few moments. "Sure you'll be okay?"

"Of course I'll be all right. Just don't be too long...I might go back to San Francisco," she added, a smile on her face, knowing that that was the last thing she would do.

Craig quickly threw some papers into his briefcase and gave Shanna a passionate kiss. He turned back when he reached the door. "We'll go out for lunch when I get back."

"That sounds good. I'll probably be hungry by that time."

Shanna unpacked her bag, put her toiletries in the bathroom and her cosmetics on one side of the long dresser. She glanced to the other end of the dresser where Craig's things were lined up neatly. She picked up a bottle of Calvin Klein cologne and unscrewed the cap, inhaling the delicious scent. "So this is what Craig uses," she said aloud and replaced the bottle in the same spot.

Surveying the rest of his belongings, Shanna knew they both would probably learn a lot about each other before their weekend ended.

Too excited to sleep much the night before, Shanna welcomed the chance to take a short nap. She was still asleep when Craig returned. Even the door opening and his calling her name did not awaken her.

Craig walked over to the bed and planted a kiss on her forehead.

Shanna awakened with a start and rubbed her eyes, then the warm spot above her eyes. Smiling shyly, she sat up and slid to the edge of the bed.

"Ready for some food?"

"I sure am. Just give me a minute." She smoothed out her shorts, put on her sandals, drew a brush through her hair and applied a tinge of tangerine lipstick. She was ready by the time Craig came out of the bathroom, having changed into shorts and a polo shirt. The sight of his brown muscular legs below his shorts sent shivers down her spine. She grabbed her bag and slung it over her shoulder, anxious to get out of the room before her longing for him took over.

Craig picked up a tourist's guide from the hotel. While having lunch, they planned what they wanted to see. As soon as they finished, they headed for Cannery Row, the oceanfront strip made famous by John Steinbeck's novels, *Cannery Row* and *Sweet Thursday*, although it was now quite different from the descriptions in Steinbeck's books. They wandered in and out of various tourists' shops and attractions, wax museums and antique shops, cheese and wine shops, and looked in the windows of some of the small restaurants.

They ended up at the Monterey Bay Aquarium. After standing in a long line several minutes to purchase tickets, they got inside and walked hand-in-hand first to the display tanks that held more than six thousand fish, mammal, bird, invertebrate and plant specimens representing nearly six hundred species, many of them native to the Monterey Bay.

Amazed by the display, Craig gazed for quite a while before commenting, "I've never seen anything like this. It's really something!"

They walked on to a ninety-foot-long glass enclosure filled with sharks, brilliant reef fish, and creosote-oozing pilings. They marveled at the kelp forest exhibit which towered three stories above their heads, the tallest aquarium exhibit in the world, according to a sign, where schools of fish wove among the swaying kelp fonds.

At a two-story sea otter exhibit, they watched the otters' antics for several minutes before wandering on to the special walk-through aviary of shorebirds. Craig marveled at everything he saw, asking questions as they moved from one place to another.

Shanna remembered the times she'd taken the boys to the aquarium and had read up to answer their questions. Now an old pro, she had answers for most of Craig's questions.

Leaving the aquarium, they decided to have dinner at their hotel. As soon as they reached their room, Shanna announced, "After all that walking, I need a shower." Quickly shedding her clothes, she threw on a short robe and headed for the bathroom, unaware of the pulses beating in Craig's throat as he gazed at her.

Turning on the shower full force, she stood under the jets with closed eyes as the pulsing water fell on her body. Caught up in the refreshing moment, she did not hear Craig open the sliding glass door of the shower.

"May I come in?" he asked softly. Not waiting for an answer, he stepped inside and slipped his arms around her waist, pulling her close to him. Oblivious to the water cascading around them, they kissed for several long moments.

Feeling his wet skin against hers was a sensation she'd never had, and she reveled in the emotions surrounding her. Finally breaking from his embrace, Shanna gazed up at him. "You take my breath away," she murmured against his chest.

Craig's body almost sagged from the passion she aroused in him. He reached for her sponge and slowly began to soap her breasts, continuing down her body, methodically touching each intimate curve. "Turn around, sweetheart, and I'll do your back."

As if in a trance, she turned slowly, thinking his hands moving against her skin was the most erotic thing that had ever happened to her.

Feeling her tremble as his hands soaped her bottom, he had difficulty with his own body, trying to hide his erection. Giving her a kiss on her back, he handed her the sponge. "You're finished, now let me get on with my own shower," he said as he opened the shower door for her.

"Don't you want—"

"Go," he ordered, "before I seduce you right here."

Smiling when she glimpsed the state of his body, she deftly stepped out of the shower and wrapped a long towel around her body. She dried off and fluffed out her hair while Craig finished his shower.

Emerging from his shower a few minutes later, Craig noted how gorgeous Shanna looked in her short turquoise robe. "Let's have dinner up here, sweetheart."

"Way to go, Craig. I won't have to change my clothes again."

Craig donned a short white terrycloth robe and picked up the menu for room service. He sat down in one of the deep lounge chairs beside Shanna. "What would you like?"

Shanna answered quickly. "Any kind of seafood, a caesar salad, and a glass of white wine, please."

"Dessert?" he asked.

"No, only coffee."

"Maybe we can have some dessert later on tonight." Craig smiled at his own suggestion. He knew she was the only dessert he wanted.

Their dinner arrived in a matter of minutes and they watched the waiter remove the metal covers and open the bottle of wine cooling in a container of ice. The delicious odor of food assailed their senses and both dived in as soon as the waiter left.

Craig glanced over at Shanna devouring her food. "All that walking must have made you hungry also."

Shanna nodded her head. "I didn't realize how hungry I was until I smelled the food."

Little more was said until they finished their dinner. Craig refilled their wine glasses and leaned back in his chair. "Now I feel a lot better."

They sipped their wine, glancing at each other surreptitiously every chance they got.

Looking at her, Craig knew he couldn't wait much longer.

Shanna thought how she longed to feel his close-shaven cheek next to her face, his body pressed against hers.

Craig rose, took Shanna's empty glass from her hand and put it on the serving cart and pushed the cart out into the hallway. He didn't want them interrupted by the waiter coming back for it.

Shanna walked over to the window, looking out of the long expanse of glass into the fast approaching night. The sky was almost cloudless and stars were beginning to dot the sky. She looked up at the slowly ascending moon. What a lovely romantic night it was going to be. She called out to Craig, "Come over to the window. The sky is so clear you could almost see forever."

As he crossed the room, Craig leaned down to turn

off the lamps. Moonlight immediately flooded the room.
He put his arms around her waist, drawing her back
close to his stomach. They stood like that for a few
moments, each reveling in the nearness of the other.

Craig turned her around to face him, whispering softly, "I can think of better things to do tonight than look at
the sky, sweetheart."

Craig's warm breath on her face was too much. She
drew his lips down to hers, kissing him with a passion
she'd held in all day.

Craig drew in a deep breath as he scooped her up
and laid her gently on the bed. Before untying the belt of
his robe and throwing it across to the nearest chair, he
retrieved a foil-wrapped packet and laid it on the nightstand.

Seeing his naked body sent spirals of pleasure
through her. She gazed at his dark brown muscular legs
and thighs, his almost flat stomach and the dark curly
hair on his chest. She unbuttoned her robe and tossed
it on top of his.

Craig pulled her up from the bed with one hand and
with the other pulled back the comforter and the sheet.
Climbing into the bed first, he pulled her down beside
him, letting out a soft groan.

Shanna drew a ragged breath and moved closer to
him. Her heart sang when she felt his hands exploring
her breasts, then his mouth on first one then the other.
She ran her hands down his broad back, marveling at the
hardness of the muscles she felt under her hands.

She gasped when he lowered his head from her
breasts to her stomach, leaving kisses which seared her
flesh before he moved back to capture her lips. She
fought to control the heat she felt rising lower in her body.
She wanted all of him so desperately she felt swept away
in an agony of desire.

Craig raised his head and gazed down into Shanna's

dark, glazed eyes, knowing she wanted him as much as he wanted her. She wrapped her arms around his neck, forcing him closer, feeling the heat that came from flesh against flesh. He lowered his lips to hers and their kisses grew in intensity for several exquisite moments until neither could stand any more delay.

They needed each other in the most fundamental way. She closed her eyes and let out a deep sigh when she felt him expanding inside her.

Later they lay in each other's arms, breathing heavily, satiated for the moment. For the next few hours they lay snuggled together in the moonlight, both deep in dreamless sleep.

It was almost morning when Shanna awakened. She cautiously slipped out of bed, careful not to awaken Craig, and tiptoed to the bathroom, then crawled quietly back into bed.

Craig moaned and pulled her against him, kissing the top of her head. Touching each other awakened their desires again. They reached the pinnacle of their passion again before they turned from each other to sleep the rest of the night.

The sun was high in the sky Sunday morning when Craig awakened, surprised he had slept so long. He reached across for his watch on the nightstand and sat up on the side of the bed when he looked at the time. Turning around, he saw Shanna still curled up, sound asleep. He decided to shower before she awakened.

He was halfway through his shower when Shanna pushed back the shower door and climbed in with him.

"It's my turn to do you," she informed him when she saw the startled look on his face.

He pulled her under the warm stream of water. "There's nothing like kisses under water," he informed her before lowering his lips to hers. They held each other tightly while the water pelted their bodies.

"Turn around and I'll do your back," she offered a minute later, taking the cloth from his hands and reaching for the soap. She marveled at his physique as she soaped his back and buttock.

"That felt great. I suppose you want me to do you again." Not waiting for her answer, he reached for the soap and started at her shoulders and breasts before soaping her stomach and thighs. She could barely contain her pleasure as his strong brown hands massaged her body.

Turning her around, he started on her back. When he reached her bottom, he used his soapy hands to rub vigorously. "You have the nicest buns I've seen in a long time," he said as he pulled her toward him.

Shanna pulled back. "How many buns have you viewed?"

For an answer, Craig slapped her gently on her backside.

By the time they finished their shower, they realized they didn't have much time left before they had to head back to San Francisco.

"Let's pack and have breakfast on the way out," Craig suggested.

Shanna agreed.

She looked up at him with her eyes shining. "It's been a great weekend, Craig. Thanks for asking me to come down."

"Don't look at me like that or we'll never get out of this place." He pushed her softly away from him. "You don't know what you do to me."

They quickly dressed and packed and had a quick breakfast at the hotel restaurant.

When Shanna's car was brought around to the hotel entrance, Craig announced that he would drive, which suited her just fine. They said little on the drive back to San Francisco, each absorbed in remembering the precious hours they had just spent together.

Craig thought he would have to find a way to convince Shanna that they were truly meant for each other. She'd awakened something in him and he would never be the same.

Shanna thought it had been the most marvelous weekend she'd ever had and wondered what she would do when Craig went back to Chicago. How would she ever settle down to a life with only her boys after the heights of ecstasy she had reached with him the last couple of days?

Early in the evening Craig turned into their driveway and turned off the motor. He reached for their bags before opening the door for her, then walked across the lawn with her and waited until she unlocked the front door. He pulled her to him and kissed her softly. "I'm going to take my bag upstairs and open my windows. I'll be down in a few minutes," he promised before turning around to make his way to his studio.

Shanna left her bag at the foot of the stairs and walked through the house, turning on lights and checking the rooms. Satisfied that everything was okay, she picked up her luggage and headed to her bedroom.

All at once she felt guilty that the boys hadn't entered her mind the last couple of days. What kind of a mother was she turning into? Looking at her answering machine, she saw the blinking light and the indication that there were two messages. Pushing the message button, she heard an unfamiliar voice asking her to call a phone number in Massachusetts. She replayed the first message, wrote down the number hurriedly and went on to listen to the second message which indicated it had come in only a half hour ago. It was the same voice explaining that her son Phillip had had an accident earlier in the evening and was in the local hospital.

With shaking fingers, Shanna managed to dial the

camp's number. She sat tensely on the edge of the bed
as the director explained that the camp nurse, who
thought Phillip had severely injured his leg, was now at
the hospital with him. And they needed her permission in
case surgery was necessary.

"Surgery?" she screamed into the receiver and
jumped up from the side of the bed. "What kind of surgery are you talking about?"

"We don't know the extent of his injuries at the
moment, Mrs. Taylor. So we're taking all the precautions
we can. His leg might be broken and if it is, it would, of
course, have to be set and put in a cast," the director
explained calmly. "He isn't—"

She cut him off. "I'll be there on the next plane. I'll call
you back about my time of arrival. Can someone meet
me at the airport in Springfield?"

Again sitting down heavily on the bed, Shanna glared
at the phone as if it were the culprit. She glanced at her
watch and placed a call to the same airline the boys had
flown on, having no idea what time she could get a flight.
Luckily, she found she could leave before midnight and
arrive in Massachusetts late Monday morning after a
short layover in New York. She called the camp again,
giving the director the time of her arrival. He assured her
that someone would meet her plane and take her directly to the hospital.

Hanging up the receiver, she looked at her trembling
hands. "I can't panic," she said aloud to the empty room.
"I have to get to Phillip."

Checking the time, Shanna realized she had only a
short time to pack and get to the airport. She grabbed
the bag she had taken to Monterey and dumped everything out on the bed. Not knowing how long she would
be away, she rushed to the closet and started throwing
into the bag everything she thought she might need, wiping away tears as she worked. Suddenly she thought

about Craig and rushed over to dial his number.

Craig answered immediately.

Without any greeting, Shanna cried out, "Oh, Craig, I just had a call from camp...Phillip is in the hospital...and I have to go there right away...and I—"

"Whoa, slow down. Take a deep breath, Shanna, and then tell me what happened," Craig said more calmly than he felt.

Shanna felt the strength in his voice and did as he asked. She gave him the few details she had, ending with the time of her flight to Massachusetts.

"I'll drive you to the airport. There's no need for you to leave your car there since you don't know exactly what day you'll be back," Craig said sensibly. "Just throw your things in your bag and call me when you're ready—that is, if you don't need me to help you pack," he added.

Shanna thought for a moment. She needed to let her boss know not to expect her in the office the next day. "Could you please call Rick for me and explain where I'll be? You have his home number, don't you?"

"Of course," Craig assured her. "Anything else I can do?"

"Nothing I can think of at the moment," she replied with a rush of gratitude.

Shanna felt a rush of gratitude toward Craig as she hurriedly changed her clothes and finished her packing while wiping away the tears that continued to fall.

❦

Little was said on the short drive to the San Francisco International Airport. Craig glanced anxiously at Shanna several times, knowing her mind was on Phillip. He pulled up to the curb of the terminal, letting her out to purchase her ticket and check her luggage while he parked. There was little time to spare by the time he joined her at her boarding gate.

Shanna looks like she hasn't a friend in the world,

Craig thought as he walked toward her. When he reached her, he took her in his arms and held her tight against his chest, kissing the top of her head.

"Everything will be all right, sweetheart," he said softly, noticing a tear sliding out of the corner of her eye. "Don't worry until you know you have something to worry about, honey. Relax on the flight and try to get some sleep."

Shanna nodded her head in understanding as she pressed as closely as she could to his body. How I wish Craig could go with me, ran across her mind. She was getting used to handling emergencies by herself, so she knew she could handle this, but even so...

Before Shanna could thank Craig for helping her, she heard the last call for her flight and reached up to pull his face down to hers. She kissed him deeply before she turned and hurried down the corridor to the plane, not once looking back. She didn't want him to see the tears streaming from her eyes.

But somehow Craig knew she was crying.

CHAPTER FOURTEEN

A driver from Camp Atwater met Shanna at the airport. She insisted that they pick up David before going to the hospital, knowing he was probably as worried about Phillip as she was.

David was waiting in the main building of the camp when they drove up. As she watched him run up and get into the car, Shanna swore he had grown a couple of inches in the past week.

"How's Phillip?" he asked as soon as he opened the door and climbed in.

"We'll soon find out, David. So how are you?" she asked as she rumpled his hair.

"I'm okay, Mom," he answered nonchalantly before adding, "but I sure did miss Phillip last night."

"And I've missed the two of you this past week. Did you see what happened to Phillip?"

"Oh, a stupid guy let a bat fly out of his hand, and it hit Phillip on the shin. Real hard. We guys think his leg is broken, but the camp nurse wouldn't tell us for sure." A disgusted look crossed his face. "I guess she didn't want us to worry."

Shanna looked out of her window and saw they were entering a hospital zone. "Well, we'll soon find out."

The moment the driver drew up to the front entrance,

Shanna jumped out, followed closely by David. They gathered her luggage and rushed inside to the nurses' station.

"I'm Phillip Taylor's mother," she informed the nurse on duty. "How is he...where is he...can I see him?" she asked in a tremulous voice.

"Glad you're here. He's been asking for his brother." Glancing at a chart, the nurse informed Shanna, "Phillip's leg is being x-rayed. You can see him as soon as he returns to his room in an hour or so. In the meantime, I have some forms to be completed." She looked at Shanna's trembling hand. "Do you feel up to taking care of them now?"

Shanna nodded her head and reached for the clip-board. Turning to David, she asked, "Do you want to go to the waiting room while I take care of these forms?"

David looked at her bags. "Want me to take these with me?"

Shanna turned back to the nurse. "Is there some place I can leave my luggage for a while?"

"No problem," the nurse replied. "I'll put them here behind the counter until you're ready to leave."

After Shanna completed all of the forms, she went across the hall to the waiting room and sank down on a sofa beside David.

David looked up questioningly when she sat down beside him.

"Someone will call us as soon as Phillip returns to his room. Then we can talk to his doctor."

"Will he have to go home if his leg's broken?" David asked anxiously.

"I don't think Phillip would have much fun here if his leg's in a cast, do you?"

David thought for a moment. " Well...he couldn't play some of the games, but there are other things he could do," he answered wistfully. After a moment, he added,

"And what would he do at home since I won't be there?"

Shanna hadn't thought that far ahead, but it was clear to her that David wanted Phillip to remain at camp if that were possible.

"We'll see what the doctor says, David," Shanna answered noncommittally. She glanced around the room, really seeing the other people in the room for the first time. She cringed when she saw a doctor enter and approach an elderly couple who became distraught after his whispered consultation with them. The doctor put his arms around them and led them from the room. She wondered what tragedy had occurred in their lives.

For a few minutes she forced her mind to observe the activity in the hallway. She saw white coated men and women bustling by, nurses carrying trays of medicine, blue-coated men and women who evidently were volunteers at the hospital. They all walked with purpose, she thought, all having tasks and schedules to meet.

David reached across his mother to pick up a magazine. He sat for several minutes, staring at its cover, not opening it.

Shanna looked over at him after a while, aware of his frequent twisting and squirming on the well-worn sofa.

When David became too restless, Shanna suggested, "Let's walk down to the cafeteria, David. I'd like some coffee. Would you like some orange juice or something else to drink?"

David nodded, eager to get out of the depressing room where so many people were so stressed out.

After inquiring at the nurses' station, they made their way down the bustling corridor until they reached the cafeteria. Standing in a long line for a few minutes, she finally got her coffee. David ordered a large glass of orange juice and two glazed doughnuts. They found a small table near a window and looked out over the well-manicured lawn for a few moments. Sipping her coffee slowly, she smiled as David wolfed down his doughnuts and gulped his orange juice.

"Can I get some more juice?"

Teenagers, she thought. Where do they put all the stuff they eat?

Determined to keep her anxiety about Phillip to herself, Shanna tried to focus on the tables of nurses having lunch while they carried on subdued conversations. White coated interns were flipping through charts while drinking their coffee around a long table near the window. At a small round table, a young girl was trying to console a tearful older woman, patting her hand and supplying her with tissues. Others scattered around in the large room showed the tension and anxiety of probably long waits for information about loved ones.

Glancing at her watch, Shanna squirmed in her chair. Time passed so slowly. She needed to see Phillip.

Glancing up at David when he returned to the table with his second glass of juice and two more doughnuts, Shanna raised her eyebrows. "Didn't you have breakfast?"

David looked at her sheepishly. "Yeah, but these doughnuts are so good. I haven't had any since I've been here. Most of the camp food's pretty good, but their desserts are usually some gook, like chocolate pudding. Yuk!" he finished, a grimace on his face.

"So tell me about camp, David." Maybe that would take her mind off Phillip. She listened carefully as David talked about his and Phillip's first week at camp and their friends who also had returned. She leaned closer to him. She swore he had more dark fuzz on his upper lip! Could that possibly be? she asked herself, before remembering again that, after all, he would soon be fifteen. She shuddered at the thought. He was growing up much too fast for her peace of mind!

"What's wrong, Mom?" he asked. "Is there something on my face?"

Shanna leaned back and smiled inwardly. Far be it from her to embarrass him by mentioning her observation. "No. I...I guess I just like to look at you. Let's go back to the waiting room. Maybe the nurse will have some information now."

They approached the nurses' station again, only to be told that Phillip had not returned to his room. They went back to the waiting room with its blaring television set that no one watched and the magazines that no one read. Most people only blankly leafed through them. They had only a few minutes' wait. A young white-coated figure appeared in the room and called her name. Jumping up, Shanna approached the doctor and introduced herself and David.

The doctor smiled at them and took her hand. "Dr. Mayhew."

"How's my son?" Shanna asked anxiously.

"He's going to be fine. He has a fracture in his left leg, but the bone is not broken clear through, so I've put on a light cast. It will certainly inconvenience him for a short time, but he'll be able to get around quite well. Won't be playing softball for a while, though," Dr. Mayhew ended with a smile.

He turned to David. "Your brother has been asking for you. He doesn't know you're here, Mrs. Taylor. He's in for a pleasant surprise. If you'll come with me, I'll take you to his room."

Phillip let out a yell when he saw his mother in front of David. "How'd you get here so fast, Mom?" he asked, in between their hugs and kisses.

"I'll tell you about that later. Let's talk about you. Does your leg hurt very much?"

"Nah, not now, but it sure hurt last night. Do I have to go home, Mom?" Phillip asked plaintively, almost like he'd forgotten about his leg. "David will help me get around if I stay here, won't you, David? And there're lots of things I can do except play ball. Isn't that right, David? We could—"

Taking hold of Phillip's hand, Shanna interrupted. "Hey, slow down, Phillip. Let's take one day at a time. We'll see what the doctor says before we make any plans."

As if on cue, Dr. Mayhew walked back into the room, and the three looked toward him expectantly. "So what have I done to deserve all of your attention?" he kidded.

All three started talking at once until Dr. Mayhew held up his hand. The boys looked toward their mother, surrendering the floor. Shanna explained to the doctor that Phillip wanted to stay at camp. "I'd like your professional opinion before this discussion goes any further."

Dr. Mayhew consulted Phillip's chart for a few minutes before replying. "Of course we have to consider what the camp director thinks about this. Medically, I see no reason for his not remaining at camp for the rest of the season." He looked over at the anxious expression on Phillip's face. "In my opinion, the time will probably go faster for him if he has a program to follow each day rather than sitting at home watching television. Suppose you talk to the director, Mrs. Taylor, and we can go from there."

"Well, that makes sense to me, Dr. Mayhew," Shanna acknowledged.

"I sure hope Phillip can stay here, Mom," David chimed in.

Dr. Mayhew looked over at Phillip and saw a glazed look in his eyes. "I think our patient needs some sleep now. He was awake most of last night. In any case, I want to keep him here until tomorrow. He has to be fitted for a crutch, and he needs some much-needed uninterrupted rest at the moment. There's not much else you can do here today except watch him sleep, so maybe you can get out to camp and get things straightened out there, Mrs. Taylor," he suggested, turning to leave. He patted David on the head as he walked out of the room.

Shanna kissed a drowsy Phillip and David patted his shoulder. She looked back before she closed his door. Phillip was already sound asleep, totally unaware that they were leaving.

"Let's go back to the waiting room while I make some plans," Shanna suggested to David. "I'm going to stay a couple of days until I see that Phillip is settled if he does get to stay here. I'll call and get a room at that motel not too far from camp. That is, if they have a vacancy. Remember the one we passed this morning? What's the name of it? And then we have to get back to camp. I want to talk with the camp director in person rather than over the telephone. And then—"

"Mom, I think everything else will fall into place if we do those first two things," David said sensibly.

Slightly surprised, Shanna looked over at David, thinking he was being more rational than she was. She guessed he really was becoming more mature and independent than she gave him credit for. "You're right, David. Let's pick up my luggage at the nurses' station, and then we will phone the motel."

Shanna was in luck in securing accommodations. After checking into the motel, she went to her room to change from her suit into some linen pants, a cotton top, and a sweater while David waited in the lobby. She phoned the camp and was told that someone would pick them up within the hour.

Shanna joined David and shared that information with him.

"Can I get something to eat before we leave? Lunch is over at camp," he informed her, "and I'll really be starved before supper."

Shanna glanced at her watch. Although it was past

lunch time, she didn't feel the least bit hungry. But then I'm not a growing teenager, she thought, as they made their way to a small restaurant near the entrance of the motel. She ordered only a glass of iced tea. Her nervous stomach couldn't hold anything else at the moment. She gulped when David ordered two double cheeseburgers, french fries, and a large soft drink, but she managed to sit through his wolfing it all down without comment.

Shortly after, the camp car arrived and they climbed in for the short drive to camp.

"How's your brother, David?" the driver asked.

"He's doing okay. Might be back at camp tomorrow. But we have to get a couple things straightened out before we know for sure."

Shanna instructed the driver to take her to the camp director's office after letting David out in front of his cabin. When it stopped in front of the director's building, she climbed out and hurried up the walk to knock on his office door.

"Come in," a pleasant voice called out.

Shanna walked in to face a young man with a wide smile on his face. She liked him immediately. He got up from his desk and approached her with his hand extended. "Ron Myers. You must be David and Phillip's mother. I'm glad to meet you. You have two fine young boys, Mrs. Taylor. They've made quite an impression on our counselors as well as on the other campers. But how is Phillip now?" He remembered his manners. "Please sit down." He motioned her to a long couch opposite his desk and sat down on the other end, facing her.

Shanna could see why her boys were so taken with this young man. His enthusiasm must rub off on everyone in the camp, she thought. Filling him in on her conversation with Phillip's doctor, she added, "Phillip will have a light cast on his leg. The doctor wants your opinion on whether Phillip should stay here the rest of the season. That is, would he interrupt your program? Could he still join in on some of your activities and ..."

Without hesitating, the director put Shanna's mind at ease. "There's no reason why Philip can't enjoy the other weeks here, Mrs. Taylor. We have so many different activities that even a broken leg wouldn't inhibit him too much, except for some of the athletic games, of course," he assured her. "That is, if you're comfortable in leaving him in our care. We have an excellent infirmary here. It's staffed by two registered nurses, one during the day and one at night. So if Phillip needs anything, we could certainly take care of it."

Shanna didn't hesitate in making her decision. "David wants Phillip to stay. I know Phillip would be devastated if he can't finish out the next two weeks. And after meeting you, I'm sure he'll be in good hands. I'm going to be at the Holiday Inn in Sturbridge for at least a couple of days." She handed the director her telephone number. "Phillip will not be discharged until tomorrow. I can bring him here as soon as the doctor says he can leave," she explained, worry suddenly drifting away from her mind.

"I'll put a camp car at your disposal, Mrs. Taylor. You may take it back to the motel with you this evening, if you wish, and then you'll have it to pick up Phillip tomorrow."

Shanna thanked the director profusely and rose to leave.

"By the way," Ron said, "if you'd like to join us for supper, you're welcome."

"Thank you," Shanna responded. "I want to see David before I leave. I'm not sure I'll be here for supper, but I'll try to join you."

Ron directed her to where she might find David. "I'll have a car parked here when you return. The secretary will have the keys."

David was engaged in a wild volleyball game when Shanna finally located him. She watched for a few minutes and waved to him before she left, not wanting to disrupt his concentration since his team was winning. She walked around the grounds for the next couple of hours, met and talked with some of the campers as well as with two of the counselors. Luckily, and quite by accident, she met the waterfront director who turned out to be Craig's friend, Frank Kerr.

"I'm happy to meet any friend of Craig's, Mrs. Taylor," Frank told her enthusiastically. "Craig's a great guy. He called me a few days ago and asked me to look out for the Taylor boys. As it's turned out, they need very little looking out for. They're the two most popular campers here. They take to camping like a duck to water."

That news warmed Shanna's heart. After a few more minutes of conversation with Frank, she walked back to the director's office to pick up the car she was going to use. She decided not to stay for their evening meal.

By the time Shanna reached her motel, her stomach was growling from lack of food all day and her head felt light. She rushed to her room to freshen up before going to the motel's restaurant. By the time she finished a large bowl of chowder and a caesar salad, her stomach felt better and her head no longer ached.

CHAPTER FIFTEEN

Glancing out of the window of the restaurant, Shanna saw the sun approaching the horizon. She signaled for her check and left some bills on the table. Before settling in for the night, she decided to run a few blocks. She hurried to her room, donned her jogging suit and running shoes, happy it was such a warm and balmy evening.

When she returned, Shanna stopped in the motel lobby to pick up an evening paper. before going down the hallway to her room. Unlocking the door, she exhaled a huge sigh of relief. The run had done wonders for her body as well as her mind. She stretched out and clicked on the television and lay back to relax before preparing for bed. She fell asleep in a matter of minutes.

Shanna awakened with a start. With dismay, she saw it was nearly midnight and she hadn't called Craig. Then she remembered that it was three hours earlier in San Francisco. She quickly dialed Craig's phone number, almost praying for him to be home. She needed to hear his voice.

Shanna's heart beat faster when she heard his deep, husky, familiar voice say "Hello," and she drew in her breath sharply before she spoke.

"Hello, Craig...this is Shanna," she said stupidly, as if

he wouldn't recognize her voice.

"I know. I was wondering when you'd call. I've been worried about you. Did you have any trouble getting to camp? How's Phillip? And David? And how are you? Where are you? It must be midnight there." He knew his words seemed to be falling over each other, but he was so glad to hear her voice he couldn't stop talking.

"Whoa, Craig. I can answer only one question at a time. You're so impatient," she teased. She told him about the boys and about her day. "So Phillip will be released from the hospital tomorrow, and I'll take him back to camp. The camp director thinks it'll be okay for him to stay until the end of their three weeks. I'm going to be here a couple more days to make sure Phillip can handle it."

"That means you won't be back until Wednesday or Thursday, I guess," Craig stated rather petulantly.

"Probably," Shanna replied. "On second thought I may stay until Friday. Sturbridge is really a fascinating place to explore. Such interesting little stores and antique shops. It's quite an historic place as well. And then I'm not too far from Boston. I might drive there for a day. If I stay, I'll get a rental car and a map and do some of the other tourists' spots."

"That sounds like a good idea, Shanna, but I want you to know I already miss you like sin. It'll be a long week if you're not around." His voice was low and his last words were spoken so softly she barely heard them.

"I miss you, too, Craig. I wish you were here with me this very moment."

"Don't tempt me. I just might get a flight out of here and appear before you know it."

Thinking Craig might do just that, she cried, "Oh, no, Craig. You can't come here! What would the boys think? They haven't a clue about us. I don't think it's wise to have them speculating about something so...so temporary." Now why did I say that? she wondered the moment the words were out of her mouth.

"Temporary? Is that how you think about our relationship, Shanna? We're going to have a long talk when you get back," he said earnestly, "so be ready to defend that remark."

Shanna decided to change the subject. "Just one more thing. Will you call Rick and tell him I decided to stay longer? "

"Of course. Anything else I can do? Will you let me know when you'll definitely be back? I'll meet you at the airport." He gave her his office number in case she didn't have it with her. She gave him the telephone number of her motel.

"By the way, Craig, I met your friend Frank at camp. And of course he asked about you. He had some very complimentary things to say about David and Phillip."

"I'm not surprised, sweetheart. They're great kids."

Craig's words warmed Shanna's heart and shortly afterward they hung up.

Craig was confused. Temporary? What did she mean, temporary? The word bothered him the rest of the evening. It was his last thought before he fell asleep.

Temporary? Why did I ever say something like that? she asked herself a dozen times before she pulled up the blanket to her chin. She knew she wanted everything else but a temporary relationship with him. So why did she mention it?

🪴

Shanna and David picked up a happy Phillip at the hospital the next day. She marveled at his ease in getting around on his crutches. When the doctor signed Phillip's release form, she told him about her conversation with the camp director. "Do you really think Phillip will be all right if he stays at camp?" she asked.

The doctor raised his eyebrows and looked over at

the anxious expression on Phillip's face. "I see no reason why Phillip can't manage most things very well.
Since the camp director goes along with the idea, I'm
sure he'll monitor Phillip's progress. Naturally some of
Phillip's activities will be restricted, but if he doesn't mind
that, then he'll be okay. If he has any difficulty, which I
don't foresee, he can always contact me."

Shanna thanked the doctor and went to the office to
sign the papers for Phillip's release. As soon as all three
were in the car, Phillip handed David a magic marker.
"You get the honor of being the first person to sign my
cast, David," he said solemnly, but she saw the twinkle in
his eyes.

David signed with a flourish and handed the marker
to Shanna. "You've got to do this, too. But don't write
anything mushy, Mom. The guys would never let Phillip
live it down."

Phillip agreed.

"Can't I even write 'Love, Mom'?" Shanna asked,
amused at her sons' macho behavior.

"Yeah...I guess that's okay if you can't think of anything else," Phillip finally relented. "But make it small and
put it on the back...A lot of guys have to sign this."

Well, she thought as she signed the back of his cast,
this certainly lets me know where I stand at the moment.

By the time they reached camp, Shanna felt like a
fifth wheel since most of the conversation was between
the boys. Phillip insisted on knowing everything that had
gone on since Sunday evening, and it took David the
whole time to give him a blow-by-blow account.

They're going to be okay, Shanna decided. She was
glad Phillip would finish out the season there. She drove
the boys to the cabin they shared with other campers.

After a quick peck on her cheek, they hopped out of
the car to join a group gathering firewood for a bonfire.

Shanna drove around to the camp director's building

to leave the camp's car and ask whether someone could take her back to the motel.

On her way to the motel Shanna was deep in thought, torn between staying and seeing part of Massachusetts while she was there or going home to be with Craig.

Massachusetts finally won out and Shanna informed the motel clerk she would be staying until Friday. She called the airline for reservations and was confirmed for an early morning flight on Friday. She then contacted an agency to rent a car.

While Shanna waited in the motel lobby for her car to be delivered, she collected some tourist guides on dis- play and glanced through them. The rental car agency also sent tourist information.

Shanna spent the next couple of hours looking through the brochures, making notes of the tourist spots within driving distance.

When her stomach reminded her she had eaten little during the day, she walked to the restaurant and took her time over a leisurely dinner. Back in her room, she watched the clock, eager to call Craig again.

Thinking he would probably be home by eight o'clock, she dialed his number at eleven. When she got no answer, she left a message on his answering machine. A couple of hours later, she laid aside her book and called again. No luck. She left another message. Strange, she thought. He's usually home by this time of the night. She knew she would sleep better if she could talk with him for a few minutes. She longed to hear his husky voice telling her again that everything was going to be all right. And she wanted to tell him about her deci- sion to let Phillip stay. She was sure he would have an opinion about that. But she couldn't keep her eyes open too long and soon fell into a restless sleep.

๛

Shanna was not alone in spending a restless night on Tuesday. Early in the evening Craig received a call from New York. His ex-wife, Ann, informed him she would be in San Francisco early Saturday morning and wanted him to meet her for a talk over lunch.

"What's this all about, Ann? Why are you flying out here?" Craig knew she must hear the anger in his voice.

"You're always so inquisitive, Craig. Just wait until I get there."

Craig drew in a deep breath. "All I'm asking, Ann, is your reason for coming here. Is Danny coming with you?"

"Of course not. I just need some time away from here. See you Saturday." With that Ann hung up before Craig had a chance to speak again.

"Damn her," he almost shouted. "That woman is impossible to deal with!"

For several minutes after talking with Ann, Craig thought of all the hoops she had put him through while they were married. And then her vindictiveness in not wanting him to contact Danny after their divorce.

Craig shook his head to clear his thoughts and returned to the work he'd brought home. Soon finding his mind was on everything but his work, he stuffed the papers back into his briefcase and got a jacket from his closet and his keys from the table. He had to get out of the house for a while—to a movie or a bar, or any place where he could get his ex and whatever the hell she wanted off his mind.

Craig did not return until after midnight, still almost as upset as when he left the studio earlier in the evening. As soon as he got to his apartment he checked his answering machine and listened to Shanna's messages a couple of times. He knew he shouldn't call her since it was almost three o'clock in the morning in

Massachusetts, even though he desperately wanted to hear her voice. He slowly undressed and climbed into bed, knowing the rest of the night was going to be a long one.

❧

Shanna rose early Wednesday morning, eager to be on her way to check out some tourist attractions. At each stop she made she wished Craig were with her to enjoy the gorgeous Massachusetts countryside.

Returning late in the afternoon in time to drive to camp and have supper with the campers, she stayed for the evening activity of story telling around a huge bonfire. She talked again with Craig's friend, Frank, who assured her that everything was going well for Phillip. When she looked across the circle at her boys' happy faces as they sat side-by-side, she was satisfied that she had made the right decision in letting Phillip stay at camp. His cast was almost filled with names and short messages, and he seemed to enjoy all the attention he was getting. She stayed until the bonfire was doused with a hose, and then walked back to the boys' cabin, telling them about her day and learning they had been to some of the same places on field trips the camp frequently sponsored. When the first bugle call sounded, which meant that all campers were to be in their cabins to get ready for bed, she started for her car. She'd walked only a few feet, however, when she heard Phillip call out to her.

"Have you talked to Mr. Boyd? Does he know about my leg?" Phillip asked.

"Yes to both questions, Phillip. He told me to tell both of you to behave yourselves and practice your basketball shots while you're here since he intends to be ready for you when you return."

"He's got to be kidding. We can beat him any time," Phillip boasted.

The mention of Craig's name reminded her how

much she was looking forward to talking to him again. As soon as she got to her room, she threw her purse and sweater on a chair and went to the telephone beside the bed. The red message button was flashing. Craig had called while she was out. Immediately she dialed his office number, thinking he was working late again.

Shanna heard his deep voice. "Why are you still at the office, Craig?"

Craig hesitated. How could he tell her that he was trying to make work an antidote for the apprehensive and confused feelings he had since his ex-wife's call? It also kept him from missing and thinking about her so much. That he missed the boys' antics, and that it seemed too quiet and lonesome when he was in his studio. None of that did he explain to her, however.

"Are you there, Craig?"

Shanna's voice cut into his thoughts. "Sorry, Shanna, I was in the middle of a problem when you called."

Disappointed by Craig's unresponsiveness, Shanna went on the defensive. She glared at the phone. "I'm returning your call, Craig, but I can always call tomorrow if you're too busy to talk now."

Craig ran his fingers through his hair. Now what had he gotten himself into? He wanted so much to tell Shanna about his problem. But how would she take the news that his ex-wife would arrive on Saturday? He couldn't take the chance of explaining over the phone. She might get the wrong idea. So he switched to another topic. "What time will you arrive Friday evening? I want to pick you up."

What is wrong with Craig? Shanna wondered as she listened to the casualness in his voice. Had he decided that he should cool it with her? If so, why? Was he now getting cold feet when, in fact, he had initiated the times they had been together?

"I'll be in around ten-thirty Friday night. But I can

easily get a taxi," she offered.

"I'll be at the airport, Shanna," Craig stated decisively. After a moment's silence, which seemed like an hour to Shanna, he said softly, "I've really missed you." He wanted to tell her oh so much more, but couldn't let down his guard to express himself at the moment. He had too much else on his mind, and he knew he wouldn't be the same until he learned why Ann was coming to San Francisco to talk with him. After that, he would be able to get back into Shanna's good graces. He had probably confused her no end during his conversation tonight.

Hurt, Shanna hung up the receiver after a few more words. Her first thought was, maybe I shouldn't have had sex with him. Some men act peculiar once a woman gives in. She and Angela had discussed that on several occasions, but until now she hadn't put Craig in that category. Maybe she was wrong in thinking she meant as much to him as she now knew he meant to her. Her mind was telling her one thing, but her heart refused to believe it.

Shanna sat on the bed for a while in deep thought, her self-esteem slowly ebbing away. Maybe Craig was just having a fling with her. Was he that kind of guy? But how could that be after their emotional weekend in Monterey when she became sure Craig was the man for her? On second thought, however, had he said anything about love last weekend? That thought really put her down in the dumps!

While Shanna was having doubts about their relationship after their last telephone conversation, Craig turned out the light on his desk and made his way home, heavy hearted that he didn't dare tell Shanna what was going on in his life.

❧

Shanna spent Thursday driving around during the day and stopping by camp to spend her last evening with her boys. She was not in the best of moods after she told her sons good-bye and returned the rented car. She made arrangements with the motel to take her to the airport early the next morning.

Shanna purposefully ignored the red message signal on her telephone while she undressed to take a hot shower. Tired from her day of driving and walking, she looked forward to getting a good night's sleep. Curiosity got the best of her, however, as she climbed into bed. She called the front desk for her messages and was told that a Mr. Boyd had called to remind her that he would meet her plane Friday night. Nothing else.

❦

Friday night Craig was walking down his stairs on his way to pick up Shanna when he heard his phone ring. He rushed back up the stairs and picked up the receiver. A frown appeared on his face when he heard his ex-wife's voice.

"I'm at the Fairmont Hotel on Nob Hill, Craig. We can have lunch around twelve-thirty tomorrow. Meet me in the Venetian Room."

Craig hit the side of his head with the palm of his hand. Ann was so bitchy—not asking if that would fit into his plans—just expecting him to go along with what she wanted!

"Okay, okay, Ann. Whatever," he told her wearily.

Craig banged down the receiver and rushed to his car for the short drive to the airport, worrying the whole way there whether he should tell Shanna about his meeting with his ex-wife the next day, or whether to wait until he found out what Ann wanted.

By the time he parked and got to the terminal gate, he had decided on the latter approach. He hoped he was making the best decision. Surely he could explain everything to Shanna after Ann left.

Craig's heart soared when Shanna walked through

the gate, glancing around the waiting area for him. He hurried to her and took her in his arms, holding her tightly to his chest for a few moments. "I've really missed you," he murmured against her hair. "It seems like you've been gone for weeks instead of days."

Shanna drew back and looked up at Craig. He seemed the same, yet different. For one thing, he looked slightly haggard, almost as if he hadn't eaten much the last few days or had been keeping late hours. But there was something else...

"Have you been eating regularly, Craig?" Shanna asked, concern on her face.

Craig knew he didn't look quite up to par, but hedged his answer. "Yes...well, most of the time...I've been working late and..." His voice trailed off.

"And probably not getting enough sleep, either," she finished for him.

"You're right about the sleep part," he acknowledged, thinking of the past three almost sleepless nights.

Craig took Shanna's carry-on bag from her, and they headed down to the baggage claim area to pick up the rest of her luggage. They said very little but held hands tightly as they walked. They glanced sideways at each other several times, emotion written on both of their faces. Craig didn't ask about the boys until they got into the car. Shanna gave him a full report and had just finished giving him all the details when he pulled into the driveway.

Reaching for Shanna's luggage piled on the back seat, Craig touched her shoulder and had to call on all his willpower to keep from pulling her into his arms again. But he didn't want to start anything he knew he couldn't finish in his present state of mind. He captured the bags, and she slid across the front seat to get out on his side.

"Gee, it's good to be home," Shanna exclaimed as they walked across the lawn to the front door. She took out her keys and opened the door. He reached around her to set her luggage inside. Though he looked at her longingly, he only gave her a soft kiss, turning quickly and backing onto the porch.

Perplexed, Shanna did not close the door. She watched Craig head across the lawn to open the garage door. He didn't look back.

Shaking her head, Shanna closed the door slowly, more confused than ever. Something surely was wrong. She only wished she knew what it was. "Maybe he's got a lot on his mind," she said aloud as she made her way up the stairs to her bedroom.

CHAPTER SIXTEEN

L Late Saturday morning Craig had not gotten across the lobby of the Fairmont before he noticed Ann sitting in one of the soft leather chairs, a fashion magazine half covering her face. But he would have recognized her coifed hair above her broad forehead anywhere. She still wore it in the same meticulous style as she had when they were married. She looks as chic as ever, if not more so, he thought as he approached her. Everything about her screamed sophistication, from her designer suit and blouse to the imported leather pumps on her feet.

Ann sensed Craig's presence and lowered her magazine. She looked up at him, a wide smile on her perfectly made-up face.

Uh-huh, Craig thought as he looked down at Ann. That woman has something up her sleeve for sure. He remembered that when she smiled at him like that she usually had ulterior motives. He'd become aware of her devious ways shortly after they married and still hadn't forgiven her for some of the tricks she had pulled during the time they were together.

Getting up from her chair, Ann remarked, "You're looking as handsome as ever, Craig. The women out here must be treating you very well."

Craig did not miss her slight smirk but decided not to feed into her cutting remarks. "I don't think you came all the way from New York to discuss how the women are treating me here, Ann. You mentioned you made reservations for lunch here, so why don't we go in and get seated?" He wanted to hear why she was here so he could get back home.

Ann glanced at him sideways while she gathered her magazine and purse, wondering how she could dispel the slight frown she noticed between his eyebrows and put him in a better mood.

Craig followed her into the restaurant. They had a short wait for their table, and neither spoke until they were seated at a table with snowy white linen and flowers in a vase in the middle.

The wine steward approached with the long wine list. Without looking at it, Ann spoke up. "I'll have the usual, Craig."

"The usual what, Ann?" Craig asked innocently, as though he didn't remember she always had a dry martini with two olives.

"A dry martini, of course. With two olives," she added. "Don't tell me you don't remember that, Craig." She tossed the wine list aside and started tapping her well-manicured nails on the table, a habit he remembered she indulged in whenever she was the slightest bit upset about something.

Inwardly Craig smiled as her tapping continued. I'm really getting to her, he decided, but she deserves it. What other woman would make the outrageous demands she made on him during their marriage? Which became worse after their son Danny was born.

Ann moved her hands to her lap and pasted another smile on her face when Craig asked about their son.

"So how is Danny? I haven't had a letter from him in the last three or four months. Does he still worship his grandfather?" he asked, remembering and hating the way Danny had put his love for his grandfather before his feelings for his father.

"Danny's at that difficult pre-teenage stage. Other than his grandfather, I don't think he loves or respects anyone. Certainly not me," she added, "as he refuses to do anything sensible that I ask him to do." Lowering her head as she spoke, she tried hard to get a tear to trickle from the corner of her eye. She was not successful.

Craig could read between the lines. Ann had never taken the time with Danny that he deserved, not even when he was an infant. Danny was an afterthought only when there was nothing else interesting around. Older now, he'd probably grown away from his mother. If Danny now refused to act like a dutiful son, it was basically Ann's fault, Craig concluded. She was really the loser now.

"That's all the more reason you should agree to shared custody, Ann. It's not fair to either Danny or me to deprive him of spending at least part of the year with me. You and your family got full custody on some trumped-up charges, and you know that is true." He stopped for a moment, thinking it was useless to talk with her about custody of Danny.

The waiter arrived with their drinks and left a long, embossed luncheon menu. They looked at it while sipping their drinks. He decided on the crab cakes and mixed vegetables while she ordered a Caesar salad with black coffee.

Still concerned that she doesn't gain an ounce, Craig thought as he looked over at her trim figure.

Twirling her wine glass several times before speaking, Ann finally said, "I know Danny really needs a full-time father at this stage in his life." After a slight pause, she added, "And I need you too, Craig."

The wine Craig was in the process of swallowing

went down the wrong way. He began to sputter. He set down his glass and raised a large napkin to his face, slightly embarrassed when he noticed others looking at him. He finally took a gulp of water which went down easily and the coughing subsided.

Aghast, Craig looked across the table at her; had she just grown another head?

"That's about the most asinine thing I've heard in a long time, Ann. How can you sit there so calmly and tell me something like your needing me? You've never needed me. You made that quite clear shortly after we married, if you remember. You just liked the idea of being married, not the actual reality of it. Most of your friends were married, and you wanted to be in their circle of activities for—"

"Please keep your voice down, Craig. After all, we're in a public place. I have no intention of being humiliated."

Craig wasn't aware of raising his voice. He continued quietly, "And you had Danny for the same selfish reason. So you could compare notes with all the other new mothers about who was the tallest, the smartest, the quickest child to take to potty training. You couldn't stand being left out of their group. Admit it, Ann."

Ann thought for several moments before answering, "But I was much younger then, Craig. I know I used to be selfish, wanting everything to go my way...but I've changed. I'm older now and I want to settle down and do what married women are supposed to do. I want to..." She stopped speaking and looked over at him, finally managing a teardrop in each eye. They were ready to spill over onto her rouged cheeks any moment.

Craig continued to stare at her in amazement. How can she possibly think she could now walk back into my life just as though the intervening years hadn't occurred? He would never consider taking her back. Impossible.

No way. Not in this life.

"What you're asking is one of the most absurd things I've heard in a long time, Ann. I've made a life of my own these past few years, and I'm happy with it. I have my work which takes up most of my time, and I'm free to do whatever I want with the rest of it. And one way or another, I'm going to have Danny at least part of the time."

Craig watched a pout form on her face. Her usual reaction when things didn't go her way, he thought. But that didn't bother him in the least now. At one time I might have given in to her but that time has long past, he told himself as he looked at her dispassionately.

Ann stared at Craig. She refused to give up. "You can't possibly mean what you just said. You can't forget all about that love unless there is someone else now in the picture."

Craig sat in silence, refusing to even look at her.

"So I suppose you're tied up with someone else, then. Is she here or in Chicago?" Ann asked slyly.

Craig took a deep breath before looking across at her. "I don't think it's any of your business what my current love life is like, Ann, and—"

Craig stopped speaking when the waiter arrived with their lunch. He began on his food immediately, but noticed Ann merely toyed with her salad, pushing it around with her fork.

Ann finally gave up all pretense of eating and looked across at him. "I came all the way out here, hoping we could arrive at a reconciliation. I've been doing a lot of thinking the past few months. We belong together, Craig, whether you—"

Craig held up his hand. "Save your breath, Ann. We didn't get along the few years we were married. What makes you think it would be any different now?"

Craig looked at her in amazement. He laid down his fork very carefully across his plate, folding his hands in

his lap. He stared down at his plate a few moments
before he spoke. "Ann, you're merely wasting your time
as well as mine. Don't you understand what I've been
saying to you? Or are you so self-centered that you think
you can get whatever you want, regardless of what the
other person thinks?"

Ann would not be outdone. "You'll change your mind,
Craig, if you think about what I've just said."

Craig glanced over at her again, a sad expression on
his face. "You still can't face facts, can you, Ann?"

"I was going to suggest—"

Craig interrupted her. "And I suggest we finish our
lunch so I can get back to my apartment."

With that said, Craig finished eating in silence and
sat until Ann finished part of her Caesar salad and drank
her coffee, a spiteful look on her face. When she finished, he motioned for the check and left several bills on
the tray before leading the way out of the restaurant.

Before Craig reached the door, Ann clutched his arm
to detain him. "Let me go with you, Craig. There are still
some things I'd like to talk to you about. I know you live
not too far from here; your secretary told me so. I can get
a taxi back to the hotel when we finish talking."

Craig turned to face her. "I have nothing else to discuss with you, Ann, except to say that what you propose
is out of the question. Why can't you understand that?"
he asked, anger clearly evident in his voice. He saw the
pout again appear on her face and said in a softer tone,
"Sorry, Ann, but that's the way it's got to be." With that
he went through the revolving door of the hotel's
entrance.

Ann watched Craig standing outside until his car was
brought around. He climbed in and drove away without
a glance in her direction.

Ann turned away, a smirk twisting her face, and
headed for the elevator to her floor. She decided that

that was not the last he would see of her. She planned to use the information she had wormed out of his secretary.

Leaving the hotel, Craig was in no mood to run into Shanna. Instead of going home, he headed for his office and worked until after nine o'clock. He then spent another hour or so having a late supper at a restaurant near his office. When he finally drove into the driveway, he was relieved to see that Shanna's downstairs was dark. The only light was in her bedroom.

Before Craig could flick on the garage door opener, he heard someone calling his name. Turning around, he recognized his former wife approaching him halfway up the driveway. He stared at Ann, hoping she was an apparition.

Ann spoke before Craig could say anything. "I've been sitting across the street a couple of hours waiting for you, Craig," Ann said petulantly.

"What are you doing here, Ann? I thought I'd made it clear this afternoon that—"

"But, Craig," she cut in, "now that I'm here the least you can do is invite me in. Or are we to carry on this conversation in the middle of a driveway?"

That did it! He definitely didn't want Shanna to see or hear Ann! He quickly opened the garage door and took her upstairs.

In a glance Ann took in the studio and its furnishings. "This is quite a change from your Chicago apartment, isn't it, Craig?"

From the tone of Ann's voice Craig knew she was being critical as usual, and he hated her for it. He was very happy with his quarters and with the people who surrounded him. Happier than I've been in a long time, and I'm surely not going to let Ann jeopardize that.

Craig did not answer her question but asked one of his own. "Would you like something to drink? There's some wine, beer, or juice."

Ann turned up her exquisite nose. "I'll take the wine, if that's all you have."

Craig turned from her abruptly and went into the small alcove which served as his kitchen. He took his time to pour the wine and open a beer for himself.

When he walked back into the large room and faced his ex-wife, he almost dropped both drinks.

Ann had discarded her wrap and was seated on the sofa, dressed only in a black garter belt and a black lacy bra.

"What the hell are you—"

"Oh, sit down, Craig, and enjoy the scenery." She smiled up at him, licking her lips like a kitten cleansing its whiskers after lapping up milk.

Craig's rage suddenly hit the boiling point. He set the drinks down so hard on the coffee table that the liquid sloshed out. He moved over to her, his fists clinched at his side. "I'm not into playing games, Ann. Get your clothes on and get the hell out of here."

Craig's words had little effect on her.

She reached for her glass and took a long sip, watching him over the rim of the glass. "You used to be turned on when you saw me like this. Don't tell me you've forgotten all about those torrid nights we had when—"

He wiped the back of his hand across his forehead, at a loss as to what to do next. All he wanted was to be rid of her.

He took a step toward her. "Cut the crap, Ann. Are you going to leave on your own or shall I throw you out?" he asked through clenched teeth.

The threatening tone of his voice and the wild look in his eyes were not lost on Ann. She said nothing while she walked seductively across the room to get her clothes, putting them back on slowly. When she was fully dressed, she turned to him with fire in her own eyes. "By the time I get through with you, you'll be glad to take me back."

Craig's voice rose again. "Hell will freeze over before that happens." His hands were still balled into tight fists. "And, furthermore, I'm going to fight to get Danny, so just be sure you can defend your right in court."

Ann flounced down the stairs and waited until he opened the garage door. She started down the driveway, then turned around to face him, a mean expression flitting across her face. "Believe it or not, you're going to regret treating me like this!"

Craig closed the garage door and wearily walked back upstairs. Any kind of confrontation always upset him. In a way he was sorry he'd acted so uncharacteristically. He'd almost gone ballistic on her.

Craig would have felt much worse had he known that Shanna heard the garage door open and had gotten up to see a woman walking down the driveway.

CHAPTER SEVENTEEN

Shanna was in the middle of her routine weekend chores when she heard Craig's garage door late Saturday morning. She walked into the living room to look out her window and saw him walking toward his car. She noticed he didn't have on his usual casual Saturday attire but instead he was dressed in a dark gray suit. Was he going to a business meeting? She frowned as she turned away from the window. He certainly was acting mysterious again. What in the world was happening? She turned back to her dusting, remembering Craig's aloofness when he'd brought her home from the airport the night before.

Continuing her work in the living room, Shanna tried to rationalize Craig's sudden change in his behavior toward her, why he was acting in such a withdrawn manner. Maybe he was building up for the classic brush-off. But how could he do that so casually, especially after last weekend? Of course, no commitments had been made. The least he could do was to tell her he had found someone else, if that were the case. But his sudden ignoring of her hurt too much to think about. Resolving to put him out of her mind, she quickly finished her work in the house and drove to the mall to do some shopping.

Shanna completed her shopping earlier than usual

with no one to buy food for but herself. In a short time all her purchases were put away, and there was nothing else that needed her attention. She looked out of the kitchen window at the bright sunshine and decided to drive to Golden Gate Park to jog for a while, needing something to make her miserable feelings go away. She ran raced upstairs to change her clothes.

A couple hours later Shanna collapsed onto a bench near her car, physically exhausted but feeling better emotionally. Checking her watch, she saw it was still early evening and decided to take in a movie. No way did she want to go back to her empty house until it was time to go to bed.

Remembering she hadn't eaten since early morning, Shanna first stopped at a small restaurant which served food at small tables on the outside patio. She found a seat and sank down in the chair. Looking around while waiting for her order to be taken, she felt even lonelier since most of the other customers were couples. When her sandwich and iced tea arrived, she ate slowly, hoping the hour would pass quickly before it was time to drive to the movie. Though it had received excellent reviews, when she walked out, she knew she had wasted her money because she barely saw what was happening on the big screen. Her mind in was in too much turmoil.

When she drove into her driveway around nine o'clock, Craig's car was not there. Her anxiety level rose again, wondering where he was on a Saturday night. Not turning on any lights downstairs, she went straight to her haven, her bedroom. She turned on her television and flicked her remote through the channels until she found a classic movie she liked, though she had seen it several times. She settled down on the chaise longue, figuring she was less likely to fall asleep there than if she were in her bed. During the commercial break she took a quick shower and put on her night clothes, threw back the comforter and sheet, and settled back on her pillows to watch the rest of the movie.

Around midnight Shanna was startled by the sound of the garage door going up. Then she heard muffled voices. Glancing at her clock, she got out of bed and tiptoed to the window. A woman was walking down the driveway. Then she heard the garage door being lowered. Just as she thought! Craig did have another woman in his life!

Shanna felt anger rising in her throat. Then she was powerless to stop the tears that formed behind her lids and finally coursed down her cheeks. Picking up the remote, she turned off the television before getting back into bed, burying herself in the pillows, giving them several thumps as if they were the cause of her discomfort and feeling of abandonment. What had happened to that perfect control she worked so hard to build after her divorce? How had she let someone walk into her life and take over that control? She hadn't realized how lonely she had become, how hungry she was to be held in a man's arms until Craig came along.

Blaming her present situation on her foolishness in renting Craig the studio in the first place, she berated herself. She remembered having doubts the day she met him—the vibes between them even then were unbelievable. She should have followed her first intuition and turned him away. Flopping over onto her other side, she threw one of the pillows aside, wishing with all her heart that she was back in that safe period of her life, no intrusions, no commitments—no love.

How long she lay awake she didn't know, devastated by what she saw earlier. She vowed to not have anything else to do with Craig. The miserable two-timer! Her ego had been battered enough and never again would she even give any man the time of day. She tossed and turned until she could no longer keep her eyes open.

🍂

Shanna slept later than usual Sunday morning. The sun was high in the sky when she awakened. The events of the past night immediately flooded her memory. She listlessly climbed out of bed, threw on her robe, and went downstairs to start the coffeemaker while she thought about what she wanted for breakfast. It will really be brunch, she thought, as she looked at the clock on the stove. She decided to make herself a hearty breakfast to carry her over until it was time for a late afternoon meal. She got bacon and fixings for an omelet out of the refrigerator and was cutting up a green pepper when she heard a knock on the back door. "Just what I need with the mood I'm in," she said facetiously as she crossed the kitchen, "a visit from Angela."

She unlocked the door to let Angela in, but stopped with the door only half-open. Craig faced her, an embarrassed smile on his face.

"I...I was hoping you'd be up," he finally got out as he looked at her through the half-open door. "May I come in?" he asked softly.

Speechless, Shanna stared at him a few seconds before she moved aside to let him enter the kitchen. She took a deep breath and pasted a smile on her face. She'd be damned if she would let Craig know he had given her a bad time the last couple of days. He wasn't worth all the worry he caused her.

"Of course, come in," she finally got out curtly.

Craig had already walked past her.

Shanna followed him. "Have you had breakfast, Craig? I got up late and was just starting to make myself an omelet." She hoped her voice didn't sound as shaky as she felt inside.

"I just had a cup of instant coffee earlier. An omelet

sounds great...if it's not too much trouble."

"Of course not," Shanna assured him. She walked back to the counter to finish cutting up the green pepper, now using a whole one instead of the half she planned to use. "Do you like mushrooms in yours?"

Craig nodded. "Maybe I can help you. I could cut up the mushrooms and onions."

"They're both in the bottom of the refrigerator, and the knives are over there." Shanna pointed to them lying at the end of the counter, even though they were in plain view.

They said little of any consequence as each worked. He asked about the boys and she merely told him she had talked to them a couple of times since she got back.

Both felt the tension in the air, and both were uncomfortable. But for different reasons.

Within minutes they had breakfast ready. Shanna added another plate, cup, silverware and napkin to the table. "Sit down and I'll pour the coffee." She hoped her shaking hands were up to that.

She had noticed Craig staring at her several times while he cut up the onions and mushrooms, but she ignored him. Now she had to face him across the table, and she didn't know whether she could act as if everything was normal. Her mind was spinning around in circles, and her body was refusing to ignore his nearness.

"Ummm, this is real tasty," Craig said after he took a bite of his omelet. What an inane thing to say he thought the minute the words were out of his mouth.

"Thanks." That was all Shanna could think of. She continued eating, seemingly more interested in her food than in him.

At least that's what Craig thought.

They finished breakfast mostly in silence. Neither knew what to say to the other.

Craig had no idea how to tell Shanna about Ann.

Shanna hadn't the foggiest idea how to let him know she'd seen the woman in the driveway the previous night, and that she wanted him out of her life.

Over a second cup of coffee, Craig leaned across the table and reached for Shanna's hand. He rubbed the back of it with his thumb, sending sparks up arm. Shanna wanted to pull her hand away but was powerless to do so.

Shanna wondered whether Craig could feel the heat his touch produced in her. She glanced over at him and then let her eyes fall to her plate. He looked so miserable. The two-timing cad! She was glad he was miserable.

He continued to rub her hand.

She wanted to reclaim it, but her arm muscles refused to act.

After several moments of silence, Craig suggested, "Let's clean up the kitchen and go for a drive. It's too beautiful a day to be cooped up in a house."

In his mind Craig knew he was only postponing what he had to tell her, knew he was being a coward. Maybe a change of scenery would do them both some good. Maybe he could talk to her a little easier out of their familiar surroundings. Maybe...

Like a robot, Shanna agreed to go with him and got up to rinse off their plates before depositing them into the dishwasher. Craig carried everything else to the counter for her and rinsed out the pans that were on the stove. In no time the kitchen was in order again.

"How long will it take you to change?" Craig asked.

Shanna blushed, suddenly remembering she was still in her robe. "I haven't had my shower yet. Give me thirty minutes, and I'll meet you in the driveway."

Craig walked across the kitchen and Shanna locked the back door behind him. She hurried up the stairs for a quick shower. She could not ignore the unanswered questions that boggled her mind, but she didn't even consider refusing to go either.

He was already downstairs putting a picnic hamper in his car when she locked her front door and walked across the lawn. She looked at him with raised eyebrows.

"Surprise," Craig announced. "If you hadn't agreed to go, I'd have to eat this stuff all next week. I went to the deli early this morning and picked up things I thought you'd like. Do you like smoked salmon pate?" he asked as he walked around the front of the car to open the door for her. Purposely he didn't help her into the seat. She was grateful that he hadn't touched her. She wanted no more influences on her thinking.

Shanna nodded her head. "One of my favorites," she informed him shortly as she climbed into the car unassisted, asking herself why in heaven's name she was doing this.

Craig walked around to the driver's side, climbed in and buckled his seat belt. He looked over at her before starting the car. "I'm afraid I'm not too familiar with where to find picnic spots," he confessed. "Any place in particular you'd like to go?"

While fastening her seat belt, she had an idea. "Why don't we drive to Golden Gate Park? There're a lot of interesting things to see there. Have you been to the Conservatory of Flowers or the Japanese Gardens? Or we could go—"

"Say no more, the park sounds good to me. Golden Gate Park it will be." He couldn't have cared less where they went as long as he was with her.

The park was usually crowded on weekends and today was no exception. Craig drove around several minutes before he found a legitimate parking space, not too far from the Japanese Gardens. After opening the car door for her, he walked around to the trunk and took out the picnic basket, two leather pillows and a heavy blanket which he spread on a spot a short distance from the car. "Let's sit on the grass," he suggested.

Shanna sat down on the leather pillows and slowly began to relax, breathing in the odors of the park, the perfume of blossoms and the scent of newly mown grass that mixed in the air around them. She kicked off her sandals and stretched her legs beyond the blanket to feel the cool grass on her feet.

Smiling at her action, Craig removed his sneakers and socks and settled back on his pillow.

They were silent for several moments, not knowing what to say to each other. Both pretended to be engrossed in the scenery in front of them.

Finally Craig reached across and pulled Shanna's pillow closer to him.

Shanna tensed—one part of her wanted him to continue, the other part reminded her she was through with him.

Craig felt her resistance but did not let her go. Pulling her closer to him, he announced, "We've got to talk, Shanna."

Shanna looked up at him. "So talk," she said silently. She held her breath, wondering what he was going to tell her.

Craig waited for several seconds before he spoke again. He didn't quite know how to start. "I've been so out of it these last few days...and I'm sure you felt there was something wrong with—"

"You're right, Craig. I still feel that way. Did I do something to suddenly turn you off?"

Craig noticed that Shanna's hands were clasped tightly together in her lap, and the straightness of her back betrayed the tension in her body. Knowing he was the cause of her distress, he now had to make things right for her.

He gently turned her around and took her face between his large, warm hands. "Look at me, Shanna. Believe me when I tell you that you've done absolutely nothing to make me back off. I feel closer to you now than I've ever felt to another person. I would do nothing to hurt you. Something happened yesterday that was beyond my control," he ended softly, rubbing her cheeks with the palms of his hands.

Shanna looked at him expectantly. "What do you mean 'beyond your control'?" A disturbing thought crossed her mind. So what about the woman she saw leaving his studio? Was he involved with the woman, and now trying to let her down easy? A frown appeared between her eyebrows. He saw it and reached over to smooth it out with his thumb.

Inhaling deeply, Craig started at the beginning about his ex-wife's phone call from New York, his apprehension after her call and before her arrival in San Francisco. "I didn't want to upset you while you were in Massachusetts. So I decided to wait until I found out definitely why Ann was—"

"So that's why you sounded strange during our last phone conversation," she observed.

"At that point I was very confused," Craig admitted. He stared out across the park for several moments, a faraway look in his eyes.

Shanna waited. In her mind there was more he needed to explain.

Taking a deep breath, Craig continued. "During lunch with Ann on Saturday, she told me her sole purpose in being here was to get us back together."

"You mean re-marry?" Shanna asked, her heart sinking. She looked down at her hands, again clasped tightly in her lap. She waited patiently.

Craig took another deep breath. "I thought I was pretty convincing when I told Ann there was no way in hell I'd ever go back to her. Evidently she didn't believe I meant what I said, because late last night she waited across the street until I came home and then insisted on going upstairs with me. While I was in the kitchen getting her a drink, she undressed and actually tried to seduce me. That woman has no shame! She finally left after I threatened to throw her out, but she made some threats on her way out."

Shanna heaved a sigh of relief. "Oh...it was Ann I saw—" She stopped abruptly, knowing she had let the cat out of the bag.

"You saw Ann?" Craig asked, an incredulous look on his face.

"I ... I saw a woman in the driveway late last night and I thought—"

"You thought I had a woman in the studio? How could you even think that, Shanna, after—"

"That was a woman I saw, Craig, and after all, you had been acting so mysterious the last few days and—"

"You could have had a little more faith in me," he injected.

Shanna let that comment go right over her head. "What kind of threats did Ann make, Craig?"

He shook his head. "Vague and general. Your guess is as good as mine as to what Ann has in mind, but I wouldn't put anything past her. She can be one hostile woman when she sets her mind to it." A shadow crossing his face didn't escape Shanna's scrutiny.

"So that's it in a nut shell, except I told her I'm going to take steps to gain custody of my son. I don't talk too much about Danny—that's his name—because it hurts too much not being able to see him grow up. There has to be a way to get him, I just haven't found it yet."

Shanna's first thought was that Ann must be one self-ish bitch for putting him through this! She pushed that thought aside; there was nothing she could do to change the situation between him and Ann. Instead she reached for his hand and held it tightly a few moments before she spoke.

"Oh, Ann probably just wanted the last word when she made the threats," Shanna speculated. "Maybe she was angry that you rejected her and just wanted to give you something to worry about." Even as Shanna said the words she hoped would make him feel better, she had some reservations about their truth. She thought about the adage of a woman scorned, and shivered slightly. Placing his hand against her cheek, she rubbed it gently, hoping that would tell him she was behind him regardless of what Ann decided to do.

Craig looked down into Shanna's eyes. "I sure hope you're right, but I can't get her threats out of my head."

Shanna took his face between her hands and planted a light, quick kiss on his lips. "Let's walk over to the Japanese Gardens and forget all about this for a while," she suggested.   Craig pulled Shanna to her feet and for the next couple of hours they wandered through the paths of the park, holding hands like teenagers.

Craig was the first to suggest they return to their spot. "All this fresh air is making me hungry."

When they reached their blanket, Craig opened the hamper and Shanna helped him spread out the food on a paper cloth.

"You brought enough to feed an army," she observed, smiling over at him, as they filled their plates with pate, crackers, cheese, pickles and olives, macaroni salad, and small sandwiches with various fillings.

Craig smiled. "Save some room for dessert, it's the most delicious assortment of cut-up fruit I've ever tasted. I keep some in my refrigerator most of the time. It usually tops off whatever kind of sandwich I make when I get home late."

"Don't you ever cook anything?" she asked.

"Not if I can help it."

"But you said you liked to cook," she reminded him.

"I really do, but I don't like to cook for only myself."

What he said made sense, she thought. She had difficulty cooking when the boys were away, so she could sympathize with his situation.

They spent a leisurely hour or so with their food and the white wine he had in a bucket of ice. Feeling lazy after eating, they were too content just being close to each other to have conversation. They watched teenagers whizzing by on bicycles, families with small children tagging behind, and couples walking hand-in-hand through the park. Most of the time a pregnant silence enveloped them as they sneaked glances at each other, while supposedly watching the passers-by.

Shanna wondered where their relationship was going from there. In a short time he had filled a hole in her life she'd seldom thought about before he came on the scene.

Craig wondered how they could get their budding relationship back on track and where they would eventually end up.

They felt the air cool as the sun wended its way to the west, leaving long shadows in the park. When Shanna shivered, as much from her thoughts as from the chill in the air, Craig suggested that they leave. They gathered up all of the leftovers of the picnic and headed home. About half-way home, he pulled over to the curb, left the motor running, and went into a deli. When he returned with a package, he put it in her lap. "You liked my fruit so much, I thought you might like some to take home with you."

"What a nice thing to do," Shanna said sincerely, giving him a wide smile which went straight to his heart, making it beat twice as fast.

Craig pulled into the driveway and shut off the motor but made no move to open his door. He turned to face her. "I want to hold you, Shanna. I need to know—"

"Let's go inside, Craig, and light the logs," she interrupted, knowing she wanted to be held just as much as he wanted to hold her.

He walked around to get the picnic hamper from the trunk and started toward the garage door. He halted when he heard her voice.

"Why don't we have another picnic in front of the fire later on?" she asked. "There's enough left for three or four people and—"

"Now why didn't I think of that? I surely wasn't looking forward to having this stuff in my refrigerator for days."

"—and I haven't cooked anything since I've been home except breakfast this morning," she finished. "We'll probably be hungry ...later on."

CHAPTER EIGHTEEN

A Shanna unlocked her door and Craig carried the hamper into the kitchen, depositing it on the counter by the sink. "Some of this should be refrigerated," he announced and proceeded to put cartons in her refrigerator.

Shanna got down two crystal glasses and put them on a tray with the half bottle of white wine to take to the living room.

While Craig lit the kindling under the logs, Shanna gathered some pillows from around the room and piled them on the floor in front of the fireplace. She selected a compact disk of romantic music and inserted it, turning the volume down low. Pulling up a low table beside the pillows, she put the wine and glasses on it.

They plopped down on the pillows in front of the flames at the same time. Craig reached over and pulled her closer to him. Shanna looked up at him and Craig noticed that some of the sadness in her eyes earlier in the day was gone, her smile wider than it had been since her return from Massachusetts. They listened to the fire crackling and watched the flames leap and spread among the logs until the heat caused them to move their pillows back.

Craig reached across her to fill the wine glasses.

Handing one to her, he held up his glass. "To a new start for us," he toasted.

Shanna looked at him questioningly when she raised her glass.

"Let's forget the last two or three days, act as if they never happened," he added.

"I'll drink to that," she said, taking a slow sip of her wine. She looked into his eyes and felt reassured that that was possible.

They sipped their wine in silence for a few moments before Craig took the glass from her hand and set both glasses on the table. He turned back to her and pulled her gently into his arms.

"I've been aching to do this all day," he murmured, pelting her face with small kisses before he pressed his lips tightly against hers in an almost desperate kiss, causing a reaction in her from the top of her head down to her toes.

Shanna wound her arms around his neck and pressed against him, pulling his head down until their lips met again. She ached with the need to be close to him. In that moment she knew she had been fooling herself the last couple of days. She could no more give him up than she could give up food. For her that was an alarming thought. She pushed to the back of her mind the possibility that he might soon go back to Chicago. She would deal with that when it happened.

"Shanna." His voice was a low growl as he held her tightly to his chest. He tried to be gentle, but his passion for her was getting in the way.

For both of them, tenderness soon gave way to their desperate need for fulfillment. He pushed aside the pillows with one hand while he held her with the other. He rolled her over onto the deep-piled carpeting and leaned over her, clumsily unbuttoning and removing her blouse. Seeing her breasts full above her bra, he freed both breasts and took one into his mouth. She moaned and shuddered with pleasure as he went from one to the other.

She reached down and loosened the top of her shorts and slipped them off, along with her panties. He gazed at her as she reached across to pull his golf shirt over his head, running her hand across his furry chest and down to the top of his shorts. Before he unzipped his shorts, he took a foil-wrapped pack from his back pocket and then pulled his shorts off with his underwear.

He pushed her down again and clasped her buttocks to pull her closer to him. She gave a low cry and arched against him, running her hands along his sides, his back, the muscles in his arms. Her hands touched every place she could reach while he planted kisses on every part of her body his mouth could find.

As the sexual tension between them stretched to the breaking point, he moaned, "I want you so, Shanna," and entered her with a hard thrust.

She cried out from the shock of his sudden entrance, but soon her body was moving with his in an erotic rhythm she hardly recognized as her own. As she arched towards him again and again, she knew that making love had never been like this. Their passion for each other became almost unbearable as they reached the pinnacle together. They held each other tightly like drowning swimmers in the afterglow of their passion.

It was some minutes before they turned to face each other, their breathing returning to normal. He reached over and took her face between his hands, planting tantalizing kisses on her eyelids, her cheeks, her lips before lying back down on the soft carpeting.

Glancing over at her, he knew that he had never known a woman in his life like her. He felt so close, so much a part of her.

What has she done to me? he wondered. How can I

even think about the rest of my life unless she's in it?

He rose up on his elbow and looked down on her. "You're so quiet. Are you okay?" he asked softly, brushing her hair back from her face.

"Ummm," was all the answer he got, but that satisfied him and he turned to stare at the flickering flames until he felt her sit up.

"I'm hungry," she announced, feeling around for her clothes. "Want me to get what's left of our picnic?"

"That's about the best thing you've said so far...well, maybe the next best thing." He qualified his statement when he saw the look on her face.

"I'm glad you added that. Otherwise you might have had to get the food yourself." She got up and pulled on her clothes.

By the time Shanna got back with a large tray filled with the rest of the picnic food, Craig had his clothes on and was tying his shoe strings. He pulled the glass coffee table close behind them and she set the tray on it.

By the time they finished eating, most of the food and wine had disappeared, including some of the fresh fruit he'd bought for her. He leaned back on his pillows, sighing with pleasure. "Now that just put the right finishing touch to a beautiful day," he said softly, taking her hand in his and pressing a kiss on her palm. "Thank you."

"It's not finished yet," she said, smiling at him. "We've got to clean up all this stuff."

Craig stood up and reached for the tray. "You drive a hard bargain. But I can be easily manipulated...most of the time," he added as he headed for the kitchen.

What little food was left they soon had put away, and the glasses and silverware were arranged in the dishwasher. He glanced at the clock above the stove. "I hate to leave you, but I've got a long day ahead of me, and..." He stopped when he saw a shadow of disappointment cross her face.

He pulled her into his arms. "If I stay here, Shanna, neither of us will get much sleep, and we'll both feel like hell when the alarm goes off in the morning."

In her mind Shanna agreed that he was probably right. Deep down inside she wanted to go to sleep in his arms.

She walked to the front door with him, reluctant to let him go. She raised her face for his kiss.

"I'll probably not be back until late tomorrow night, but I'll call you," Craig said before he pulled her to him, holding her close to his body for several moments. He kissed the top of her head, resisting the urge to spend the night with her. He drew back, shut the door and was gone.

The house Shanna loved had never seemed so lonely as it was after Craig left. She walked back slowly to the living room, gathered the pillows from the floor and threw them where they belonged. She checked logs in the fireplace and the fire screen before turning out the downstairs lights. Slowly walking up the stairs she wondered what it would be like to always have Craig around.

❧

The next evening Shanna had just stepped into the kitchen from a long day at work when she heard her neighbor Angela's voice at the back door.

Unlocking it, she admitted a smiling Angela carrying a covered dish. Handing it to Shanna, Angela announced, "Our dinner. It's that shrimp salad you like so much. Clifton is out of town again for a couple of days and I know your boys are away, so we'll just have us a relaxing evening of woman talk since we've not seen each other for quite a spell."

Uh huh, Shanna thought as she took the dish and put it in the refrigerator. I just know Angela's up to something. Probably wants to know more about Craig, her guilty conscience told her.

"Let's have a glass of wine while I get some crackers and stuff together," Shanna suggested as she reached to the back of the refrigerator to get an unopened bottle. "Want to get the glasses down?" she asked her friend.

Shanna poured the wine and handed Angela a glass before she sat down across from her at the table.

"So how're the boys doing at camp? I miss seeing them under that basketball hoop. You must miss them, too," Angela suggested.

"Yeah, I'll be glad when they get back." She told Angela about Phillip's accident.

Angela murmured sincere words of sympathy and promised to bake Phillip's favorite cookies as soon as he came home. Taking another sip of her wine, Angela looked slyly across at Shanna over the top of her glass a few moments before she spoke. "By the way, you've been keeping things from me."

Shanna looked at Angela questioningly. "Oh? What are you talking about, Angela?" In her heart she knew Angela was referring to Craig, but she wasn't going to make it easy for her friend to be nosy.

"Well...I...uh...late last night I was getting back from taking Clifton to the airport, and I...uh...saw your tenant coming out of your front door," she finally got out. She swallowed a large gulp of wine before looking over at Shanna.

Shanna twirled her wine glass around several times, gathering her thoughts before she spoke. "So now you want to know what's going on," she stated rather matter-of-factly, not the least bit offended by Angela's frankness. She'd found out early in their friendship that Angela was perhaps a little too direct, but she was also honest as well as being one heck of a good friend to her and to the boys.

Angela had the decency to look slightly embar-rassed, a first for her. "I thought you'd sworn off men in general after your divorce. At least that's the impression you've always given me."

"I know," Shanna admitted, thinking back to her reasons for marrying Paul. Marriage and a family were the big attraction in her life at the time she met Paul, even though she knew Paul was not her dream man. In spite of that she had looked forward to marrying him, to settling down, getting pregnant, and doing the mother thing. That's what she'd always wanted, but she also wrongly assumed that Paul wanted the same kind of life. But Paul had wanted more, and soon after their marriage he went looking for it.

Shanna shook her head to dispel her thoughts and drew her mind back to Angela. "Craig is a great guy. We've been out a couple of times," she said, crossing her fingers in her lap at that small lie, "and I've learned we like to do a lot of the same things."

"Ummm," Angela murmured, studying her friend with an expression that plainly said she thought there was much more than that going on. She decided to tell Shanna that her ex-husband had called her, asking about "that guy that lives in the studio."

"I didn't mention it to you, Shanna, but a few days ago Paul called me wanting to know what the hell—his words—was going on. Seems he saw you and Craig and the boys at a picnic."

Shanna bristled. "So what business is that of his? He's evidently now happily married. And he was never that concerned about me when we were married," she ended rather vehemently.

"Oh, grow up, girlfriend. You're so naive. This is all about male ego. Paul probably fancies you're still in love with him—at least he hinted at that when he called me— and that makes him want to keep an eye on you while going his own merry way. Probably can't imagine anyone else in your life."

Shanna snorted and pushed her wine glass across the table. "That's absurd. And I'm sure as hell going to tell him so when I see him again if..."

"Whoa, Shanna! Don't even go there! If I were in your shoes, I'd ignore Paul completely, act like he really didn't exist. I think that would surely make him think twice before he meddled with you again."

Before Shanna could reply, the doorbell chimed. She stomped through the hallway to the front door, prepared to get rid of a salesman or whoever was disturbing her conversation. She flung open the door to do battle and almost fell into Craig's arms.

Craig walked through the doorway and caught her. "Hold it! You look like you expected the devil himself to be waiting outside. Why the stormy expression?"

Feeling like the proverbial fool, Shanna pulled away. "You told me you would probably work late tonight," she ended lamely.

"I know, sweetheart, but I wanted to see you more than I wanted to finish my work. It'll be there tomorrow when I go in," he said and drew her back into his arms, pasting a firm kiss on her lips and ruffling her hair.

Shanna felt warmth spreading through her before she remembered that Angela was waiting. "Oh, Craig, Angela is in the kitchen. Come say hello."

Shanna patted her hair into place. Craig raised his eyebrows when she wiped the lipstick from his lips. She was still flushed but her breathing was almost back to normal by the time they got to the kitchen.

"Angela, this is Craig," she said very simply.

Angela took his outstretched hand. "Nice to meet you," she said meekly, all the while admiring his tall, handsome frame. He is more of a hunk than I thought, ran through her mind.

Craig pulled out a chair and plopped down just like he belonged there. This did not escape Angela's eyes.

"So you're Shanna's neighbor. I wondered when I'd get to meet you. Shanna told me you're a really good friend."

Angela threw a look at Shanna as if to say, what else did you say about me?

Shanna returned Angela's stare, shrugged her shoulders and turned to Craig.

"Some wine, Craig?" Shanna asked.

Not waiting for an answer, she went to the refrigerator to get the bottle and another glass from the cabinet. Craig took the bottle from her hand, refilling their glasses before pouring a glass for himself.

Angela's eyebrows went up a bit higher. "So how do you like San Francisco?" Angela asked innocently, while thinking he really was a handsome brother.

Craig gave Angela his best smile. "I love the city, and Shanna and her boys have been showing me some of the tourists' spots." He took a long sip of his drink. "I think this is the kind of place I could call home for the rest of my life. I even like the fog. And the temperature suits me fine, neither too hot nor too cold the year round."

Angela slanted her eyes toward Shanna, who seemed to be hanging onto Craig's every word. I think she's a goner, Angela thought, probably more so than she even knows.

"Feeling like that will probably make it harder to go back to Chicago," Angela observed. "That's where you're from, isn't it?"

"I've been working in Chicago for several years, and you're right about my not wanting to get back to the midwest weather, summer or winter." Craig lifted his glass to his lips and took a big swallow before he spoke again. "I may be here longer than I thought, however. In fact, the powers in Chicago have been feeling me out about permanently transferring out here and heading up this office as well as the others in California."

Shanna almost choked on her drink and started coughing. He didn't mention that to me!

Craig knew that his news was the cause of Shanna's momentary distress and turned to her. "That's what I came in to discuss with you tonight, Shanna. If I do stay longer, may I keep the studio?"

Not daring her voice to sound normal, Shanna merely nodded, refusing to look at either him or at Angela.

For the next several minutes, the three carried on a conversation about some people Angela knew in Chicago, Craig's long hours at the office, and, of course, Shanna's boys.

Shanna said little. Just thinking Craig might be there longer than he'd planned threw her mind into a turmoil. She was glad when he announced that he had some reports to finish and left the two friends to their own devices.

Immediately after Craig closed the front door, Angela pounced.

"You might as well admit it, Shanna. You're more than just a friend with that guy. I could almost feel the sparks in the air between you two." When Shanna did not answer, Angela asked softly, "You're afraid, aren't you?"

Shanna nodded mutely. "But do you mind if I don't talk about it right now?" she asked in a plaintive voice.

"Of course not. But what about our shrimp salad?"

Shanna jumped up. "I'd forgotten all about it! You must be starving," she cried as she hurried to the refrigerator. "I'll put some rolls into the microwave, you can do the table, and we can eat in a very few minutes."

Working together, they were ready to sit down to the table again in a matter of minutes, and little was said while they devoured Angela's salad.

Shanna was relieved when her friend decided to call it a night and left without referring to Craig again.

CHAPTER NINETEEN

During the boys' last week at camp, Shanna and Craig spent every possible moment together in the evenings, knowing the restrictions they would have to face when the boys returned. During their late suppers at various restaurants and their talks in bed at night they told each other about their lives, their hopes and fears, likes and dislikes, their dreams as well as their pet peeves. The sheer joy of being together made the week pass too swiftly. They had a wonderful late supper Friday night during which they planned to spend all day Saturday together doing more tourist things before they picked up the boys Saturday night.

Around mid-morning on Saturday, Craig knocked on Shanna's door, as anxious to start their day as she was. Shanna met him in tight-fitting white pants and a colorful top, a bulky white sweater thrown over her arm. Even though it was a warm cloudless day, she knew it would grow cool before they returned.

"You look good enough to eat," he said, pulling her into his arms and planting soft kisses on her forehead, her cheeks, and finally a hard kiss on her lips.

Shanna blushed. Any compliment from Craig went right to her heart. "You're looking mighty good yourself," she returned. In her eyes he was the epitome of the handsome men in most women's dreams. She pulled away from his arms. "We better get out of here now, or we may end up spending the day right here."

Craig agreed and reached for her keys to lock the front door.

Hand-in-hand, they walked across the lawn to his car and headed for Sausalito. When they reached the end of the Golden Gate Bridge, Shanna asked him to pull into Vista Point. "You can't pass this spot without seeing San Francisco from here," she pointed out as they climbed out of the car and walked to the cement wall.

"God, what a spectacular view!" Craig exclaimed as he leaned against the railing and gazed out over the wide expanse of the bay to the skyline of San Francisco close by.

After a few minutes, Craig said, "We better hit the road again." Holding hands, they walked back to the car.

They drove only a short distance on the highway to the exit for Sausalito. Driving slowly to Bridgeway, Sausalito's main street, they looked for a parking space. Tourists flooded the streets, most just window shopping in the famous galleries, boutiques, and antique shops while others were taking photos of the quaint rustic houses that seemed to hang from the cliffs, reminding some tourists of the hamlets they'd seen in parts of Europe.

Craig finally found a parking space near the Plaza Vina del Mar. He helped Shanna from the car. Walking a short distance, they stopped to admire the Plaza's elephant statues and rather dramatic fountain which seemed like a grassy oasis in the middle of a commercial district. They sat for a few minutes on a bench in Gabrielson Park, right on the water's edge, enjoying the scenery and watching the people around them.

For the next two or three hours they browsed in all of the shops that caught their fancy and window shopped in others. In one of the art galleries Craig found a small seascape oil painting by a local artist which caught his eye. "Wouldn't that look great above the sofa?" he asked and bought it when she agreed with him. By the time they reached the end of Bridgeway, they were both a bit pooped and hungry.

"Let's have a sandwich and something to drink at that restaurant we just passed," he suggested. They turned back to the famous Horizons Restaurant. The aroma of food assailed their senses and they hastened their steps.

Luckily, the popular restaurant didn't have too long a line, and they were seated within minutes out on the porch just above the waterfront. They faced a scene that was again spectacular—a full-frame view of San Francisco lying across the bay. Gazing out over the bay they watched large and small sailboats wending their way through the waves, and a ferry loaded with passengers approach from San Francisco and dock at the pier.

"I can see why this is a favorite restaurant of so many people," Craig observed. The atmosphere makes you feel like eating even if you're not hungry."

"Not to mention if you've just walked miles," Shanna quipped, glancing over at him with a smile on her face.

"I'm a bit bushed myself." He reached across the small table to take her hand. "But looking at you rejuvenates me," he added, placing a soft kiss on the palm of her hand. He smiled when he noticed Shanna blush from her forehead down to her cheeks.

Lucky for Shanna, a waiter arrived with a long menu and she dropped her head while she studied it. Both ordered a ham on rye sandwich and a soda, which they devoured quickly.

Early evening was fast approaching by the time Shanna and Craig headed back to his car. A slightly chilly breeze swirled around them as they climbed into their seats. On the ride back across the Golden Gate Bridge, both were comfortable in their small silences and just happy to be with each other. Craig held her hand in his warm palm most of the way.

This is probably the last day I'll have her all to myself for a while, he thought and let out a deep sigh.

It's the end of an almost perfect day for just the two of us since the boys will be home in a few hours, she thought.

Shanna glanced at her watch when Craig drove into the driveway. "We still have and hour or so before we pick up David and Phillip. Want to come in and wait?"

Craig declined, thinking he didn't want to start something he couldn't finish. He walked across the lawn with her and waited until she unlocked her door.

"I'll be back down in an hour or so to go get the boys." Giving her a soft kiss, he turned toward the garage door, a slight frown on his face. With the boys coming home, he had to work out some way that he and Shanna could have some time to themselves. And it bothered him that he had no solution.

Maybe he could persuade her to meet him at a hotel. Maybe her neighbor Angela would look in on the boys for her if he could whisk Shanna away for a few hours. Maybe the boys' father would take them for some long weekends. Maybe... He refused to rack his brain for other possibilities and tried to put a positive spin on their situation. Maybe everything would work out better than he presently thought. It just had to.

Disappointed that Craig didn't come in with her, Shanna walked into the foyer. She started as she bumped into one of the balloons that was drifting from the ceiling. She looked up. The rest of the balloons were all still floating above her head. They were a welcome home for her boys. She and Craig had spent an hour or so the night before blowing up the balloons with a helium contraption and tying them tightly. She smiled when she remembered the two or three that Craig burst when he first started the process. When they finished with the balloons, they spent the rest of the night making love, the last night they would have the freedom to be with each other before the boys returned. It had turned out to be a very emotional night since both were aware they would have to make other arrangements to be alone, even for a few hours.

On the way home from the airport David and Phillip entertained Shanna and Craig with stories of their exploits at camp. Someone believable, others a bit blown up.

Phillip still had his light cast on and gave her a letter from the doctor in Massachusetts for her to give to their family doctor. The cast could be removed in a few days.

While listening to the boys, Craig and Shanna glanced surreptitiously at each other several times with soulful looks in their eyes, as if each knew what was in the mind of the other.

The boys piled out of the car as soon as Craig pulled into the driveway.

"It's great to be home, isn't it, David?" Phillip asked. David nodded his head. "I sure did miss you, Mom," Phillip added, bringing a big smile to her lips.

Craig didn't linger after he helped carry in the boys' luggage. He sensed the boys wanted Shanna to themselves to finish filling her in on their camp experiences.

By the time David and Phillip unpacked all their clothes and the awards and trophies they'd won at camp, they were just as bushed as Shanna was. All three were soon in bed.

As soon as her head hit the pillow, Shanna found her mind wandering to the hours she'd just spent with Craig. She desperately wished she was in his arms now instead of lying alone in her bed, feeling more lonely as the night hours passed.

She tossed.

She turned from side to side.

Piling her pillows against the headboard of her bed, she reached for her book on the table beside her bed and lay back, hoping that reading would put her to sleep.

It didn't work.

She threw her book to the side of the bed and leaned across to pick up the phone to call Craig. Before she could dial, however, she had an attack of conscience. Maybe he was sound asleep and would resent being awakened. Maybe he would... She threw caution to the wind and dialed his number. When he answered, she could tell from his voice he had not been asleep either.

In a small voice, Shanna whispered, "I can't sleep. Can you ...?" Her voice faltered before she continued. "Can I come over for a while?"

"God, how I was just wishing you were here in bed with me," Craig said in a low voice.

That was all Shanna needed to hear. "I'll use the door down the hall. The boys are knocked out for the night, so I know I won't disturb them."

She slipped her feet into her slippers before she finished talking and quickly threw a light robe around her shoulders as soon as she hung up. Getting the key from her dresser drawer, she padded softly down the hall to open the door that led into the studio.

Craig heard the key in his door and walked over to pull Shanna into his arms the moment she stepped over the threshold. Someone up there must be in my corner, he thought as he looked down into her sparkling eyes.

He opened her robe and held her tightly against his naked body, lightly stroking her hair for several moments. The warmth of their skins seemed to mingle before he released her and removed her robe, letting it tumble to the floor.

Shanna shivered when she heard the sharp hiss of

his in-drawn breath as he drew her against him again. She spread her fingers wide over his wide, warm back and her breasts heaved against his furry chest as she held him tightly to her. For a moment she forgot how to breathe.

Still locked together, they made their way to his tumbled bed, proof that he'd also had a few restless hours. He threw aside the rumpled sheet and blanket and lowered her onto the bed, dropping beside her in a full-length embrace. The only sounds in the room were the ticking of his bedside clock and the beat of their hearts in their ears. With their mouths joined, he rolled her to her back and found her breasts first with his hand and then with his mouth.

She responded passionately and wrapped her hands around his buttocks, feeling the strength of the muscles there. Her body strained upward toward him. Sensation after sensation flooded her whole body from the pressures building within her. She shut her eyes and groaned softly, calling his name until he closed his mouth over hers in an almost suffocating kiss. She shivered in his embrace.

He gently pulled away from her, curbing his own passion for a few moments while he savored her sweet agony. His kisses caressed her breasts, her stomach, her thighs until her breath became sobbing pants.

She pulled his head back to her lips and held him tight against her, her body melting beneath him. When she no longer could stand the passion building within her, she opened herself to him and he entered slowly, easily.

Time was suspended as their bodies moved as one. Even when it was over, he still lay nestled within her and they held each other tightly for a long time, each reluctant to put any space between them.

Shanna finally stirred and sighed deeply. Looking at him in the moonlight filtering in between the venetian blinds, she murmured, "I've got to go. I can't fall asleep here. I might not awaken before the boys are up."

Craig understood but felt bereft when she slipped through his door and down the hall.

※

Craig spent a couple of hours Sunday afternoon dunking baskets with David while Phillip cheered from the lawn. Shanna made dinner for all of them later on and listened to more exploits from the boys. When dinner was almost over, David had a sudden thought. "Do we have to go stay with Dad this summer?" he asked plaintively.

Phillip put his two-cents' worth in. "We talked about it at camp and we'd rather stay here, even if we do have to go to your friend's house during the day while you're at work. Last year Mrs. Bergen took us and her son to all kinds of neat places. Remember, Mom?" Phillip thought for a moment before he added, "And if we're here with you, you wouldn't be by yourself at night."

Shanna smiled at Phillip's afterthought. Little did he know that she wouldn't be by herself if they were away again. On the one hand, she was happy they wanted to stay with her the rest of the summer. On the other hand, they would make it more difficult for her to be with Craig. The horns of a dilemma—except in this case both were pleasant choices. She glanced at Craig and knew from the expression on his face that he was having similar thoughts.

Shanna looked at the boys a few moments. "Suppose we cross that bridge when we get to it," she suggested. "I don't know your father's plans. He hasn't mentioned anything to me yet about your spending time with him."

Both boys looked crestfallen. David finally spoke up. "Why can't we tell him what our plans are? After all, we're old enough now to make up our own minds."

Shanna's eyes sought Craig's, and she looked at him appealingly: What do I do now?

Although Craig knew Shanna wanted a response from him, he felt he didn't have the right to express an opinion. He merely raised his eyebrows and shrugged his shoulders. Little did she know he didn't have any answers either.

For lack of a better solution, Shanna merely turned back to the boys. "Suppose we discuss this after I've given it some thought, guys."

David and Phillip exchanged glances before David said, "Okay, that seems fair enough...but you'll think about what we want to do, won't you?"

"Don't I always?" she retorted and reached over to ruffle his hair.

When they all finished their dinner a few minutes later, Craig volunteered to help clear the kitchen, and the boys raced to the television room, happy they didn't have that chore.

❦

The next morning as Shanna and the boys left, she noticed Craig's car was not in the driveway. She dropped the boys and their bikes off at her friend's house nearby while she was at the office, an arrangement she had previously made. Even though David and Phillip had earlier insisted they would be okay at home by themselves during the day, Shanna didn't feel comfortable with that arrangement. The boys went along with her decision without raising too much of a ruckus. Her friend's son, Roger, was just a year younger than Phillip and the three boys had been friends for a long time. Also, she knew Mrs. Bergen was glad for their company for her son and looked forward to having them during the summer weeks.

"Behave yourselves," Shanna reminded David and Phillip when they arrived at Mrs. Bergen's. She waited while they took their bikes out of the trunk. They looked at her. Did she think they were still little kids? But each gave her a peck on the cheek through the car window before she drove off.

Shanna's morning was so busy she didn't have time to think about Craig. But her heart raced when she answered the phone and heard his deep voice as she was leaving to pick up something for her lunch.

"How about a welcoming home cookout for the boys this evening?" Craig asked after greeting her. Before she could answer, he informed her it was all on him. As an afterthought, however, he added, "I guess you could make a salad if you insist on doing something. I'll take care of everything else. And I'll pick up the boys for you."

"Sounds great to me," Shanna managed to get out. "Is there anything I can get at the market for you on my way home?"

"I have everything planned. Just put on your sexy shorts and look gorgeous while I slave over the grill this evening."

"What more could a woman ask for?" Shanna teased. "I have to stop at the market on my way home this evening and stock up on juice and sodas since the boys are back. If you need me to pick up anything, call me before I leave the office."

Shanna hung up the receiver and walked out of her office to get a sandwich to take back with her, her feet barely touching the floor. It was going to be a long afternoon while she anticipated being near Craig again. The way that man gets to me is unbelievable! She thought.

CHAPTER TWENTY

Early in the evening Shanna stepped into her kitchen and stopped short, surveying the disarray facing her. "What in the world have those guys been doing to make such a mess?" she asked out loud. She heard Craig and the boys on the patio, evidently disagreeing on what should be done next.

Shrugging her shoulders, she moved pots and pans from the counter to make space for her packages. She put the fixings for a salad in the refrigerator until she was ready to cut up the ingredients.

Rushing upstairs, she threw off her suit and shoes and quickly donned the shorts Craig had mentioned during their telephone conversation earlier in the day. Smiling to herself she thought, Now I'm even dressing for him. But she had no qualms about her actions. She didn't give them a second thought as she hurried back downstairs and out to the patio.

"Hi, everybody," Shanna called as she opened the kitchen door. Craig was now mixing some ingredients in a sauce beside the grill, and the boys were putting out paper plates and napkins on the picnic table. All three looked up from their chores and greeted her.

Shanna saw a look of pure pleasure spread over Craig's face as he turned toward her, a wide smile on his face. She gazed at him, hoping he did not notice how disconcerted she quickly became. Neither was aware that David and Phillip looked from her to him before raising their eyebrows at each other.

Shanna walked toward the grill and forced herself to sound calm. "You seem to have everything under control, Craig, including the boys. How did you manage to keep them away from the hoop?"

Craig glanced over at the boys before he answered. "I had to bribe them."

"Bribe them?" Shanna echoed.

Craig smiled sheepishly. "I promised to shoot some baskets with them later on if they helped me get this together," he admitted, not looking at her.

"I see you've got a lot to learn about teenagers," Shanna pointed out, looking lovingly over at the boys. "They will try to talk you into anything if you're not careful. I caught on to their tricks when they were much younger. Now I can almost tell what they're thinking before they speak."

"Aw, Mom, you know you're exaggerating," David complained.

Phillip chimed in, looking at Craig. "Sometimes she really can. One day a long time ago she knew just..."

"Let's not tell tales out of school, Phillip," Shanna interrupted, having no idea what might come out of his mouth.

While the banter was going on between Shanna and her boys, Craig felt a dull pain deep in his stomach thinking how much he missed his own son's growing up. Under his breath he uttered an unmentionable word when he thought of his ex-wife.

Shanna saw Angela come out of her back door and called over, "Have you had dinner, Angela?"

Angela walked across her lawn to the fence that separated the two properties. "No, I haven't. I was just wondering what kind of sandwich fixings I could find in the refrigerator. Clifton is out of town, as usual."

"Come on over and join us," Shanna invited. "Craig seems to have enough for a dozen people," she added, smiling in his direction.

"Yeah, Mrs. Montgomery, and he makes great hamburgers," Phillip chimed in. "I'll even set another place for you."

"Who could refuse such an invitation?" Angela called back. "I'll be over in a few minutes."

Shanna went inside to make the salad while Craig finished grilling. In only a short while they were ready to pile the food on their plates. Shanna and Angela kept up a running conversation during most of the meal, with Craig and the boys doing most of the listening.

Craig finally leaned back to relax for a few minutes. "I'm stuffed clear down to my toes."

The boys looked over at Craig. "But you promised to shoot some baskets with us," David reminded him.

"Angela and I will clean up since you three did most of the work," Shanna volunteered, much to Craig's dismay.

Craig uttered a low groan. "Oh, no, guys, you're not going to hold me to that, are you?" he asked, giving the women a woe-is-me look before he got up slowly. He followed the boys around the house to the driveway.

As soon as Craig left, Angela asked, "So how is it going? And don't start acting naive again, Shanna. Anyone with two eyes could tell there's some heavy stuff going on between you two."

Shanna's first instinct was to deny Angela's accusation, but on second thought she really wanted to talk about the newfound passion she had for Craig. "You're right, Angela. Craig and I are having an affair, albeit a temporary one. I had no intention of getting so involved. I don't know how much longer he'll be out here, so I'm

just taking it one day at a time," she stated rather plaintively.   She rose to gather up the utensils and pans from
the grill while Angela cleared the table. "Let's finish this
and then we'll talk."

The two friends had the kitchen in order in no time.
Shanna made a pot of tea, and the two sat down at the
table to finish their conversation.

Angela sipped her tea and waited patiently for
Shanna to fill her in on whatever had been going on.

"So?" Angela finally prompted.

"So I think I've fallen in love with Craig. But he does-
n't know that. I'm sure he considers our little affair just a
temporary thing. He's really a decent, thoughtful guy.
He's great to have around—we like to do a lot of the
same things. I can relax with him and talk if I feel like it
or say nothing. And he seems to understand my moods,
just as I understand his. He has truly been a friend to me
in many—"

"Whoa, girlfriend. Maybe he is all that, but the looks
that pass between the two of you have little to do with
friendship," Angela observed quite candidly. "And there's
no need for you to start blushing. Sex is quite a normal
thing between two people," she added.

"Okay, okay. Since you always worm everything out
of me sooner or later, yes, even our sex is great," Shanna
admitted, feeling a warm glow just mentioning the act.
"But I don't know how he really feels about me. Seems
he had a pretty unhappy marriage. I don't know whether
he has gotten to the point of trusting women again. He
still has some bitter feelings about his ex-wife and the
way she's kept his son from him. So whether he's just
taking advantage of my situation here or whether he has
other motives...I just don't know," she ended lamely and
looked over at her friend.

Angela moved her cup around in her saucer several
times before she spoke. "Girl, the way his eyes follow

you would make anyone believe that for him this is not just a casual affair you two are having. He doesn't seem to be the love 'em and leave 'em kind of guy, either. Maybe you better start thinking about that."

It was Shanna's turn to be thoughtful. After a short pause she declared, "I can't afford to think about the future, Angela. After all, my first priority is my boys. It'll be a few years before they're not my total responsibility. At the moment I'm just going to enjoy the time Craig and I have together."

Angela had a ready comeback. "I hear what you're saying, girlfriend, but have you thought that the boys are growing up mighty fast? And I don't think it'll be a few years before they'll have their own interests. David is just about at that stage now, in case you haven't noticed. And where will that leave you?"

Shanna looked down into her cup for a few moments. "Things have a way of working themselves out, Angela. For the time being, I think I'll just go with the flow."

Angela glanced at her friend. Perhaps Shanna has the right attitude after all, she thought to herself. But she didn't want to see her hurt again. She got up and took her cup and saucer to the dishwasher. "Thanks for dinner. You kept me from having a lonely sandwich in front of the TV. And thank Craig and the boys for me," she called back as she headed for the back door.

Shanna sat back down at the table and stared out of the window. What was she going to do about Craig?

No miraculous solution came out of the blue by the time Craig and the boys burst into the kitchen asking for something to drink.

Craig looked like he'd been hit by a freight train while the boys were still bursting with energy. He slowly sank down into a chair at the kitchen table and wiped his forehead with the back of his hand. "Those two are going to be the death of me," he quipped as he looked at them fondly. He finished his drink and looked over at Shanna. "I'm going upstairs while I still have the energy to climb the stairs."

Shanna walked with Craig to the front door.

Looking back to make sure the hallway was clear, Craig drew Shanna into his arms and kissed her soundly before he closed the door.

The boys were having some cookies with their soda when Shanna floated back to the kitchen. Both boys looked up at her very smugly and then smiled at each other when she walked in, but neither spoke and she ignored their peculiar actions.

"I think Mr. Boyd likes you and is—" Phillip finally blurted out.

David interrupted, looking at him scornfully. "You snitch! You've got the biggest mouth on the block. I'll never tell you anything else. What we talked about was just between us, you goon!"

A little chagrined, Phillip, not to be outdone, retorted, "But Mom oughta know that Mr. Boyd likes her. Maybe she'll start liking him and then—"

"Oh, shut up, Phillip." David glanced over at his brother with a disgusted expression on his face.

Shanna listened to that interchange between her sons with her mouth open, aghast at what she was hearing. "Don't talk that way to your brother, David. I'm sure he didn't mean to say anything, it probably just slipped out. And about Mr. Boyd, he's a very nice person and he certainly seems to like you guys, so why shouldn't he like me, too?" The minute the words were out of her mouth, she knew that while Phillip might accept her explanation without question, David was not about to. She could tell by looking at him.

David didn't. He looked at her out of the corners of his eyes, a weird expression on his face.

Oh, God, she thought, Craig and I will have to be

doubly careful when we're around the boys from now on. I keep forgetting that David is not a little kid any longer. He's old enough to know the score, and he's at the stage to be attracted to girls. So why wouldn't he be able to recognize the actions of others?

Forcing a smile on her face, Shanna said cheerfully, "How about calling it a day? You may look at television in your rooms until you're ready to go to bed if you want, but try to keep the volume down. I'm going to turn in and read for a while."

No way was she able to read. Wanting Craig was too much on her mind. She thought about the way he handled the cookout. The way he looked in his shorts. The surreptitious glances he threw her way most of the evening. The way he handled the boys, playing with them even though she knew he must have been tired after a day at the office and then preparing for the cookout.

And not too far away, Shanna was disturbing Craig's night as much as he was disturbing hers.

❦

The minute Shanna picked up her boys the next evening she knew something was up. They sat in the backseat not looking at each other, nor were they talking to her except answering her questions in monosyllables. As soon as they got in the house, David went to his room while Phillip followed her to kitchen and sat at the table while she started preparations for their dinner.

Shanna glanced over at Phillip several times, but each time he refused to meet her eyes, his hands evidently more interesting than she was.

After a few minutes, Phillip could no longer stay quiet. In a rush, he burst out, "Mom, David's mad because he saw Jennifer with another guy this afternoon. I told him last week I'd seen her with that same guy, but he didn't believe me, and now..." His voice trailed off.

Shanna walked over to the table and sat down, putting a hand on top of his. "Oh, Phillip, thanks for telling me. I thought you two were angry with me for some reason." She hesitated a few seconds. "And David will be okay in a couple of days. He'll soon forget all about Jennifer and look around at all the other girls who like him. Let's not mention this around David, though. I'll act like I don't know. If he tells me, okay. If he doesn't, that's okay, too. He needs to be able to have his own privacy, so don't kid him about it." She reached up and ruffled Phillip's hair before she went back to the sink.

"Huh! I'm not going to like any girl for a long, long time. They're all pains in the...ah...stomach," he stated vehemently.

With her back to him, Shanna smiled widely, knowing "stomach" was not his first choice of words. She also knew he was suffering for his brother.

"Wait until you're a little older, Phillip. I'll remind you of those words, young man," she advised.

All Shanna got was another "Huh!" before Phillip headed for the television room. She was not looking forward to a silent David at dinner, but he surprised her. David came down, showing no signs of languishing from unrequited love, and joined in the conversation at the table as usual. He even kidded Phillip about something that had happened during the day while they were at Mrs. Bergen's.

Shanna smiled at their antics, happy that David was his usual self.

Later, while tidying up the kitchen, Shanna thought she would certainly feel better if she could get Craig out of her thoughts as easily as David let Jennifer leave his. On second thought, however, she knew that that was the last thing she wanted to do at the moment.

CHAPTER TWENTY-ONE

S hanna and Craig were able to survive having others around the following week, but both were forlorn since they couldn't arrange time to be together. They spoke briefly in passing early in the morning or in the evening, each time looking longingly at each other. Topmost in both their minds was how they could manage to be together while keeping their secret from the boys.

By Friday Craig had hatched a plan to take the boys for an all-day outing at the zoo on Saturday. He phoned Shanna at work and asked what she thought of his idea.

"I think the boys will really like that," Shanna told him. "We haven't been there this summer. We usually go to the zoo two or three times when they're out of school."

"How about you?" Craig fished for an answer, wanting her to tell him she also would like to spend the day at the zoo with them.

"Oh, I'd love to tag along. I guess that's part of the kid still in me," she confessed.

"Don't ever lose that part of you. I like it."

Craig's voice was doing things to Shanna's psyche. She felt tingles inside as she listened to him.

"At least we'll be alone part of the time while they do some exploring on their own," Craig explained. "I don't know how I'll keep my hands off you, but I'll give it my best shot. You don't know how I've missed you."

"I've missed you, too," Shanna confessed.

"Every night I twist and turn, wanting you beside me when—"

Shanna did not let him finish. "Oh, please, Craig, let's not talk about that. It only makes me feel worse."

After a few more comments they hung up. Both stared at nothing several moments before they turned back to their work.

❧

Saturday finally arrived and they all piled into Craig's car and headed for the San Francisco Zoo. The boys were excited and tussled with each other in the backseat, arguing where they would go first.

Craig tossed a coin back to them. "Use this. Whoever calls 'heads' two times out of three tries wins and can decide where you will go first."

Shanna looked at Craig in amazement. What a great way to settle an argument, she thought, and turned around to watch the coin tossing.

In two out of three tosses, Phillip won and gleefully laid out their itinerary. David reluctantly went along with it.

"But what about you guys?" Phillip asked, addressing his question to the front seat. "Where are you two going first?"

"Oh, we'll just wander around and stop wherever Craig wants to park for a while," Shanna answered, thankful for once that the boys wouldn't bug her to go every place with them.

It was a beautiful, clear day with a slightly warm breeze, and the zoo was crowded by the time they arrived. "I should have warned you about the tourist crowd on the weekends," Shanna observed while Craig hunted for a parking space.

"No problem," Craig returned. "I feel like I'm as much

a tourist as they are." He finally saw an empty space and quickly pulled into it, much to the chagrin of a driver who wanted the same space. They had quite a walk to the front gate, but they didn't mind the trek.

The boys started off on their own as soon as they paid the admission fee. Craig called them back. "Look, guys, we need to set a time to meet this afternoon." He looked around. "Let's meet at that restaurant over there around two o'clock. Not that we have to leave at that time, just check in with each other." The boys agreed and took off again.

Shanna glanced over at Craig when he took her hand. "You think of everything."

Craig looked down at her. "Lately most of my thinking is about you," he teased and squeezed her hand.

"We can't go around holding hands like two teenagers," she reminded him as she withdrew her hand. "What would the boys think if they saw us?"

Craig led her over to one of the empty benches and they sat down. "They've got to know sooner or later, sweetheart," he said softly.

"At the moment, I think it had better be later," she replied. Since their future was uncertain, she didn't want the boys to get too attached to him being around.

"Whatever you say," Craig said and got up from the bench. "Let's go see some of the animals." They weren't able to get too close to many of the enclosures because of the crowd, old and young people straining their necks to see. Shanna told Craig some of the background of the zoo while they walked, and she could tell he was interested by the questions he asked.

"Zoos have always fascinated me. While I was growing up, my parents always took us to the zoo whenever we visited a new city." He was quiet for a few moments. He wished he had his son Danny here with him.

"I'll bet you used the boys as an excuse to get here

yourself," Shanna teased, giving Craig a soft punch on his arm.

He caught her hand. "You're getting to know me too well. I'll have to stop telling you my secrets."

They were not halfway around the grounds when Craig glanced at his watch. "It's almost time to meet the boys. We better start in that direction. We can see the rest after lunch."

By the time they met the boys at the restaurant, Shanna and Craig were a bit bushed from all the walking and were glad to sit down to have a sandwich and a drink while the boys regaled them with their adventures the past two or three hours.

"We'll leave around six, so meet us back here. We'll stop for dinner when we leave here," Craig promised.

Both boys nodded their heads, eager to take off again.

Shanna was amazed at how Craig had taken over their day. She willingly went along with his suggestions, for once happy not to have to make any of the decisions herself.

They said little as they walked around the huge grounds, but each was conscious of the other. They didn't hold hands in case they ran across the boys. It was late afternoon when they decided to sit for a while on one of the benches.

Craig noticed the sun was much lower in the sky. "It's about time to head back to our meeting place, but before we meet the boys, I have another proposition for you."

Shanna's heart jumped up into her mouth. Another proposition? What in the world was he getting at?

"It's about later on tonight, sweetheart. I want to hold you in my arms, kiss you to distraction, make love to you until you cry 'uncle.' Will you please come to my room after the boys are asleep? I don't care what time it is, I'll be waiting."

Shanna promised she would be there without giving his proposition a second thought, except to wonder how she could get through the next few hours without revealing the anticipation building in her. She drew a deep breath. "After all their excitement today, David and Phillip will probably turn in early. What about any time after eleven?"

Craig brightened at her reply. He leaned closer to her. "I want to kiss you right now, but I guess I can hold off."

He got up and pulled her to her feet. "You look a bit pooped, sweetheart. Let's go find the boys and head out of here."

The moment they were all in the car, David and Phillip asked if they could have pizza for dinner. Shanna turned around and gave them a "mother" look. She knew they had planned that while they were at the zoo. She also knew that Craig would go along with their request as he was as much a pizza lover as they were. She sighed loudly. "Sure looks like I'm overruled again. So I guess it's pizza, but we're absolutely not going to stay long enough for you to get involved in those video games," she warned the boys.

Winning one out of two was good enough for David and Phillip, so they didn't protest her decision.

The restaurant was crowded by the time they arrived. They had a long wait for a table, and an even longer wait to get service. The boys pleaded to play the video games while they waited, and Craig promised to get them when their turn came to be seated. The wait was longer than they anticipated, so the boys had several minutes at the games and didn't protest when Craig finally called them. By the time they'd finished their meal, it was getting dark outside. Which was fine with Shanna because that meant it wouldn't be too much longer before she would be in Craig's arms.

❦

Shanna got through the rest of the evening pretending everything was normal, even though her anticipation built with each passing hour. As she predicted, the boys were in their bedrooms sound asleep shortly before eleven o'clock.

After checking on them again, she went to the telephone. "I'll be there in about twenty minutes," she informed Craig, hanging up and rushing into the shower. She finished her shower and threw on a light robe. Slightly unnerved just thinking about him, she got the key and padded softly down the hall to unlock the door to his studio.

Craig waited for Shanna in the darkened room with only the moonlight shining through the half-closed blinds for what seemed to him several hours. After she called, in his vivid imagination he visualized her in the shower, all her curves and her breasts dripping wet and her drying all her body parts with a large fluffy towel. He turned over on his bed, groaning from the flood of heat in his loins. He glanced at his watch again, for about the tenth time, or so he thought.

When Craig finally heard Shanna's key in the lock, he quickly rolled out of bed and met her when she opened the door. He enfolded her in his arms, holding her to him for several moments before he released her and drew off her robe. He threw it over the back of a chair on their way to his bed. Lowering her onto his bed and lying down beside her, he murmured, "It's been a long night, sweetheart. I thought you'd never get here."

She pulled his head down to meet her lips and kissed him passionately before she let him go. "I know. I felt the same way. I could hardly wait until the boys went to bed."

He felt her nipples standing at attention against his chest. He reached down to cover her breasts with his broad hands, kneading her soft skin before moving his hands down farther to her stomach, to the inside of her thighs. Each spot he touched sent electric impulses through his body and his loins felt like they were on fire. He felt her tremble as he massaged her thighs, and his chest and throat tightened at the pleasure he was able to give her.

Shanna writhed from side to side, whispering his name. When she could no longer stand the torment of his hands, she pulled him up to her and buried her face in his shoulder. "Now, now," she whispered. She reached down to guide him into her.

Her touch was almost his undoing as he swallowed hard and plunged deeply, feeling her muscles caress him as he eased in and out, her hips moving in tune with his.

Time stood still for both of them, and finally the silence of the room surrounded them as they lay back, satiated with the passion they felt for each other.

Craig's breathing returned to normal. He drew her close to his side. She snuggled against him, her head on his chest, wishing with all her heart that she could stay in that position the rest of the night.

The ringing of the phone shattered their silence. Both sat up and stared at the insistent intruder.

"Aren't you going to answer it?" Shanna finally asked when she saw he made no move to pick up the receiver.

"Damn! Who is calling this time of the night?" Irritable, he reached for the telephone. Picking up the receiver, he said angrily, "Craig Boyd here."

Craig didn't say anything else for a few seconds. Shanna looked across at the deep frown forming on his forehead as he listened. He shifted the receiver to his other ear, clearly aggravated at whoever was on the other end.

Uh huh, Shanna thought as she watched Craig's body tense, this must be trouble. She reached out to touch his arm.

Craig turned to smooth her hair as he asked the caller in an exasperated voice, "Why didn't you at least have the decency to give me a little warning before you made such a decision? This is such a bitchy thing to do—not only to me, but how do you think Danny feels?"

Shanna was sorry she couldn't hear at least part of what was going on at the other end of the line. She saw Craig getting more upset each minute he listened, now rubbing his temple with his thumb.

Craig finally shouted, "Of course I'll meet his plane." He banged down the receiver. It dawned on him that this was probably one of the pay-backs Ann had threatened him with.

He took several deep breaths and ran his fingers through his hair a couple of times before he turned to Shanna, a weary look on his face. "Now I've really got a problem. Ann has put Danny on a plane that arrives late tomorrow morning at San Francisco International. Seems she's going to Europe with some friends for part of the summer and she's not taking Danny with her. She also thinks Danny would be better off here with me rather than spending the summer with his grandparents." He grabbed one of his pillows and threw it across the room. He wished he could do the same to the caller.

Shanna looked at Craig in astonishment for several seconds. *What can I say or do to calm him down? He's really in a blue funk!*

"Damn her! And I don't even have a place for Danny to sleep!" he exploded. "What kind of a person does things like this?" he shouted, not expecting an answer. "I don't know why I said that. This is typical Ann behavior—not thinking about anyone but herself."

"Sssh, Craig, keep your voice down, you'll wake up the boys."

Craig ran his hand over his hair. "Sorry, Shanna, I'm just so damned put out with that woman. She never considers how her actions might affect others." He glanced across at Shanna and she saw a flicker of emotion cross his face. He looked like he felt better. "The one good thing about all of this, Shanna, is that I'll get to have Danny for a few weeks. I'll have to think of some kind of arrangement for him, though."

Shanna climbed over him to sit on the side of the bed. She took his hand in hers, rubbing it gently. "Calm down, Craig. The world hasn't come to an end yet. I'm sure we can think of some way to handle this." The second the words were out of her mouth it dawned on her that he would need a larger apartment now. He would be moving out! That thought was devastating! What would she do without him?

Shanna got up from the bed and walked over to the chair to get her robe, her brain spinning a mile a minute. When she got back to the bed, her mind was made up. "Listen to me, Craig. Maybe Danny could stay in the television room downstairs until you can make other arrangements. There's a pull-out sofa he could sleep on. And there's a closet for his clothes that's not being used except for some of the boys' junk, which they could easily move out."

Shanna held her breath. Maybe Craig wouldn't go for that idea. She added, "Besides, Danny is about the same age as Phillip, isn't he? Maybe Danny would feel less of a stranger out here if he had someone around his own age." She knew she had struck the right chord with Craig when she saw his face brighten. Then a shadow passed over it again.

"Oh, honey, it's big of you to suggest that Danny stay downstairs, but I can't ask you to take in a stranger. And besides, how would the boys react to such an idea? It's almost an invasion of their privacy."

Shanna was touched by Craig's concern for her boys, but she had an answer. "Suppose we talk it over with them in the morning before you pick up Danny," she suggested.

Craig studied his hands for a few moments before he agreed. "What you say makes a lot of sense, that is if the boys go along with the idea, but what can I do with Danny during the week while I'm at work?"

Shanna hadn't thought that far ahead, but all at once she had another idea. Perhaps her friend who took care of Phillip and David during the day wouldn't mind having Danny also. At least she could ask her.

"It's possible Danny could stay with Phillip and David at my friend's house. We could check it out and go from there. It's a good thing tomorrow—or rather today—is Sunday. It gives us time to make some phone calls."

Craig pulled her back into his arms. "You have an answer for everything, don't you? What would I do without you?" he asked as he nuzzled her neck before planting passionate kisses on her forehead, her cheeks, and finally her mouth.

After a few moments Shanna drew back to catch her breath. She glanced at the clock on the beside table. "Oops, do you see what time it is? Much as I hate to, I've got to go if I expect to wake up in my own bed this morning. Why don't you come down around nine o'clock, and we'll see what the boys have to say about our plans."

Craig held her tightly for several minutes before he walked to the door with her, kissing the top of her head before she slipped out into the hallway.

CHAPTER TWENTY-TWO

S unday morning David and Phillip were on their second helping of pancakes when Craig knocked on the back door before entering. Shanna greeted him and asked him to sit down while she put more pancakes on the grill. The boys looked at each other with raised eyebrows when Craig joined them at the table.

"Looks like I'm just in time before you guys do away with all the pancakes," Craig said as he sat down and took the mug of coffee Shanna brought to the table.

Little was said while they all finished their breakfast. When the boys asked to be excused, Craig interrupted. "Sit for a few minutes, guys. Your mother and I have something to run by you. And by the way, we both want your honest opinion after you hear what we've got to say. I mean that."

Looking at the stern expression on Craig's face, the boys knew he was not in a kidding mood, that he meant exactly what he'd just said.

Puzzled, David and Phillip glanced across at their mother, who remained silent, having decided to let Craig handle the explanation since it concerned his son.

Clearing his throat a couple of times, Craig explained in detail about his son's arrival at the airport later on in the morning and the temporary arrangements that had been discussed about his sleeping in the television room until something else could be worked out. When he finished, he looked at both boys. "So, you see I need to know how you feel about Danny's staying down here for a few days."

David started to speak but Phillip interrupted him. "Danny's almost as old as I am, isn't he?" he asked.

"Only a few months younger," Craig replied.

"Does he like to shoot baskets?"

Shanna was not surprised when David asked that. Basketball was still the current love of his life.

Craig looked down into his coffee mug for a few seconds before he answered. "I can't really answer that, David. You see, I don't know Danny very well. I haven't had much contact with him these past few years, except letters, of course. And most of his letters were short, just saying he was okay, that school was okay, and his mother was okay—which really didn't tell me a heck of a lot about him. So I'll have to get to know him just like you will have to do if you agree you don't mind his staying here."

The boys exchanged looks again. "It's okay with us if it's okay with Mom," David said. "Isn't that right, Phillip?" he added.

Phillip merely nodded. He didn't say he really would like to have the guy around, but he thought his enthusiasm might make David feel a little jealous. He knew his brother pretty well.

Craig felt like a great load had shifted from his shoulders. "Well, the next thing on the agenda is to meet his plane. Want to go with me, guys? And how about you, Shanna? I'd like it if you three would go with me, and then we all can get acquainted at the same time."

"That's cool," the boys agreed, and Shanna went along with their sentiments.

"We should leave about ten-thirty, which doesn't give us too much time. I'll meet you in the driveway," Craig informed David and Phillip before they scooted out of the kitchen to get the basketball.

The minute the boys were out the door, Craig reached across the table and lifted Shanna's warm hand to his lips. "Want some help with the kitchen?" he asked as he rose from the table, carrying his dishes to the sink to rinse them before depositing them into the dishwasher.

"I can manage these few things," she informed him. "Besides, you only upset me when you're around," she added coyly.

"That goes double for me, sweetheart." Craig gave her a long look before he pulled her into his arms, holding her close to his chest for several moments before planting a soft kiss on her lips. "I'd better get out of here before I carry you back upstairs." He released her and headed for the back door.

&

A little later all four waited apprehensively at the gate for the plane's arrival, but each for different reasons.

Shanna wondered how Danny's arrival would eventually affect all their lives.

Craig worried that Danny might be too estranged from him after so many years with only letters to bind them together.

The boys wondered what they could do with Danny if he didn't like basketball.

Little did they know that on the plane Danny was the most apprehensive of all. Whether or not his father would be happy to see him was uppermost in his mind.

Passengers started filing through the gate. Craig scanned the corridor for Danny. He was almost the last passenger to de-plane, and he walked slowly through the gate with his carry-on, looking lost and forlorn.

Spying Danny, Craig rushed forward, calling his name. When he reached his son, he hugged his thin shoulders. "Hi, son," he greeted Danny. "Welcome to San Francisco. Come meet some friends."

While David and Phillip greeted Danny noisily, Shanna gazed at the tall, slender, brown-skinned boy in a red up-scale prep school jacket and dark pants. He looked like he'd just lost his best friend. Her heart went out to him. He was the spitting image of what she thought a young Craig must have looked like—the same pretty black hair and wonderful dark eyes.

David and Phillip immediately took over Danny and the three boys chatted excitedly as they walked through the terminal to the baggage claim area. Craig and Shanna followed, looking lovingly at each other, remembering the passion-filled hours they'd spent together the previous night. They longed to touch each other but didn't dare take the chance.

Shanna was amazed when Danny finally collected all of his pieces of expensive initialed luggage. Had his mother sent everything he owned? she wondered. Not all of his luggage would fit into Craig's trunk, so the boys piled a couple of bags in the back seat with them.

On their way to San Francisco, Craig explained the temporary living arrangement to Danny, who at first seemed confused until David chimed in. "And we can dunk baskets in the evening." Danny brightened at David's words, suddenly feeling a little less lonely.

As they neared the house, Craig turned to Shanna. "How about my treating everyone to dinner later on this afternoon?"

"Can we have pizza?" Phillip asked.

"Yeah, let's have pizza," David and Danny chimed in

"That's up to your mother," Craig answered. "Whatever she says."

Shanna did not have the heart to object to having

pizza again if that would keep the boys happy. But she couldn't resist asking, "Is that all you guys ever want to eat? I guess I will survive having pizza again since I don't seem to have a choice."

"Cool," David and Phillip said in unison and Danny agreed. All three boys continued to interrupt each other until Craig drove into the driveway.

Craig turned to Danny. "Come on upstairs and talk to me while the boys take your luggage to the television room."

Danny reluctantly handed over his carry-on and bags in the backseat to David while Craig and Phillip gathered the rest of his luggage from the trunk of the car.

Hesitantly, Danny followed his father up the stairs, thinking the studio was a neat place to live. However, he was in no hurry to have a talk with his father. He'd rather shoot baskets with the boys. How could he tell his father that being in San Francisco was as much a surprise to him as it was to his father?

Thinking about his mother, Danny remembered she had always done some dumb things where he was concerned, but this was about the dumbest. The least Mom could have done was to give me a choice of being in San Francisco or staying with Grandma and Grandpa in New York. But, no, she just had my things packed and shipped me out.

Maybe Dad might not even want me around for a few weeks. Who knows what goes on in the minds of adults any more? If they didn't want children around they shouldn't have had them in the first place. He gave a start when his father asked, "Didn't you hear me, Danny?

"Uh...uh...I guess my mind was somewhere else," Danny finished lamely. "What did you say?"

"I asked about your mother."

"She's okay," he answered shortly and walked across the room to the back window. "That's a neat back yard.

There's a barbecue pit and everything down there. Where's the hoop?"

"Above the garage door. You walked right under it when we came upstairs," Craig informed him.

"Oh...I was thinking about something else and didn't see it," Danny explained.

Craig sat down on the end of the sofa and called to Danny. "Why don't you sit down for a few minutes? You seem so antsy. Is something bothering you?"

Danny approached the sofa slowly and sat down at the other end, all of a sudden more interested in his hands than in talking. Craig was at a loss as to what his son might be thinking, so he approached head-on what was on his own mind.

Craig moved to the middle of the sofa. Danny seemed so far away. "Didn't you want to come out here, Danny?" he asked in a low voice.

"Well...uh...I knew you'd be busy at the office and I'd probably be in the way and I—"

"Look, son, I know your mother did a rush job on you to get you out here, but I'm really glad you're here. We haven't spent any time together the last few years. I've often wondered how you were getting along and what you were interested in and—" Danny attempted to interrupt but Craig held up his hand and earnestly continued. "I know you've written and sent me pictures from time to time, but that's not the same as seeing you in person. We need to get to know each other, son, and this is a great opportunity for that to happen. Your being here does not interrupt my life one iota. I intend to spend every free minute I have in doing things with you."

Craig was gratified when he saw some of the tension leave Danny's expression and a shadow of a smile cross his face.

"The one fly in the ointment, so to speak, is that I don't have a room up here for you, but the Taylors are really great people and I think you'll make out just fine sleeping in their television room for the time being." He moved closer and laid his hand on Danny's knee. "Feel better now?"

Craig saw Danny brighten and the hesitancy disappeared from his speech. "I'm okay with not staying up here with you. I can see you don't have any room." He stopped and looked around the room. "It's just that most of the time I always seem to get in Mom's way at home. She's always going out with her friends or different guys, and she doesn't ever ask me what I'd like to do or plan anything for me to do. Most of the time I go to Grandpa when I want to do something and he tells me whether I can or not." He had another thought. "Maybe David and Phillip will watch some of the TV programs with me."

"You boys will probably be like three peas in a pod before you know it. They're great kids and get along well together. I'm sure you'll fit right in with their plans."

Craig was rewarded with a wide smile from Danny. "Can I go down to my room now and get out of these clothes? I want to put on some jeans like David and Phillip."

Uh, huh, Craig thought, what have I gotten myself into? Now I have three boys to contend with. He smiled at the thought. "Come on, then, son. We'll both go down. Maybe I can help you get settled."

Danny liked the prospect of having his father help him.

Shanna opened the door before they rang the bell. "I was just coming from the kitchen and saw you on the porch. Come on in." She put her arms around Danny's shoulder and led him down the hall. Craig followed. They found the boys in the television room. Danny's luggage had been dumped in the middle of the floor and David and Phillip lay on their stomachs, their eyes glued to the television set. The minute they saw Danny, however, they sat up.

"Want to dunk some baskets?" Phillip asked.

Craig smiled. "Do you expect him to play in those clothes?" he asked, pointing to Danny's jacket.

"But I can change in nothing flat," Danny said. "I know the suitcase my jeans are in." He proceeded to pull out one of the smaller pieces and opened it with his key.

"What about unpacking the other bags?" Craig asked.

Shanna pulled on Craig's sleeve. "Oh, Craig, that can wait until Danny has nothing else to do. This is his room now. Maybe he can even maneuver the boys into helping him put his things away later," she said with a big wink at Danny.

In just a few words Shanna, having no inkling of Danny's feelings, had won a place in Danny's heart.

Shanna pulled Craig out of the room, leaving the three boys hunting for Danny's jeans.

When they were out of earshot of the boys, Craig looked at Shanna in amazement. "How do you always manage to say the right thing to the boys?"

"Remember, I've had more practice than you've had. I've learned how to handle my own boys without them knowing what I have in mind. Usually they think they've made the decisions," she said smugly.

"Does that work with big boys, too?" he asked, pulling her into his arms.

"I can't claim much experience with big boys, but that would probably work with them, also," she said as she lifted her face to be kissed.

After moments of holding and kissing each other passionately, he drew away from her. "Let's go outside and watch the basketball fanatics. I'll be in trouble if I stay in here with you any longer."

Shanna and Craig sat on the edge of the lawn while the three boys vied for their parents' attention in making baskets. Danny was barely holding his own, but his competitive spirit and determination helped him. It took some time, but Danny finally was able to break away from the other two and actually made a dunk. David and Phillip cheered, and Danny held up his right thumb. Craig and Shanna clapped, both thinking the three boys were going to get along just fine.

Watching Danny, Craig felt happy that his son was with him. He was going to be all right for the few weeks he was staying.

"I'm glad Phillip's cast is off," Shanna said. "He'd be very unhappy now if he couldn't compete with the other two."

Craig nodded. "I only hope Danny can keep up."

"Give him some time. He'll adjust quicker than you think."

When the breeze from the bay cooled, Shanna announced it was time to wash up and go out for dinner.

"Do we have to change clothes?" David asked, a disgusted look on his face.

"Yeah, do we?" As usual, Phillip chimed in.

Danny just looked, but Shanna could tell he sided with the other two boys.

"We're just going for pizza," Craig reminded her.

"Okay, okay. Wear what you have on, then. I see I'm going to really be outnumbered around here. I'll have to get me an ally to survive."

Danny sidled up to her. "I'll be your ally, Mrs. Taylor," he said in a low voice.

Shanna looked down on Danny's dark hair and brushed a few strands off his forehead. "Thanks, pal, I'm glad I have at least one person on my side."

"Huh!" David uttered. "Big deal, Danny. Mom usually gets her way. You'll see. I don't know how she does it, but that's the way it mostly turns out."

Craig looked over at Shanna, a mischievous grin on

his face. "Seems like I've heard something like that before," he quipped.

Shanna refused to be baited. "I'm going in to get a sweater. You boys better take a jacket also."

"But I thought it was always warm in sunny California." Danny looked from one to the other.

"I think that applies to every place except San Francisco," Shanna informed him.

Danny looked confused.

"San Francisco has a climate all its own. It's surrounded on three sides by water. Even when its really warm during the day it usually gets cool when the sun goes down," David explained to Danny. "Come on, I have a jacket you can wear for now, and we won't have to go through your stuff again to find one."

That suited Danny just fine.

By the time they finished their pizza and salad and cold drinks in between a lot of teasing among the boys, Craig suggested they take a short drive to let Danny see some of the city. They drove to a vista point in the Twin Peaks section of the city and parked the car. They all climbed out to have a better view. For several minutes they looked down at the Financial District and part of San Francisco Bay.

"Wow!" exclaimed Danny. "I'm glad I brought my camera with me. I'll have some humdingers to show Grandpa when I go back home."

They all piled back into the car. Danny asked, "Can we come back here when it's sunny, Dad?"

"Of course, son," Craig answered. "But you haven't seen anything yet. Wait until the boys tell you about some of their favorite spots. They introduced me to a lot of the city." He looked over at Shanna. "Shanna helped, too," he added but didn't elaborate.

Craig turned around and headed out Market Street, ending up in the Sunset District of the city. "The zoo is not too far from here," Craig said. "I'm sure you'll want to go there while you're here."

On the way back to the house, David and Phillip regaled Danny about some of their exploits at the zoo the previous day, a couple of which made Shanna raise her eyebrows at Craig as she listened to the chatter in the backseat.

When Craig pulled into the driveway, the boys jumped out of the car as soon as he cut off the motor. Danny turned to his father. "Dad, I think I'll go to my room and get that luggage out of the middle of the floor. I'll come up before I go to bed, if that's all right with you."

"Of course, Danny. I have a couple of reports to read before tomorrow morning, so I think I'll leave you guys to your own devices," he said as he turned to open the garage door. He threw Shanna a special look that said, "I don't envy you having the three of them."

The last bit of conversation Craig heard was Phillip and David offering to help Danny put away his things, explaining to him that they each had to take care of their own rooms and that their mother always checked after they cleaned it on Saturday mornings. Craig smiled as he went up the stairs. "I think everything is going to be all right," he said aloud. He looked upward to thank his lucky stars or whatever was up there helping him out.

CHAPTER TWENTY-THREE

The next few days went by quickly in some ways and dragged by in others for Shanna and Craig. Both were happy that Danny was adjusting so well to all of them. The three boys were becoming inseparable, almost as though they were related or had been friends for years.

Craig bought Danny a bicycle and when the three weren't at the hoops in the evenings they were riding their bikes around the neighborhood.

On the other hand, Shanna and Craig were devastated by not having time to themselves. Craig never knew when Danny would be in the studio, so he and Shanna could no longer plan to spend time with each other there.

Craig managed to leave his office early several evenings to take Danny sightseeing with the help of David and Phillip. On other evenings they shot baskets until dusk and then had dinner together. Danny spent some evenings upstairs with his father, and, with very little effort on the part of either, the two forged a bond in a very short time.

One night Shanna heard Danny groaning downstairs in the TV room and rushed down to check on him. She found him sitting up on the side of the bed, a look of ter-

ror on his face. Sitting down beside him, she took his
hand in hers. "What in the world is wrong, Danny?" she
asked softly.

"I...I had a nightmare...seemed so real," he finally
stammered, looking rather sheepish. "I wanted to go up
to Dad's, but I don't have the garage opener."

Shanna stayed with him for a few minutes until she
saw that he was all right. She got him back to bed and
tucked the blanket around his shoulders. "Okay, now?"
she asked softly.

Danny nodded his head.

From that night on she left the upstairs hallway door
to the studio open for Danny.

Danny's contentment with being with his father
showed in everything he did. He no longer had that lost
feeling in his eyes that was noticeable when he first
arrived. Now whenever he was with his father, he hung
on to every word Craig spoke, and there was an almost
worshipful look in Danny's eyes when they talked to each
other.

During these conversations Craig learned his son
was not happy in New York, even though he adored his
grandparents. Craig lay awake many times at night wondering how he could deal with sending Danny home
when his mother returned from Paris. It was during one
of those sleepless nights that Craig faced the fact that
Danny's mother evidently neglected him and concocted
a plan to gain custody of him.

Craig contacted some friends who were lawyers in
Chicago. After several conversations with his lawyers,
Craig knew there was no way he could allow Ann to continue raising his son. They'd dug up some damaging
information about his ex-wife. He kept this to himself,
hoping he would be able to develop a plan to keep
Danny with him.

❦

Shanna and Craig were becoming desperate for time for themselves, beyond a stolen kiss or a quick hug when the boys were not around. Late one evening, they were sitting at the kitchen table having coffee, and the boys were in Danny's room watching a re-run of a Star Trek episode. Craig looked across the table at Shanna and guessed she was just as unhappy about their situation as he was. "Am I going to have to kidnap you, sweetheart? I want to hold you in my arms, I want to kiss you until both our heads spin, and—"

"Oh, Craig, I know how you feel. But what can we do?" she asked plaintively, not expecting an answer. "I can't risk coming to your studio any more. You never know when Danny might burst into your room since we now leave the hall door unlocked for him."

"But doesn't your bedroom door have a lock?" Craig asked. "Have you thought about that?" He stopped talking for a moment and looked down at his hands. "We've got to work out something. I've got to have you all to myself...or I might do something desperate."

"Oh, Craig, you're always exaggerating."

"Who's exaggerating? I'm dead serious. So what about your bedroom?" he asked again.

She halfway believed him as she was getting a bit desperate to see him also.

"Oh...I...I hadn't thought of my bedroom," Shanna stammered, feeling skeptical of his suggestion, even though her door did have a lock on it. "But what if one of the boys has a stomach ache or something in the middle of the night and comes looking for me?" she asked.

Craig smiled as reached across the table to capture her hand. "I could hide under the bed," he said facetiously.

"I'll have to think about that," she said, still not convinced they could pull it off. "Besides, how—" She didn't have a chance to finish her thought when the three boys bounded into the kitchen.

"Mom, can we make some popcorn during the commercial?"

"Where's the popper?"

"Get the package of popcorn on top of the refrigerator while I melt some butter."

"Where do I plug this thing in, Mom?"

Shanna sat back in her chair. "Well, guys, since you three seem to have the issue settled, why ask me?" She turned to Craig. "Let's go into the living room, Craig. I don't want to watch while they wreck my kitchen."

"What's the world coming to when your own mother won't—"

Smiling, she turned back from the doorway. "Don't you dare finish that question, David." She followed Craig down the hallway.

"Want me to light the logs?" He walked over to the fireplace and reached for the matches on the mantle.

Shanna pulled some pillows over in front of the fireplace. They watched the flames from the kindling quickly engulf the wood. She rested her chin on her crossed arms and stared into the flames. Craig hugged his knees. Both had private thoughts.

Craig was thinking he probably should tell her about his plans to gain custody of Danny, even though there was nothing definite settled at the moment. If he did get Danny, what would she think of adding another boy to her family?

Shanna was thinking she needed to come to terms about what she would do when Craig was finally called back to the main office in Chicago. Why did even the thought of losing him cause such an ache deep inside her?

Both kept their innermost concerns to themselves.

After a few moments, they turned as one, a sad

expression on both their faces. Shanna gulped down the lump in her throat and forced a tight smile to her lips as she stated very matter-of-factly, "The boys have become almost inseparable, haven't they? They act like they've know each other all their lives. They even fuss with each other and then immediately make up, like David and Phillip have always done."

Just like a real family, she added silently, and a small tear formed in the corner of her eye knowing they all were living in such a temporary arrangement. A sudden longing for Craig's touch overwhelmed her and she rubbed her upper arms vigorously when she felt a shiver go through her. She looked at his handsome profile as he stared into the flames. She wanted to pull him close to her, to feel his arms around her, his kisses on her lips. It took all her will power to resist pulling his face down to hers. She was so engrossed in her own thoughts that she started when she heard Craig's voice.

"I don't know what you've done to Danny, Shanna, but he seems to idolize you," Craig said softly. "Haven't you noticed how he hangs on your every word? He even told me a couple nights ago that he wished his mother gave him just half the attention you give your boys."

Shanna looked over at Craig in amazement. "Danny really said that? But then, on second thought, I did notice when he first got here he looked more like a little lost lamb than a soon-to-be teenager. And now he gives Phillip and David a run for their money in dunking baskets. And the bike you got him really puts him in competition with them. Just a couple of days ago I had to threaten to ground all three of them if I caught them racing three abreast down the street again."

For a while they exchanged their experiences with the boys when they'd had them alone. Craig had spent more time with the three when David and Phillip suggested taking Danny to their favorite haunts. He smiled to himself when he thought how he'd not be sorry if he never saw Fisherman's Wharf again in this life. "I shouldn't tell you this, Shanna, but last week when I took the guys to the Wharf again, I turned them loose on their own for a couple of hours. I sat on a bench, perfectly content to watch the sailboats on the Bay."

"You've got to be kidding!" Shanna exclaimed. "They certainly never mentioned anything like that to me! They could have gotten into anything, Craig."

"The point is, they didn't. You've got to give them some space sometimes, honey, to make their own mistakes."

"So now, all of a sudden, you're an expert on parenting?" she asked rather spiritedly.

He smiled down at her and reached for her hand. "Calm down," he said softly. "No, I'm certainly not experienced at being a parent, but I was once a boy their age."

Shanna glanced at Craig out of the corner of her eye but refused to return his smile. She was at a loss to refute his argument, but didn't want to give in entirely. "They're still too young to make a lot of their own decisions," she finally got out.

"I agree with that," Craig said, not wanting to pursue the topic.

What both really wanted was to be in each other's arms, but since that was not possible at the moment, they looked at each other longingly while they exchanged stories about their own childhood and families until the boys trooped in to say goodnight.

Craig got up to leave, saying goodnight while the boys were in the room. He let himself out the front door, leaving Shanna feeling more lonely than ever as she followed the boys upstairs. She slowly undressed and put on her night things. She reached for her novel when she got into bed, knowing she would have a hard time going to sleep with Craig not too far away.

It was way past midnight. Shanna had been tossing restlessly since she'd gone to bed. Then she lost the battle between her conscience and her heart. In a moment of madness, she reached across to the telephone on her nightstand and dialed Craig's number, waiting breathlessly for his deep voice to come on the line.

Before he could say anything, she whispered, "I want to see you and—"

That was all he needed to hear. "Are the boys all asleep?" he asked in the same hushed voice and hung up quickly when she told him that they were.

Shanna locked the door quietly after Craig entered her bedroom and led him across the moonlit room to her bed.

Craig threw off his robe on the way and pulled her naked body to his in a bear-like hug as they sat down on the side of the bed. Brushing aside a tendril of hair from her temple, he planted a soft kiss there, then let his lips drift down her cheek to her mouth. "I couldn't sleep. All I could think about was you in my arms," he murmured between kisses. He wanted to take things slowly, but his self-control was getting out of hand as he nuzzled the sensitive spot on her neck and on down to her breasts.

She tried in vain to control her own rising passion, but her body was making its own decisions, and she groaned as she savored the warmth of his lips and felt his labored breathing.

"Are you okay?" he asked.

For an answer she wrapped her arms tightly around his neck and pulled his head up to meet her lips in a long, hot passionate kiss, as explosions of desire rippled through her body.

Craig lifted his head and looked deeply into her eyes. "It seems like years since I held you in my arms. What you do to me is unbelievable," he murmured as he claimed her lips again, his tongue reached inside her mouth, touching hers as he inhaled deeply.

A tingling coursed through her from her head to that secret place that ached for him. She arched her hips against him and moaned again when he slid his hands down over the curve of her derriere, pulling her even tighter against him. She gasped when she recognized how aroused he was, and her body quivered with her own need and heat. She murmured his name softly over and over as she spread her fingers wide over his muscled shoulders, his smooth back, his round tight buttocks, and down the back of his firm thighs.

His heart pounded as her body strained against him, and he drew some ragged breaths, trying to keep control. When he could no longer resist, he closed his mouth over hers and groaned as he entered her slowly, gently, thrust after thrust...again...and again...and again...until they both were sated and exhausted. When it was over, he remained nestled inside her. It took a long time for them to recover.

With a heavy sigh, he rolled off her to his side and pulled her gently to him. His mouth made love to hers while he stroked her body before he whispered, "Being with you is incredible, but I'd better get out of here before we both fall asleep."

She reluctantly agreed.

❦

A few nights later Craig was awakened at two-thirty in the morning by his phone's insistent ringing. Drowsily he reached across the bed and picked up the receiver, thinking it was probably Shanna. The sound of his ex-wife's voice shrilled through the telephone. He sat up, instantly fully awake. "Where are you, Ann?" he asked, as soon as he could squeeze in a word.

"At the airport outside of San Francisco. I want you to pick me up." As usual, her voice that was almost a command really irritated him.

"It's the middle of the night, for heaven's sake! I'm not getting up and driving out there when you can easily get a cab into the city."

"So wait up for me. I'll be there in an hour or so. We've got some things to settle."

"You mean you expect to stay here?" he asked in an incredulous tone of voice. How could she possibly think she would be welcome in his apartment after their last fiasco?

Ann was not one to be put off so easily. "Where else would I stay? I didn't have time to make reservations," she declared.

Craig paced around the bed with the receiver in his hand. Her question stopped him dead in his tracks. No way was she staying with him, and he didn't want her within a mile of their son, since he'd already filed for permanent custody but hadn't yet mentioned it to Danny.

"There's no way you can stay here, Ann. I'm sure you can get reservations at a hotel. It's the middle of the week, so you shouldn't have a problem. Try the Fairmont or the St. Francis or—" The slamming of a receiver echoed in his ear. Slowly returning the phone to its base, he ran his fingers through his hair in exasperation. Typical Ann behavior! Everyone was supposed to jump at her command. Well, he wouldn't! The least she could have done was to telephone him before she left Paris. And he might have made reservations for her. One thing he hoped he'd made perfectly clear: she wasn't staying with him. Knowing he wouldn't get back to sleep, he padded across the room and removed some files from his attaché case.

It didn't take long for him to realize he couldn't keep his mind on his work, either. What did Ann have up her sleeve? he wondered. Was she here to take Danny back to New York? He hadn't gotten legal custody of Danny yet, but maybe what he knew about her at this point would keep her from cross-filing. Whatever. He would keep her arrival from Danny until he talked to her. Maybe...maybe...maybe he could talk some sense into her. But if that didn't work, what could he do? He couldn't let her near Danny again. All kinds of scenarios crossed his mind until he became too exhausted to keep his eyes open, and he stretched out on the sofa. He slept through the ringing of the alarm clock the next morning and awakened a half hour later than usual. "Damn!" he said aloud when he looked at the clock. He rushed to the bathroom and showered, shaved, and dressed in record time.

The past night's events came to his mind, and he uttered another mild curse under his breath while he gathered up his papers to take to the office. He rubbed the back of his aching neck. "Damn that Ann. Now I'll have to spend time hassling with her today."

He was ready to leave for the office when his phone rang. He knew it had to be Ann.

"I'm at the Fairmont. Shall I meet you at your office or your apartment?"

No way would he see her at either place! He would meet her where he would have half a chance of keeping her under control. "I'm on my way to the office, Ann. I'll meet you for lunch. I'll call you later and tell you where." Before she could reply, he quickly hung up the receiver and stared at the phone for a few seconds, expecting it to ring again. She usually did not give up easily. When it didn't ring, he rushed out the door.

❧

Ann arrived at the restaurant in the financial district before Craig. He noticed the hostile look on her face when he slid into a chair opposite her. He glanced at her manicured nails tapping the table top.

Without so much as a greeting, she asked, "So what

is this nonsense about you having permanent custody of Danny? What in heaven's name makes you think you can carry out something like that? Have you lost your feeble mind completely?"

Craig took a deep breath. He had no intention of getting into an argument with her. He didn't need to. He had done his homework—thanks to his lawyer friends in Chicago—and was prepared to counter any arguments she might present against his having Danny. Knowing that her ego was too big to deal with any damaging gossip among her friends, he had gathered more information than he needed about her affairs with men the past couple of years. His ace-in-the-hole was the indisputable evidence he had about an affair she was presently having with a married, well-known Washington politician, who he knew would certainly brook no publicity about his illicit affair with her.

"So how was Paris?" he asked in his most casual tone of voice.

"I didn't run out on my friends to discuss Paris with you. I—"

The waiter arrived to take their order.

"About Danny—" she tried again when the waiter departed.

He cut her off. "I refuse to discuss anything serious on an empty stomach, Ann. I missed breakfast this morning, and I'm starving, so save whatever stringent remarks you may have until later."

The look she flashed at him was filled with venom, and her fingernails started tapping again, in fact louder than before.

Good, he thought. I'm really getting to her, and there's not a thing she can do about it without making a public spectacle of herself. And that she will never do. He swirled the liquid in his glass. "These are the best martinis in town." He didn't expect a reply; thus he wasn't surprised when she just stared at him. "How's your room? You evidently had no problem getting a reservation."

Silence. Except for the tap, tap, tap of her long nails. Finally Ann leaned toward Craig and said softly, "Damn you and double damn you!"

He smiled at her engagingly as if she had just whispered words of love.

The look she sent his way was sparked with hatred.

If looks could kill, I'd be dead right now, he thought to himself as he glanced at the expression on her face.

The waiter arrived with their lunch and they ate in silence for several long minutes. As soon as their dessert arrived, Ann pushed aside her plate and burst out, "Now, about Danny. How in hell do you think you can now have custody of him when for the past years you barely had visiting privileges?"

It was evident to Craig that she thought she held the winning hand and wasn't prepared to give an inch in his direction. He slowly and carefully laid down his dessert spoon and pushed the sherbet aside. Crossing his arms on the table top, he spoke very softly. "I want you to listen carefully to what I'm going to say, Ann. By the time I'm finished, I think you'll be happy to get the next plane back to Paris and your friends—and without Danny. I've had my lawyer and friends doing a little detective work since Danny's been here." And he proceeded to tell her about all the dirt he now had on her. "So, I don't think you'll even consider contesting my having custody of Danny," Craig ended.

During the few minutes that Craig laid out several of her transgressions during the past years, Ann's expression turned from surprise to anger, from disbelief to hate. How or where he had gotten all of his information about her private life she didn't know. What she did know when he finished speaking was that there was no way she could prove him wrong. Her shoulders slumped, and she sat quietly for several moments, looking down at the fork she slowly turned around on the table.

Finally, in a low vehement voice, she declared, "Okay, you bastard, you win—I'll be in touch when I return from Paris. I'll ship Danny's things out. I won't contest whatever action you've taken." She pushed back her chair and, without any further comment, she reached for her bag and rose, not once looking at him again.

Craig watched her profile as she wove her way through the crowded restaurant, no sign of remorse on her face. She'll survive, he thought. More than likely she's glad not to have the responsibility of Danny any longer. Her past selfish actions in keeping Danny to herself were probably just to hurt me. He shook his head. What kind of a woman is it that will give up a child so easily? She didn't even ask about him!

Shaking his head to clear his thoughts, Craig took out his wallet and laid some bills on the table. He walked out of the restaurant with a lighter heart than he'd had when he entered it. He broke out into a tuneless whistle when he reached the street. He would not have whistled all the way back to his office had he known that Shanna had entered the same restaurant during the time he was in deep conversation with Ann.

Shanna spotted Craig and the back of his blond female companion while she and her co-workers waited to be seated. Her hand flew to her mouth, stifling a cry. When she abruptly turned and made a hasty exit, leaving the rest of the group to celebrate the birthday party she had planned for her secretary, her mystified co-workers looked at each other, wondering what had gotten into her. No one noticed her tear-filled eyes as she blindly made her way out of the restaurant and back to her office.

Minutes later Shanna slammed her office door shut

with a vengeance and sank down heavily in her chair. She opened a drawer and drew out a box of tissues while she took some deep breaths, trying to stop the flow of tears. For the rest of the afternoon she felt she was on an emotional roller coaster that hit valley after valley.

She tried to rationalize her feelings toward Craig after the fiasco in the restaurant. She had no doubt in her mind that she had been used while he was pursuing someone else. She didn't know whether to be angry or heartbroken. Or be grateful for the memories of their times together, memories that would stay with her forever.

It was mid-afternoon before Shanna got her emotions under control enough to keep her mind on her work the rest of the day. By the time she picked up the three boys in the evening, she knew she had to get through the evening without showing the turmoil she felt deep inside.

Shanna saw Craig sitting on her porch when she and the three boys drove into the driveway. Before she could gather her purse and open her door, the boys bounded out of the car and started toward him, thinking he was waiting for them to shoot some baskets.

She called after them, "Have you forgotten that your bikes are in the trunk?"

"We won't need them this evening," David called back and hurried across the lawn until he stood in front of Craig. "Want me to get the basketball?"

"Sorry to disappoint you, David, but I was waiting to talk to your mother. But sit down. There's nothing secretive about what I want to tell her."

"Tell me what?" Shanna asked when she reached the porch, her heart in her mouth.

"I'm going to be out of town two or three days this week and next week also. The Chicago office wants me to check out the other branches here in California. I'll be doing the same as I did with the Monterey office when you—" He caught himself before he revealed her spending the weekend with him. "Remember my telling you about it?" he amended.

David detected some funny business going on but kept quiet. When he looked at the flush on his mother's face, he knew he was right—right about what, he didn't know, but he was sure something was going on. He glanced at Phillip with a I-told-you-so look in his eyes and both boys suddenly found their hands very interesting. Danny wondered what was going on. The boys' actions did not escape Craig or Shanna and they looked at each other, shaking their heads.

"Uh...oh, yes, Craig, I remember you mentioning Monterey," Shanna finally got out, her face flushing from the memory.

"Sit down, Shanna. My main concern at the moment is leaving you with these three. Think you can manage? It'll only be for a couple of days and I—"

Shanna held up her hand. "Of course I can manage. Besides, what do you think they're going to do without you around? All three know the rules and they've been pretty good at sticking to them." She reached out her hand and brushed back Danny's hair from his face.

"Uh...I guess what I meant is I'm sorry I have to add Danny to whatever you have to do," Craig ended lamely.

Phillip spoke up. "Danny's no problem. Is he, Mom?"

"Of course not," Shanna answered, smiling at the boys. "So why don't you three go do...whatever."

They raced to get the basketball before the words were out of her mouth.

Craig rose. "I'm leaving directly from the office later on this evening, so I'll pack a couple of things now and take them back with me," he said, his love showing in his eyes. "I'll call you and—"

"We'll be just fine, Craig. Go do what you have to do." Shanna looked at Craig with mixed feelings. He had become so much a part of her life and now that part was in jeopardy. She didn't know what to do about it. She couldn't get out of her head the fact that she'd seen him with that blond. Maybe by the time he returned she would have her thinking straightened out. Maybe. What she wanted at the moment was to be in his arms again. She was certain her emotions showed on her face and she turned to go into the house. "Have a good trip, Craig," was all she could manage. She wondered about the perplexed look she saw on his face before he turned and walked across the lawn to open the garage door.

All during the time Craig was packing his small bag, he couldn't get Shanna out of his mind. Why was she acting so distant all of a sudden? Had he done something to provoke her into acting so strange? He shook his head slowly. Women! he thought. You could never tell what was going on in their heads.

CHAPTER TWENTY~FOUR

Shanna was devastated. The man who fulfilled all of her romantic notions of the opposite sex was attracted to someone else. It was just that simple. She felt like the proverbial ostrich, that she'd buried her head in the sand the last few weeks. She thought of all the emotion and passion she'd put into their affair. Evidently that's exactly what it was to Craig, only an affair. She hated to admit it, but knew it was jealously—pure and simple jealously—causing the hard knot in her stomach.

She tried to put on her happy face as she drove from work to pick up the boys on her way home. She succeeded in being her normal self on the outside while she made their meal. She even kept up her side of the conversation while they were eating.

The boys quickly finished their dinner and rushed outside while there was still light. She heard their kibitzing with each other, and wondered how Danny would feel when he had to leave. He seemed so happy here with his father, and Craig had turned into the ideal father to him. Even her boys now looked up to Craig in ways they hadn't done before. Evidently it was just a matter of time until the lives of all of them would change. She hoped they all would survive without too much pain when

Craig went back to Chicago.

She finished cleaning the kitchen and sat down with a cup of tea. A sudden thought went through her. She wanted to talk with Angela, bounce some of her frustrations off her friend. She reached for the phone and dialed Angela's number. When Angela came on the line, Shanna said, "I want to run something by you, Angela."

"You really sound down, girl. Are you okay? I'll be right over." Angela hung up and in a few minutes knocked on Shanna's back door.

"Sit down while I get you some tea," Shanna said when Angela entered the kitchen, a slight frown on her face.

"This must be serious, girlfriend," Angela quipped, and was immediately sorry when she saw tears form in Shanna's eyes. "Come sit down. You can get the tea later. You're as jittery as a teenager on her first date. What's wrong?"

Shanna continued getting down a cup and a tea bag. She methodically poured hot water into the cup, dunked the tea bag, and placed it in front of her friend, a devastated look on her face.

Waiting for Shanna to speak, Angela observed, "You look like you've lost your last friend, Shanna. Nothing could be as bad as you seem to be making it." From her own experience she supposed Shanna was having man trouble. That was about the only thing she knew that would put a woman as low in the dumps as Shanna seemed to be.

Shanna took a long sip of her tea and looked at Angela over the rim of her cup a few seconds. "I hardly know where to start ...but it's Craig."

"Ah...I've already guessed that, girlfriend. So what about him? Where is he now? And what about Danny? Didn't I see him playing with the boys out front?"

Shanna stared at her. "Give me a chance to get one

thing out before you ask a zillion questions, Angela. You always do that to me," she ended irritably.

"Okay, okay. So what about Craig?" Angela leaned back in her chair and watched various emotions flit across Shanna's face before she spoke again.

"Well, you might as well hear the whole story," Shanna began. "I'm more in love with him than I ever dreamed possible. I thought I was just having an affair until he went back to Chicago. Now I don't know what to do."

Shanna played with her cup for a few seconds before she continued, frustration etched on her face. "There's a kind of magic between us when we're together...it's almost like the air around us sizzles when we touch and—"

"You've really got it bad, haven't you?" Angela asked, an element of surprise in her voice as she began to look at her friend a little differently. "So how does Craig feel?"

"Well...he...he hasn't come right out and said he loved me. I guess I was just hoping he did. Maybe he's just not aware of how he feels. You know how men are— they don't express their emotions too easily."

"Men aren't like some women who wear their hearts on their sleeves," Angela quipped, but was immediately sorry when she saw the devastated look on Shanna's face. "Don't mind me, Shanna, go on with your story."

"I probably made a mistake when I decided to have an affair with him. But I thought what could be so wrong about that since he was going to be in San Francisco only a short time."

Angela waited patiently for Shanna to continue.

Shanna uttered a sound that seemed like a groan. "And then when Danny's mother shipped him out here, I became attached to him. He seemed such a lonely, confused young boy. Somewhere along the way I guess I just lost my objectivity and let my emotions take over."

"Hmm. Maybe all's not lost. Maybe he just needs some time to get used to the idea of being in love—"

Shanna bristled. "But you haven't heard the other half of it! Would you believe that I saw him today having lunch with a woman who looked like...I really don't know what she looked like since I only saw the back of her head!"

Angela leaned forward with raised eyebrows upon hearing that information. Gossip was her cup of tea, but not when it concerned her friend. "You what? Did you let him know you saw them? Who was she? Anyone you know? What did you say to him?"

Wiping a tear from the corner of her eye with a napkin, Shanna jumped up and put her cup in the dishwasher before she answered. "I just hurried out of the restaurant when I saw them and went back to my office. I felt so betrayed. That's when I knew I truly loved him."

"So when are you going to have it out with him? Feeling the way you do about him, you can't just sit back and ignore something like that," Angela insisted.

Shanna shrugged her shoulders. "At the moment I haven't the slightest idea what I'm going to do. He's leaving this evening for one of the branch offices and won't be back for a couple of days." She signed heavily. "Maybe by that time I'll have my own mind straightened out."

Angela had a sudden thought. "Shanna, maybe the woman was his secretary or just a business acquaintance."

Shanna looked up with doubt in her eyes and shook her head. "They seemed to be having an intense conversation, and I don't think it was about business."

Angela thought a few moments. "You say you're in love with this guy, so how can you give up so easily without at least confronting him about this? It seems to me he owes you some sort of an explanation."

Shanna did not answer that question. "I've got to think about this, Angela. At the moment I'm just so damned confused. I'll think about what you said. I don't want to make a fool of myself. Maybe my head will be clearer tomorrow," she added hopefully.

Angela wondered how that could happen, but she didn't voice her opinion for once. She knew that in reality Shanna had to sort out her emotions by herself, and she changed the subject for a few minutes. Shortly afterward she gave Shanna a big hug and said goodnight.

"Thanks for listening," Shanna said as she followed Angela to the door.

"What else are friends for?" Angela retorted before she closed the door.

Feeling lonely, Shanna walked into the television room where the boys were arguing over the remote control. At least that is something I can understand, she thought. She sat down on the sofa to watch whatever program they finally decided on.

❧

While Shanna was agonizing over her plight with Craig, he was having disturbing thoughts about her in his hotel room in San Jose. He wondered why she'd acted so distant toward him the evening he left San Francisco. Was she having second thoughts about their affair? He couldn't let that happen, he was too much in love with her, even to the point of re-locating to San Francisco permanently if he could have her. He had made up his mind about accepting the management of the California offices, even though nothing official had yet been announced by the Chicago firm. Also, he was certain he was getting custody of Danny. He knew his life would be complete if he could convince Shanna of his love and total commitment. Now he just wanted to complete his work in San Jose and head back to San Francisco.

Later that night Craig placed a call to Shanna, but got

her answering machine. Thinking she was probably out with the boys, he waited until after midnight to call again. The answering machine was still picking up her calls. He became more confused. What was going on with her? She had his number if anything had gone wrong, so why didn't she return his calls? All kinds of negative thoughts ran through his mind while he tossed and turned beneath the sheet. It was some time before he fell into a troubled sleep.

Craig called Shanna's office the next day and was told she was in a meeting both times. He suspected she was avoiding him for a reason—what that reason was, he hadn't a clue. He decided to have it out with her as soon as he got home. Every thought he'd had recently revolved around her and the boys. He surely wasn't going to give up his hopes and dreams so easily.

❧

Both Shanna and Craig would have temporarily forgotten about their concern about each other had they known what was going on with their boys.

All three boys were lying on the floor engrossed in one of their favorite television programs when Danny suddenly jumped up, shouting, "I've got it! I've got it! I ... think," he ended lamely.

David and Phillip sat up and stared at Danny and then at each other, their mouths open.

"Think he's losing it?" Phillip whispered to his brother as they continued to stare at Danny, who now had a wide smile on his face.

"He's been acting kinda weird the past few days, hasn't he?" David whispered back as the two brothers watched Danny sit back down on the carpet and slap his knees.

"You know what, guys?" Danny asked. He didn't wait for an answer. "You know how I could stay out here with Dad?"

The brothers became more confused. They had no idea that Danny had been thinking about staying in San Francisco with his father.

"How?" the brothers asked in unison.

"It's real simple, guys. Dad could marry your mom, and then we'd all live together." Danny felt he'd just solved the world's problems.

Phillip gave Danny a punch on his arm. "You're off your rocker, Danny. People have to be in love before they marry each other. Don't they, David?" he asked, turning to his brother.

"Why are you asking me, Phillip? I don't know anything about that stuff," David mumbled.

Phillip would not give up. "Well...well, you know how you used to like Jennifer, and you told me you wanted to marry her some day," Phillip insisted.

"Aw, she's just a girl and, anyway, I don't like Jennifer any—"

"But women are just grown-up girls, David, and men are—"

"I know, I know—just grown-up boys. But I think there's more to it than that, stupid." David glared at Phillip disgustedly.

Danny looked crestfallen as he listened to the brothers. "But there must be something we could do to get them together," he said determinedly. He put his chin in his hands in deep thought.

David and Phillip waited...and waited.

"Haven't you come up with anything yet?" Phillip finally asked.

Danny thought some more and then started smiling.

The brothers watched Danny's grin for a few moments.

"It's going to be something weird," Phillip predicted to his brother. "I just bet he's thinking about something really far out." He turned to Danny. "So what brainstorm have you come up with?"

Danny was still smiling. "Well, I think this will work." He started to explain. "Suppose they each start receiving those I-Love-You cards you see in the supermarkets. You know, the mushy kind."

"But how can that work?" David asked, doubt clearly in his voice.

Danny lowered his voice conspiratorially. "Here's what we can do. We buy a lot of those cards and sign our parents' names like they're sending the cards to each other...and put the cards in their mail boxes." He glanced at David and Phillip, a gleam in his eyes. "It'll work, I know it'll work."

David and Phillip stared at him several moments, each thinking about Danny's outrageous idea.

"You know, as crazy as that sounds, it just might work," David finally acknowledged.

"Yeah," Phillip chimed in, "we could use our allowances to buy the cards while Mom's at work."

For the next hour or so all three boys forgot about their television program as they discussed their plan: how to sign the cards, when to deliver them, how frequently each parent would get a card.

"But how are we going to know whether the cards are working?" Phillip asked.

Both boys turned to David. He should have the answer. David shrugged his shoulders. "I suppose if they start looking more goo-goo eyed at each other the cards are working."

"Goo-goo eyed? What's that?" Danny asked.

Phillip looked over at Danny. "You'd know if you were a little older," he said with an air of superiority.

"I'm almost as old as you, Phillip. I bet you don't know, either." Danny was not going to be put down by Phillip.

"Oh, stop it, you two," David ordered. "Let's just wait

and see how Danny's scheme works after we finish it."

By the time they worked out all the details about where to get the cards, how many to get, and who would sign the names on the cards, it was time for them to go to bed.

Danny had one last thought before the boys left his room. "Remember we're all in this together if we get caught." Even that didn't dampen their enthusiasm, and they couldn't wait to put their plan into action.

CHAPTER TWENTY-FIVE

Shanna managed to get through the next couple of days while Craig was away by finally resolving to live for the moment and not think about what the future might hold. So what if Craig was seeing some one else as well as her? Maybe he was like a lot of men—they always had to have a woman on the side. For most women, making love meant making some kind of commitment, while a lot of men equated the act to simply having sex.

She remembered having several conversations with Angela on that subject, and they were in basic agreement: men and women approached love and sex from two entirely different viewpoints. For now, Craig was filling a void in her life she had not recognized she had until he came along. If he didn't love her, she could deal with that after he went back to Chicago.

Shanna knew she probably had been foolish in falling for him in such a big way. But how could she just forget about all the hours they spent together, locked in each other's arms? He was also fun to be with, to talk to, to listen to. She liked having him around. Danny had become almost like a member of her family in such a short time, and her boys had taken to Danny as if he were another brother.

Shanna decided she would just enjoy Craig and
Danny as long as they were around and get on with her
own life when they left. But during the long hours at night
when thoughts of Craig tormented her, she wondered
how she would survive without him.   This isn't the
first mistake I've made, Shanna finally told herself, and it
probably won't be the last. That's life, but it's better than
living in a vacuum, which pretty much described my life
before Craig came along. With that settled in her mind,
it was easier to look forward to his coming back from San
Jose.

On Wednesday when she got home after picking up
the boys, she followed her usual routine of picking up the
mail and taking it to the kitchen to be sorted out later. All
three boys followed her through the hallway, plopping
down at the kitchen table while she started their dinner.
She glanced over at them several times, thinking they
had something up their sleeves. She wondered what in
the world they were up to. She kept her silence as their
eyes seemed to follow her as she went from the refrigerator to the counter. She started when she heard Danny's
voice.

"Aren't you...aren't you going to open your mail?" he
stammered.

Shanna looked over at Danny, wondering why he
was suddenly so interested in her mail.   Then she
thought maybe Danny was expecting a letter from his
mother. She walked over and picked up the letters and
junk mail. She noticed the interest in the eyes of the
other two boys as she shuffled through the envelopes.

"Open that one," Phillip instructed, pointing to a
square envelope that looked like an invitation.

Shanna slit the envelope and pulled out a card with
two colorful love birds on the front, their necks entwined.
She opened it and silently read the words expressing a
deep love for her. She smiled and then blushed when

she saw who it was from. It was signed "From your lover, Craig."

The boys were all looking at her reaction. "What is it, Mom?" Phillip asked.

"It's nothing, Phillip," she explained as she slipped the card into its envelope and then into her pocket.

The boys gave a thumbs up to each other behind her back. They suddenly had the urge to play basketball and rushed from the room, satisfied smiles on their faces.

As soon as the boys left the room, Shanna took out the card again and re-read it, ecstatic that Craig had thought about her while he was away. She was so thrilled to receive the card she didn't notice that the envelope had no postmark.

On Thursday the boys beat her to the mailbox and again waited until she opened all of the envelopes. Shanna found a card similar to the one she'd gotten the day before. She still couldn't figure out why the boys were interested in her mail. Had they suspected that something was going on between her and Craig? she wondered. But then she dismissed that thought and went on with her work in the kitchen.

Outside, the three boys discussed the look on Shanna's face when she read the cards.

"I think the cards are working," Danny declared. "Did you see how she kinda looked embarrassed before she put the card in her pocket?"

"Yeah," Phillip said, "it looked like she was blushing."

"Oh, come on, you two. Let's shoot the ball. We still don't know how your father will act when he sees his cards, Danny," David said, throwing him the basketball. David thought he had a pretty good idea but didn't voice his opinion to the other two.

❧

Shanna saw Craig's car in the driveway when she drove in Friday evening, and her heart skipped several beats as she got out. He had come home early!

The boys bounded out of her car and headed for the garage door, calling Craig's name.

She tried to contain her emotions without much luck and unlocked her front door with trembling fingers, thinking about the two cards she'd received from him. Get a grip, she admonished herself as she walked into the house and down the hallway to the kitchen. She deposited the bag of groceries she'd picked up on her way from the office.

Glad that she had something to do while she got her emotions under control, she put away her purchases and started dinner. Hoping Craig would join them, she phoned upstairs and asked him, saying dinner would be ready in about a half hour. She was elated when he enthusiastically accepted and rushed upstairs to change from her office clothes and freshen up her makeup.

"That was your mother inviting me to dinner," Craig told the three boys while glancing through his mail. The boys held their breath, afraid he wasn't going to open the ones they'd put in his mailbox. He hesitated when he came to two square envelopes and started to throw them on top of the others, thinking they were probably invitations to something he had no interest in or were solicitations for money from some agency he had no intention of supporting.

"Why don't you open these, Dad?" Danny asked, picking up the square envelopes.

Craig looked at his son curiously, wondering why he was interested in those particular pieces of mail. Then it dawned on him. Probably thinks they're from his mother. He slit the top of the envelope and pulled out a card with the words "Guess Who Loves You" emblazoned above two large entwined hearts and cupids around the border. Opening the card and seeing Shanna's name astonished him. He carefully inserted the card back into the envelope while the boys looked on. He found a similar message expressing love with the same signature when he opened the other square envelope. He quickly stuffed both envelopes into his inside coat pocket and turned to examine the other pieces of mail.

The smiling expression on his face as he read the cards hadn't escaped the scrutiny of the boys. They winked at each other and gave each other high-fives behind his back.

"Why don't you three go on down? I'll be there as soon as I change my clothes." He wanted a few minutes to compose himself after reading Shanna's messages. She really missed me, he thought as happiness flooded through him.

"We'll be in Danny's room. Call us when dinner is ready," David said as they headed for the stairs, jubilant that Danny's plan really seemed to be working.

As soon as the boys left the room, Craig reached into his pocket for the cards and sat down to re-read them. He had a glow on his face when he walked into the kitchen for dinner.

Craig carried most of the conversation during their meal, telling the boys about San Jose and how it was expanding. He noticed Shanna was unusually quiet during most of the meal, though glanced at him several times when she thought he wasn't looking. She seemed to have something on her mind. He couldn't wait much longer to take her in his arms and find out whether she really meant what her cards had implied.

They had almost finished dinner when Craig had what he thought was a brilliant idea. "How'd you guys like to go to a movie this evening?" he asked, looking around the table at the boys.

"Yeah," they cried in unison and slapped each others' hands while Shanna tried to hide her amusement. She suspected that Craig's idea was just one of his ploys to get them out of the house.

The boys quickly finished their dinner and waited impatiently for Craig to finish his.

"Get your jackets and I'll drop you off. You can call me when the movie's over," Craig said as he rose from the table. He took some bills from his pocket and handed them to David. The other boys were already on their way to their rooms for their things.

Craig turned to Shanna. "We need to talk when I get back," he said softly and moved toward her. But she avoided him with her hands full of dishes.

Shanna's stomach felt as if it were filled with butterflies as she cleared the rest of the dishes from the table and stacked them in the dishwasher. She went into the living room and lit the kindling under the logs, more from wanting a cozy atmosphere than from the heat it would produce. All her good intentions of protecting herself from having a broken heart went up in smoke when Craig walked back into the house.

"You look exhausted," she observed.

"It was a hell of a couple of days," he said as he sat down on the couch and reached for her. "But I feel better already. Let me hold you for a few minutes and I'll feel fine."

Memories of their past lovemaking flooded Shanna's mind as she went into his arms, and her heart pounded as she leaned into him, lifting her face for his kiss.

When they drew apart, Shanna looked up at him shyly. "Thanks for the cards, Craig. The messages inside were very touching."

Craig stared at her in amazement. What in the world did she mean? "Cards? What cards are you talking about?"

"Oh, stop trying to fool me. Did you really mean the things the cards said?" Shanna asked.

Craig shook his head. Something screwy was going

on. "Did you mean the things in your cards?" Craig asked.

"My cards? I...I didn't send you any cards!" she stammered. "And I didn't send you any!" he declared.

They stared at each other a few moments before it dawned on them at the same instant what must have happened.

"The boys!" they cried in unison and broke out in loud laughter.

Shanna was finally able to speak. "I thought something fishy was going on with those guys the past couple of days. They all suddenly developed an interest in my mail!"

"Come to think of it, Danny insisted that I open those particular pieces of mail, and all three of them watched me while I opened the envelopes."

They looked at each other in amazement. "I guess they call themselves playing Cupid," Shanna surmised, a look of wonder on her face.

Craig agreed and added, "Suppose we act like nothing has happened and see who breaks down first—them or us. They'll probably be watching us every chance they get to see if their scheme worked."

"Who would have thought they would think up something like that? They really must want us to get together!" A blush suddenly covered her face.

"You know what? They did a pretty good job in picking out those cards. They're like something I'd send you."

She smiled shyly. "My cards were pretty appropriate, also."

He leaned closer and took her hand in his, gently circling the back of her hand with his thumb. "I don't know how you're going to take this, but I've been doing some behind-the-scenes work the past couple of weeks and I've..." His voice trailed off as he watched her reaction to his words.

Shanna drew in her breath sharply. So here it really comes, she thought, the brush-off. I should have expected this. She felt the color drain from her face as she stared at him.

Craig looked at her. "Aren't you feeling well?" he asked, his voice full of concern.

It took a few seconds before she got out, "I'm okay. What were you saying?" She inhaled deeply, ready to face whatever it was.

"Well...for the past few days I've had investigators working on Ann's shenanigans in New York. From what I learned, she doesn't spend too much time with Danny and is letting his grandparents basically raise him. I want custody of Danny because she's been neglecting him far too long. I contacted her through friends in Paris to let her know of my intentions. She flew here a few days ago as mad as a wet hen that I would even think I could gain custody of Danny. But when I laid out all the dirt that the investigators had dug up on her, she was only too glad to agree not to contest my gaining custody. She's sending all of Danny's clothes and belongings out as soon as she gets back from Paris."

Shanna let out a long sigh. "Ann was here again?"

"Yes, we had lunch together the day I left for San Jose. I didn't want to mention it to you until I had another piece of the puzzle in place that we—"

Shanna held up her hand. "I've been such a fool, Craig. I saw you having lunch with someone and I thought—"

"You thought I was seeing another woman?" Craig asked, his voice rising. "How could you even think like that, honey, after what we've been to each other? What kind of a person do you think I am?" A note of exasperation sounded in his voice as he watched a tinge of color creep up from her neck to her cheeks.

He moved closer to her and took her in his arms, smoothing her hair with his hand. "Don't you know I love you like I've never loved another woman, sweetheart?"

Shanna didn't know whether to laugh or to cry. Craig had actually said he loved her! But he hadn't said one word about anything beyond that! What was he actually going to do about her? She couldn't control the flood of tears that sprang from her eyes. She withdrew her hand to wipe away her tears.

Craig felt a wetness on her cheeks and took out his handkerchief to dry her eyes. "Why are you crying?" he asked, frustrated to see her in such a state.

It took several seconds before her tears subsided and she was able to blubber, "But...but you've never really told me you loved me...and I thought I was the only one in love."

"You love me?" he asked, staring at her. He couldn't believe what she'd just uttered.

"From the first time I saw you, I think. I've never felt like this about anyone else. I guess I didn't handle it too well." She looked down at her hands twisting in her lap.

Craig drew the back of his hand across his forehead. "And I was afraid I would have a hard time convincing you that we belong together, sweetheart! I've spent many a night wondering how I could make you love me. You're such an independent soul that I thought you had the world by the tail and didn't need anyone else in your life except your boys."

"I did kinda feel that way...until you came along and turned my world upside down," she added tearfully.

They held each other tightly for several minutes, not saying a word, amazed that they had finally reached a plateau that both wanted to be on all along but were afraid to reach for.

Craig finally drew back. "You didn't let me finish telling you my other news."

"You mean there's more?"

"The Chicago office wants me to manage the California branches. I haven't given them a definite answer yet, but I've kinda fallen in love with this area and I think Danny would be happy here."

Indignant, she sat up straighter. "Is the area all you've fallen in love with?"

"Cool it, Shanna, I've already told you I can't live without you."

Shanna couldn't believe her ears. "Really, Craig?" was all she managed to get out before the phone rang. She picked up the receiver and listened to the voices of the boys. She turned to Craig. "They're ready to be picked up, but wanted to know if they could stop to get some Italian ice on the way home."

"Those three are going to be the death of both of us," Craig teased as he rose and grabbed his jacket to go for them. "I suppose you also want some Italian ice," he said, remembering her penchant for sherbet.

Shanna nodded her head. He kissed her passionately before leaving. "That will have to last for a while since we won't be alone, damn it." He was almost to the door when he turned back. "Let's keep what we talked about to ourselves for now, shall we? When we have everything straightened out, we'll tell the boys."
Shanna agreed. In fact she didn't want to share their conversation with anyone for a while, not even Angela.

After Craig left, Shanna sat down and stared into the flames for several minutes. She couldn't quite believe what she'd heard the past couple of hours and thought about pinching herself to be sure she wasn't dreaming. "And he loves me," she said aloud. "Craig really loves me." Her heart was too full to sit still. She got up and paced back and forth in front of the flames until she heard his car pull into the driveway.

Craig followed the boys into the house, acting like a

referee as they argued about the ending of the movie.
"So take your discussion and Italian ice into the television
room so we can enjoy ours in peace," he directed when
they entered the hallway. He walked into the living room
and gave Shanna a cup and a spoon before he sat down
beside her with his own cup of Italian ice.

Craig waited until the boys were out of sight before
he pulled her to him. "I've missed you so much these
past couple of days, sweetheart. At night I had trouble
sleeping because I wanted you so much. You even disturbed my dreams when I was able to fall asleep for a
few hours." He finished his Italian ice and set the empty
cup on the coffee table. "Could we possibly get together
after the boys are asleep? I don't care how late it is, will
you call me?" he asked, his voice almost pleading with
her.

Shanna couldn't get the words out of her mouth. Her
emotions were too near the surface. She nodded her
head and dug her spoon into her cup of Italian ice.

CHAPTER TWENTY-SIX

It was almost midnight when Craig slipped into Shanna's bed. He pulled her warm naked body close to his chest, and they held each other tightly for several moments. Craig cupped her face in his hands saying huskily, "I love you more than life itself, sweetheart. And those aren't easy words for me to say. I've been so wrapped up in my own shell for so long that I gave up hope that I'd ever find anyone I could love and trust. But meeting you has changed all that."

Shanna's eyes flooded with tears of happiness as she listened to his deep, vibrant voice. In that instant she knew she'd been fooling herself in even thinking she could give him up if she had to. No way could she do that! She wanted him in a way she had never wanted anyone or anything. Yet a feeling of uneasiness rose in her mind. Was she just clutching at straws because she'd fallen in love with him? Was he ready to make a commitment? He still hadn't said he wanted to actually marry her, to make a home for all three of their boys.

Craig touched the tip of her nose with his thumb. "You're awfully quiet. Didn't you hear what I just said?"

Shanna did not reply. Her emotions were too close to the surface. She drew his head down for a long kiss and wrapped her arms around his muscled shoulders while all her doubts vanished like a puff of smoke.

The kiss seemed to go on forever. The warmth of her mouth against his made his head spin, and he could no more control his passion than he could stop the sun from rising each morning. He rubbed his body sensually along the length of hers, and the feel of his throbbing passion on her stomach made her cling more tightly to him while their tongues played against each other.

His kisses grew more feverish, more demanding, as they clung together. He tangled his fingers in her hair, cupping the back of her head with his palm, pushing her mouth more insistently against his. He released her lips and moved his mouth to her earlobe, then moved down the side of her throat and back up under her chin, leaving hot kisses on each spot he touched.

Shanna felt powerless to control her wanting him, he was everything in her world at the moment. She arched her body to meet his, moaning his name softly.

Her voice sent powerful erotic surges sweeping through him. He drew a deep, ragged breath, and felt his muscles tense, almost quivering with desire. He wanted the moment to last and he forced his hand to move slowly down to her breasts, and his head followed, softly kissing each mound before he moved down to her stomach, planting small hot kisses wherever his head landed. The heat of her body sent shudders through his entire nervous system. Shanna could only lie still while wave after wave of sensation rippled through her.

He reached under her and gripped her hips tightly.

She squirmed against him, almost breathless from her need to have him inside her. She gave a low moan when he pulled up above her and reached under the pillow. She heard the crinkle of foil as he fumbled with a packet before lowering his body to hers again.

Craig felt Shanna moving beneath him, undulating,

writhing. Braced on his forearms, he felt her wrap her legs around him. With a slow, careful, tentative motion he entered her, and for a moment neither could move, savoring the closeness that both wanted more than anything else in the world at the moment. Their lovemaking was slow and agonizingly sensual as they became one in an explosion of feeling that reached deep within both of them. Sated, they fell asleep in each other's arms for a short time before they awakened and again started their journey together, taking their time to reach the heights of lovemaking, so in tune with each other. They made love silently. No words were needed.

❃

It was almost dawn before Shanna stirred to find Craig sleeping beside her, a contented expression on his face. Before awakening completely, she reveled in their lovemaking of the past few hours as she inhaled deeply and let her breath out slowly.

The way she felt was almost unreal, she thought, stealthily slipping out of bed. She didn't want to awaken Craig. She closed the bathroom door quietly and slid open the shower door. She put on her shower cap and turned on the shower. She stepped beneath the pounding warmth of the jets, luxuriating in the feel of the water as it pelted down on her before methodically soaping her sponge to wash away the passion of the last few hours.

Shanna was almost finished when the shower door slid open and Craig climbed in with her. "This reminds me of Monterey," she said as she moved over to make room for him.

Craig nodded and reach for her shoulders, pulling her to his wet body. "There's nothing like kissing under a shower," he said as he took the sponge from her and turned her around to do her back. When he finished, he gave her a pat on her buttocks. "Out you go so I can shower in peace."

He walked back into the bedroom a few minutes later, mopping his wet hair. "I better get back to my own room before the boys wake up," he announced and she agreed, even though she wanted him to crawl back into bed with her. He leaned over and kissed her. "I'm going to the office for a few hours." He unlocked the door and opened it quietly, peering out before slipping down the hallway to his studio.

Shanna heard the boys' voices in her sleep, at least she thought it was in her sleep until she rolled over and saw that it was after ten o'clock. Jumping up and throwing on her jeans and a top, she rushed downstairs to find all three arguing about what they wanted for breakfast.

Shooing all three boys out of the kitchen, she settled them down when she informed them she would make a breakfast of her own choice. "Go do your rooms until I'm finished," she instructed them, "because I want you to help me with some errands today." She knew the day would pass quicker if she were busy.

❦

The sun had not reached the horizon when Craig drove into the driveway. The boys surrounded his car before he opened his door. Craig sighed, knowing what he was in for. The four dunked baskets until the sun sank behind the horizon in a blaze of red-gold glory.

"Guys, put the basketball in the garage and let's go inside. We've got some things we need to talk about." Craig noticed the guilty looks that the boys gave each other, each wondering what he'd done, Craig supposed. He ruffled their hair. "Everything's okay with you guys. I've got some news and I want to know how you three feel about some decisions I'm about to make."

"What about Mom?" Phillip, the worrier, asked.

"Oh, she already knows about most of it," Craig informed Phillip and saw a look of relief cross his face.

Craig herded them into the living room and lit the kindling under the logs before he called Shanna. The boys flopped down on the carpet in front of the fireplace. Craig pulled over two large pillows for Shanna and him.

"We're going to have a pow-wow," quipped David to his mother when she came into the room.

Shanna smiled at the boys stretched out in front of the fireplace. "Looks that way, doesn't it? Except we don't need a peace pipe."

As soon as she lowered herself down on the pillow behind them, the boys sat up and turned to face the two adults. All three looked at Craig expectantly.

Craig cleared his throat, well aware of the suspense he was creating. He enjoyed every minute of it.

Shanna had difficulty keeping a straight face, well aware of what Craig was doing.

In a very business-like voice, Craig started. "First, I'll explain about a decision I need to make about my position in Chicago at—"

"Oh, no, you're not going back there right away, are you?" Phillip asked, distress showing on his face.

"Hold on, Phillip, until I tell you the rest of it. You guys know I've already visited the firm's branches in Monterey and San Jose. Well, next week I'm going to Sacramento to look over that branch. I've been approached by my bosses in Chicago to take over the management of the offices in California. If I accept their proposition, it means that I'll be permanently located here in San—"

Danny interrupted, a wide grin on his face. "Really, Dad? You're going to take it, aren't you? Then I could come back and visit some more."

"We'll talk more about that later, son." Craig ignored the shadow that passed across his son's face.

Shanna saw Danny's look of disappointment. She reached out and patted his shoulder.

Craig continued as though he were telling a suspense story. "Now here comes the best part, the best part for me at least. I hope you'll all agree."

The boys stared at Craig, tension showing on their faces. "I've filed to have permanent custody of you, Danny, and I don't—"

Again he didn't have a chance to finish his thought as all three boys bounded up to hug him, asking questions at the same time until he quieted them and turned to Danny. "How about that, son?"

Danny sat down slowly. "You mean I'll live here with you all the time, go to school here and everything?" he asked. He didn't quite believe his ears. It was too good to be true! Then he remembered his mother. "Did Mom say I could stay with you?" he asked in a hushed voice.

"Yes, son, your mother agreed that living with me would be best for you. The legalities haven't been worked out completely yet, but she's going to send all of your belongings to you as soon as she returns from Paris."

David and Phillip pounced on Danny. "See, I told you everything would work just as we..." David's voice trailed off when the other two boys turned to stare askance at him.

The adults smiled at each other.

David dropped his eyes to his hands, knowing he had been close to letting the cat out of the bag by almost revealing Danny's plan to get their parents together.

Seeing the sheepish expression on David's face, Shanna asked, "What was that all about, David?"

"Uh...uh...I'll tell you later," David finally got out, still not looking at the other boys.

Danny looked puzzled for a moment. "Will I live here with David and Phillip, Dad?" he asked, turning to his father.

Craig glanced over at Shanna.

Shanna suddenly seemed very interested in the wood crackling in the fireplace, refusing to look at him.

"We'll...uh...we'll have to see how some other things work out before I can make any more decisions, Danny," Craig said hesitantly, glancing over at Shanna again.

She still refused to meet his eyes.

Danny was not appeased by his father's vague answer. "But, Dad, what about—"

Danny stopped talking when Shanna jumped up, a sly smile on her face. "How about some hot chocolate and cookies?" she asked and made her way to the kitchen, leaving Craig to field any other questions Danny and the other boys had.

CHAPTER TWENTY-SEVEN

A The two families had settled into a routine of sorts, usually having dinner together when Craig was at home. All three of the boys were now aware of the attraction between their parents and talked about it among themselves, discussing whether adults had to wait a long time before they got married. None of the boys had an answer to that.

Late one evening Shanna and Craig were having a late snack in front of the fire, while the boys were having theirs in front of the television in Danny's room, which had become their hangout.

Shanna turned to face Craig. "All evening you've looked like the proverbial cat who swallowed the canary. Are you getting ready to go on another of your trips?" she asked, fervently hoping he wasn't.

Craig moved closer to her and took her free hand in his. "The news I have to tell you has to do with my not going on any more trips with—"

Shanna withdrew her hand and leaned back to look at him, a question in her eyes. "Don't kid me, Craig. What do you mean you're not going to have to travel any more?"

Craig leaned back and took a deep breath, thinking

how typical it was of her to ask a lot of questions. "If you just let me talk, I'll tell you, sweetheart."

"Oh, Craig, you always keep me in suspense before you get to the point," she complained.

"And you're always asking a lot of questions before I can get to the point," he teased.

"Okay, okay. What were you saying?"

"As of today I am officially the CEO of the California offices."

Shanna could not contain the joy she felt hearing his news. She stood up and raised her thumb. "Way to go, sweetheart!" Then something else occurred to her, however, and she sat back down. "But how do you feel about not traveling at all? Won't you miss it?"

"So you think you're the only one who has been concerned about that? It's been bothering me, too. No, not traveling will not bother me in the least. I'll be happy just doing my job in the office right here while others do the traveling. I'll get a substantial raise in pay, by the way," he ended, looking at her out of the corner of his eye.

"Sweetheart, the raise is great for you but it's immaterial to me. I just want you to be happy with your decision. Your being around every day is what would make me happy at the moment." Her happiness was reflected on her face.

"Really, Shanna? Nothing else would make you happier?"

Shanna did not answer. She knew there was one thing which would make her happier, but she supposed that was too much to ask for at the moment. Craig drew her into his arms and planted soft kisses on the top of her head. She felt as if she were melting in his arms and pressed closer to him.

He leaned back from her and looked into her eyes for several moments before he spoke. "You've really become the most important part of my life, Shanna. I

want to make you a part of me, to make love to you forever, to laugh and talk with you, to face life's problems
together, to cry together if the need arises." He drew her
back against his chest again, gently rubbing his chin
across the top of her head.

Turning around to face him, Shanna took his head
between her hands, softly whispering, "No one has ever
made me feel the way I feel about you, Craig. I can't
remember what my life was like before I met you."

"Does that mean you would say 'yes' if I asked you to
marry me?" he asked, his heart thudding against his
chest, eager yet apprehensive to hear her answer.

Shanna felt tears gathering behind her eyelids as she
leaned toward him, her lips slightly parted. How could
she make him know how happy he made her?

Craig saw Shanna's dark eyes glistening and pulled
her closer to him, kissing her gently, slowly increasing
the pressure of his lips on hers until they both were
breathless. Then he released her slowly and reached
into his pocket. He removed a small box.

Shanna's heart skipped several beats as she
watched Craig. Turning to face Shanna, Craig looked at
her tenderly for several moments before he softly said,
"You haven't answered my question."

She was suffocating from emotion. "I...I ..." She
stumbled over her words. "Yes...I'll marry you," she
finally got out. Tears again filled her eyes, trickling out
onto her cheeks this time.

Craig opened the small red velvet box and reached
for Shanna's left hand. Very solemnly and slowly he
slipped a large solitaire diamond onto her ring finger.

Holding up her hand, Shanna gazed at her ring
almost in disbelief. "Oh, Craig, it's gorgeous!"

"Not half as gorgeous as you are!" Craig declared.

They looked deep into each other's eyes, silently
pledging to love each other as long as they had the

breath to do so.

Smiling, Craig rose and pulled her to her feet. "Shall we tell the boys, sweetheart?"

Shanna nodded, her heart too filled up to speak.

Hand-in-hand they headed for the television room to break their news to their boys.

All three boys looked up at the broad smiles on their parents' faces when they entered the room. They held their breaths, wondering what was now going on with their parents.

Craig took over. "We've got more good news for you, guys," he started, then added more drama to his voice. "We're going to be married!"

"Wow," David said softly.

"You really mean it?" Phillip asked. He couldn't believe what he'd just heard.

Danny just stared, hoping he wasn't dreaming. Finally he grabbed the other two boys around the neck. "See? I told you my plan would work!"

"Hold on, son. What 'plan' are you talking about?" Craig asked.

The three boys looked at each other sheepishly, but no one spoke.

"Did your 'plan' have anything to do with sending some cards?" Craig asked. He looked from one to the other, smiling inside at their expressions since they knew their scheme had been exposed.

Still no one spoke.

"Maybe all three of you would like to confess later," Shanna said softly, "since no one wants to claim the credit now. We'll let you all think it over and you can tell us whenever you feel like it...or never if you prefer."

The three boys let the air out of their lungs slowly when Shanna and Craig left the room. Then they lifted their thumbs high in the air, shouting, "Yes!" before turning back to their television program.

Craig and Shanna smiled at each other when they heard the outburst coming from Danny's room.

Still holding hands, Shanna and Craig wandered out to the patio. Little was said as they sat close together enjoying the balmy breeze, knowing they all would soon be one family the rest of their lives just as surely as there would always be stars in the sky above them.

☙

Shanna slowly drifted awake and stretched lazily as she sat up on the side of her bed, wishing Craig was still beside her. But he had left for his office earlier than usual, promising to return early to help her with the packing. She slowly looked around her all-too-familiar bedroom, realizing that soon they would all move into a larger house Craig had recently purchased. She twisted the diamond wedding band that sparkled behind her engagement ring, still thinking how blessed she had been in Craig's choosing her.

She took a quick shower before awakening the boys for breakfast. They all had a couple of busy days ahead of them if they were to have all the boxes filled before the movers came.

Going down the stairs to face the day, Shanna thanked whoever was up there for the love that she and Craig had found—the link which bound together all their lives.

EPILOGUE

Shanna waddled around the large, cheery kitchen, satisfied that the dinner she'd prepared for her family would be ready when they got back. Craig had taken David to visit Stanford University, which he planned to enter in the fall, and Phillip and Danny had gone along for the ride. She thought of how all three boys had grown inches during the past two years. All three were now taller than she.

While setting the table, Shanna stopped several times and rubbed her swollen stomach. Their baby was due any day now. From all the kicking she frequently felt, she was just as eager for it to arrive as it seemed to be to leave her body.

Finally finishing the table, she slowly made her way to their comfortable family room overlooking a large expanse of lawn. A gazebo sat at the far end, surrounded by large trees. She surveyed the several varieties of plants and flowers, and beautiful mounds of trimmed shrubbery in their landscaped yard.

Standing in the doorway for a few moments, she inhaled the fragrant scent of the flowers and recently mowed grass. She wanted to walk outside, but thought better of it when she felt another dull pain. Slightly out of breath, she walked back across the room and clumsily lowered her heavy body onto her favorite sofa. She put her feet up on the low table in front of it. Feeling another dull pain, she shifted around on the sofa.

Shanna had planned today's dinner in celebration of David's being accepted to Stanford. She didn't want anything to spoil it. Lying back and breathing deeply several times as the doctor had instructed, she soon dozed off.

A couple of hours later, Shanna awakened when Craig and the boys entered the house. She slowly raised up. A pain, sharper than any of the others, shot through her, and she fell back onto the sofa, a loud gasp escaping her lips.

Craig hurried to her side when he saw the distress on her face. He silently berated himself for leaving her alone, if only for a few hours.

He tried to keep his concern from showing on his face. "Shanna, honey, what's wrong?" he asked, his stomach already tightened into knots.

The three boys stared at her in alarm.

"I think you better call the doctor and get the bag we packed," Shanna managed to get out between the pains.

Craig struggled with the panic growing inside. "Oh my God! She's in labor!" The idea terrified him.

For the next few minutes pandemonium reigned. Everyone ran into each other while they prepared to take Shanna to the hospital. The boys became more terrified than Craig when he shouted at each, telling them what they should be doing.

❧

A few hours later, although to Craig it seemed an eternity, Shanna's doctor entered the hospital's waiting room. He put his arm across Craig's shoulder. "Congratulations, Craig. You have an eight-pound boy! Baby and mother are both doing fine. Your wife is still a little groggy, but your baby is trying his lungs out in the nursery if you want to see him."

Craig sank down into the nearest chair. His legs suddenly would not hold him up. Drawing the back of his hand across his sweaty forehead, he managed to thank the doctor. He sat very still for a few minutes, trying to compose himself. Whispering a silent prayer that Shanna was all right, he thanked the powers that be for another link that had been added to their lives. Rising, he rushed down the hall to Shanna's room.

Looking up at him groggily, Shanna announced, "It's another boy." She glanced behind him. "Where are the boys?" she inquired.

"They'll be here later on, if the hospital will let them in, that is," he promised.

Craig leaned down and took Shanna's face between his hands. "You sound disappointed that it's a boy...guess we'll have to start working on a girl!"

Shanna looked up into his shining eyes. "The way I feel at the moment we might never have another baby," she declared. The last few hours caught up with her and she turned over, closing her eyes.

Craig smiled and leaned down to softly kiss the top of Shanna's head before tiptoeing from the room. He knew she didn't mean a single word she had just said.